# ON THE RUN

# Praise for Charlotte Greene

## *Legacy*

"Greene does a good job of building suspense as the story unfolds. Strange things happen one by one in increasingly spooky fashion. Background information is revealed a little bit at a time and makes you want to try and solve the mystery...I recommend this to those who like to read about hauntings, nature, history, DIY home maintenance, violent husbands, scary things in the woods, and water."—*Bookvark*

"The characters are well developed, and Greene hit just the right amount of tension between them...I rarely like every character in a book, but I loved the whole group. The creepiness never let up, the tension built steadily, and...things escalated rapidly. The ending was very satisfying! Horror is definitely Greene's forte."—*Bookish Sort*

"This is a wonderfully scary paranormal novel. The setting is perfect and well described. The characters are well-drawn and likable. The romance between Jo and Andy is especially charming and fits perfectly into the tale. This is just a wonderful story, and I'm so glad I read it, even in the middle of the night. If you love a good scary story, I believe you will love it too."—*Rainbow Reflections*

"Greene likes to take her time to work up the suspense, starting with smaller and seemingly inconsequential things that build up a suitably creepy atmosphere. Placing the characters in an isolated setting ratchets things up. This isn't a gore-fest nor is it relying on jump-scares to set the atmosphere—instead it's a well paced ghost story with strongly developed characters..."—*C-Spot Reviews*

"Greene does a great job of establishing a creepy atmosphere by setting a rather slow (but not overly so) pace, taking the necessary time to describe the woods, the uncared-for cabin, the ominous well from the cover, the sounds, the smells, the weather and temperatures..."—*Jude in the Stars*

"Very fun horror story that just touches on the creep factor without going full blown scary. There's a lot of really good elements to the book, from the menacing spook, to the mystery, and even the relationship...Great work!"—*Colleen Corgel, Librarian, Queens Public Library*

## *Pride and Porters*

"Have you ever wondered how *Pride and Prejudice* would work if it were two women falling in love with a brewery as a backdrop? Well, wonder no more!...All in all, I would say this is up near the top on my list of favorite *Pride and Prejudice* adaptations." —*Amanda Brill, Librarian, Rowan Public Library (North Carolina)*

"Greene's charming retelling of *Pride and Prejudice* transplants the Bennets into the world of Colorado craft beer...The story beats are comfortingly familiar, with the unusual backdrop of brewing and beer competitions, modern setting, and twists on the characters providing enough divergence to keep the reader engaged... Feminism, lesbianism, and class are all touched on in this refreshing update on a classic. (Starred review)"—*Publishers Weekly*

## *Gnarled Hollow*

"Greene has done an outstanding job of weaving in all sorts of layers: mysterious patterns in the gardens, missing rooms, odd disappearances, blandly boring journals, unknown artwork, and each mystery is eventually revealed as part of the horrific whole. Combined with intensely emotional descriptions of the fear the characters experience as they are targeted by the tortured spirit and this book is genuinely a page turner...not only could I not sleep after reading it, I didn't want to put it down."—*Lesbian Reading Room*

"*Gnarled Hollow* by Charlotte Greene is an awesome super-natural thriller that will terrify and entertain you for hours on end." —*The Lesbian Review*

"*Gnarled Hollow* is a creepy mystery story that had me gripped from the start. There was layer upon layer of mystery and plenty that I didn't see coming at all."—*Kitty Kat's Book Review Blog*

"Scared myself to death, but hauntingly beautiful! Had my heart beating at rapid speeds and my mind working overtime with this thought provoking story. Piecing together the mystery of *Gnarled Hollow* was both fascinating and scary as hell. It takes talent to put that much suspense and thrill into words that build the picture so vividly, painting descriptions that you can imagine perfectly and see as you read."—*LESBIreviewed*

"I really enjoyed this. This is the fifth book I have read by Greene and by far my favorite. It had some good twists and kept me in suspense until the end. In fact, I was a little sad when it ended. This would be a perfect book to read around Halloween time...I would absolutely recommend this to paranormal-crime/mystery fans. I really hope Greene takes the opportunity to write more books in similar genres. I would love to read them if she does. 5 stars."
—*Lez Review Books*

**A Palette for Love**

"The relationship really works between the main characters, and the sex is steamy but not over the top."—*Amanda's Reviews*

# By the Author

A Palette for Love

Love in Disaster

Canvas for Love

Pride and Porters

Gnarled Hollow

Legacy

On the Run

# ON THE RUN

*by*
## Charlotte Greene

2020

# ON THE RUN

ISBN 13: 978-1-63555-682-7

THIS TRADE PAPERBACK ORIGINAL IS PUBLISHED BY
BOLD STROKES BOOKS, INC.
P.O. BOX 249
VALLEY FALLS, NY 12185

FIRST EDITION: MARCH 2020

---

CREDITS
EDITOR: SHELLEY THRASHER
PRODUCTION DESIGN: STACIA SEAMAN
COVER DESIGN BY TAMMY SEIDICK

# Acknowledgments

Thanks, as always, to my lovely and supportive wife and family, and to my wonderful and dedicated editor, Shelley. I couldn't do any of this without all of you.

This is for my Grandma Lois, who always liked a good thriller.

# CHAPTER ONE

The heat, more than oppressive, was almost heavy on her skin. It had been bad enough inside the car, the weak air-conditioning going full-blast, but now, outside, the weight of the hot air almost hurt, pulling on her. The sunshine was also too much, even for her sunglasses—the bright, almost white light nearly blinding.

"Jesus Christ," Gwen whispered to herself. Why would anyone live here? Why would any human with the ability to leave submit themselves to this?

She was surprised to see that she could pay at the pump—she thought only cities had that kind of thing. She moved toward the back of the car, realizing as she did that she'd neglected to pop the little gas hatch from inside. At least I remembered to check which side it was on, she thought. The idea of having to move the car now was almost too much to imagine.

After she finally got the gas going, the little dial on the pump turned so slowly at first that she wasn't sure it was on. A few pennies finally appeared on the total line, then a few more. She put her ear near the pump and could hear something moving inside, almost groaning.

"I feel ya," she told it.

She sighed. Should she wait inside the little store? She knew it would have dusty, unappealing local snacks, a pruney old-timer with too much time on his hands, and a toilet in need of cleaning.

She dreaded the old-timer the most, the kind of questions he'd ask and the comments he'd make. She'd heard them before.

She waited another thirty seconds before realizing that if she stood out here much longer, she would fall over dead or catch on fire. Sleigh bells jangled as she opened the flimsy door, and she had to stop entirely to let her eyes adjust to the dim, almost murky light. It was cooler in here, but only a little—no air-conditioning in evidence.

"Hot enough for ya?" the old man asked.

She made herself chuckle and slid off her sunglasses. "It's a scorcher, all right."

"Sorry about the slow pump out there. Always acts up in the heat."

"No problem." Was it always acting up?

"Ladies' is in the back," he said, gesturing. "Though it's also the men's." He seemed to find this remark funny, and she forced a smile.

Still nearly blind, she almost walked into a stand of some local jerky, then staggered to the back of the little store between shelves of things she would never buy, even in her wildest, hungriest desperation.

The toilet, at least, wasn't what she'd expected. It was small, yes, smelly, yes, but the bowl had clearly been cleaned recently with a bottle of bleach sitting next to it, and she spotted a bonus: toilet paper.

"Jackpot."

Years on the job had trained her bladder to wait for hours and hours. She hadn't planned on going, so she had to sit there for a while before her body recognized what she was doing. This was good, she thought, washing her hands. Since she'd gone now, she wouldn't have to stop again anytime soon. And despite her terrible morning, she felt good, fresh. She might even make it until eight or nine tonight, if the gas held out that long. She checked her watch. Just after eleven, so maybe not. This tank had lasted only a little more than four hours.

Back in the store, eyes adjusted, she spent a few minutes

surveying the saleable goods, putting off the inevitable small talk as long as she could to give the gas pump time to finish its job. She didn't recognize most of the brands on the shelves—odd, cheap knock-offs with strange, punny names. Not that she would have bought any of it, brand-recognition or not. She didn't eat crap like this. Still, she needed to waste some more time, so she picked up a bag of bright-orange Cheese Grenades as if interested in purchasing them. The sell-by date was February 1, 1997—more than four months ago. She set them down as if changing her mind and surreptitiously wiped the dust off on her jeans.

The lone cooler was shuddering and loud, by all evidence on its last leg, and when she opened the door for the only appealing beverage inside—generic water—the air that escaped was barely cool. Knowing she could dawdle no longer, she carried a bottle up to the front counter, digging her wallet out of her back pocket.

"That all you need?" he asked.

"That's it," she said. If I needed anything else, I'd have it, she thought. She took her change, bracing herself for what would come next.

"Those are some interesting tattoos." His expression—suspicion, maybe disgust—suggested he thought they were anything but.

"Thanks."

"You have those done all at once or—"

"Over the years."

Luckily, he left it at that, but he couldn't seem to keep himself from talking, moving on to her next dreaded topic almost at once.

"So where you headed?"

"Phoenix," she lied.

He whistled. "Got a piece to go, then, huh?"

"Yes."

"You from there?"

She knew from his tone and from the careful, squinty way he was staring at her what he meant. The implication was the same no matter what city she said or who asked: she didn't look like she was from there. Some of this maybe wasn't his fault. Friends over the years had told her, gently or not, that with her mixed heritage, she didn't seem Asian or Hispanic, and not really a blend, either. She was something else, something unfamiliar. New people, especially older ones like this guy, always stared at her a beat too long, assessing her, trying to figure her out. Still, she wondered, not for the first time, where people like this man thought she *was* from.

"Yes," she said, once again bracing herself for the next question.

"Where are you *really* from? I mean, where were you born?"

"Phoenix."

"Really?"

She had to bite her tongue to keep from snapping at him. She was lying, yes, and she'd been in some version of this conversation so many times in her life she knew she shouldn't let it bother her, but it always did. It didn't matter where she was, whether at home or on the road, or who she was with—no one believed her. She was too foreign-looking for any of the places she mentioned.

"Really," she managed.

Some of her anger must have surfaced on her face, as the man held up his hands. "No offense."

She managed to nod and turned to leave.

"Have a nice day!" he called.

"No thanks to you," she said, loud enough for him to hear.

The heat was almost a relief after that exchange, and she paused outside, hands on her hips, breathing deeply to calm down. She was making progress. Six months ago, that guy wouldn't have gotten the snide, passive remark thrown over her shoulder. He would have been in trouble. Dr. Leichman would be proud of her for not kicking the shit out of him.

She smiled at the thought and pressed the slightly cool bottle of water to her forehead, realizing a moment too late that the dye from the coloring on the label had leaked onto her hand.

"Shit," she said, wiping her forehead. Her fingers came away smudged and blue.

Great. Now, on top of everything, she was probably marked

blue for life—all thanks to a two-dollar bottle of shitty, lukewarm water.

She heard the gas stop pumping as she approached the car and noticed for the first time the enormous markup on the gas here—almost a dollar higher than it had been in town this morning. Between the water and the gas, she'd dumped almost forty dollars on this one stop.

Still, in this case, she had no one to blame but herself. She hadn't been paying attention—too distracted from this morning. In fact, by the time she'd realized she needed gas, she couldn't have said how long the car's gas light had been on. Even if she'd been aware of the price of gasoline here, she'd been forced to stop at the first place she'd seen—this dump. God knew how far the next one would be. That's what you got from avoiding the interstate.

She opened the car door, and a blast of heat rolled out of it like a hot wind. She closed her eyes against it, rocking back a step, then forced herself to climb in. She immediately rolled the window down. If this morning was any indication, it would take the damn thing thirty minutes to cool down again inside. The car had no cup holders, so she threw the bottle onto the passenger's seat, unconcerned about the dye hurting the upholstery. No one would even notice in an old jalopy like this, and anyway, it wasn't her car. She used a tissue and a little spit to clean the blue off her forehead, surprised when it all rubbed away.

Doing some quick math, she thought she'd probably hit El Paso in an hour, maybe less. She'd meant to ask the guy inside how far it was, but judging from the time and her usual speed, she must be close. From there, she'd head north into New Mexico, and that would give her a little breathing room, a little time to make some choices. Getting out of Texas was the first step.

She turned the key and the engine failed to roll over, grinding and complaining. She had a hot flash of desperate panic, and then it finally sputtered to life. Her heart sputtered with relief, tight and painful in her chest. Her hands were shaking and sweaty when she threw the car into gear, and she spun the wheels, squealing out of the station and back into the little one-lane highway. She sped crazily for a few minutes and then forced herself to slow down, setting the car at a mile or two over the posted limit. No reason to get herself pulled over now—not when she was this close to escape.

The blacktop stretched out in front of her, doing that funny mirage thing in the distance. There was nothing to see on either side of the car, the sun too blinding, the landscape too bleak. A few long irrigation machines sat in brown fields, growing dirt, as far as she could tell. Only a lone bird in the sky or an occasional pickup truck indicated anything was alive out here. Finally, she spotted a mile-marker sign. El Paso: 47 miles.

"Thank Christ," she whispered, finally feeling a bit of tension seep out of her shoulders. Not far now.

Despite the hazy heat, she saw the figure long before she reached it. She even knew what to expect: a hitchhiker. She'd passed several of them already this morning. Broken men with ratty clothes, an occasional college kid with a patchy beard and a guitar. All of them held a cardboard sign with destinations, or pleas of some kind. She was usually going too fast to read them but would catch a word or two: *Help* or *Going To* and the name of some city. Not that she would ever consider stopping, not on her own, and not this close to the border, but it gave her something to think about for a while. She liked imagining their lives, what had brought them to stand on the side of the road, out here of all places. She'd been trained to make educated guesses about people from a single glance, and she was very good at it. Going by someone at 55 miles an hour didn't usually give her much to go on, but it passed the time.

This hitchhiker was different; she could see that right away. For one thing, the person was walking away from her. Usually this close, close enough to hear her car, they would turn around and hold up a sign. This one didn't. Also, she could see even from here that this person was slight, short even, and dressed inappropriately for walking along the side of the road.

It was a woman.

As her car roared past, she turned her head toward the woman outside, and their eyes met—it was less than a second, but it was enough. Gwen moved her gaze back to the road, unaccountably gripping the wheel, her knuckles so tight they drained of blood. What was that woman doing out there? Why on earth was someone like that walking alone on the side of the road? Where had she come from? Even with a glance, she'd seen that the woman's hair and clothes had been nice—formal even, as if she'd just walked out of the office for a cup of coffee. In fact, the only thing off about her had been her eyes. She'd looked terrified.

"Shit," she said, slamming the steering wheel with her hand. Already, her foot had moved to the brake, almost unconsciously, and her car gradually came to a stop as she pulled off to the side of the road. She was well beyond the woman, now a tiny speck in the rearview mirror, so she took a second to think. Was she really going to do this? Helping her would delay everything.

"Motherfucker," she said, and turned her car around.

She slowed down as she reached the woman, shooting past her slightly to turn back. This far from nowhere, she basically had the road to herself. The woman had stopped now to watch, and when Gwen got her car pointed in the right direction, the woman put up a thumb. She pulled over a few feet in front of her and rolled down the passenger window. The woman outside hesitated, still standing some ten feet behind the car, staring at her, but she finally walked over and leaned down, peering inside, her fingertips on the edge of the window.

"Hi," she said.

"Hi. You need a ride?"

The woman hesitated, her glance darting around as if searching for something. Up close, her clothes were even nicer than they'd seemed while driving past. She was like a fashion plate for a businesswoman in her dark-blue skirt-suit and stark-white silk shirt. She had a little matching purse tucked under one arm, the thin strap over her shoulder. Her blond hair was pulled up into a neat, stylish coif, and she wore tasteful, delicate makeup. She seemed fresh and clean despite the heat, only a thin sheen of sweat on her upper lip reflecting some slight discomfort. Finally, she stopped her nervous search of the car and rested her gaze on Gwen's face, assessing, reading it.

Finally, she nodded. "Yes. Please."

"Get in."

The woman continued to stare at her evenly for a moment longer, and then she stood up and opened the door. She was about to sit down when she spotted the water bottle on the seat.

Gwen grabbed it. "Sorry. Forgot that was there."

"No problem," the woman said. She was wearing low, white heels, and she climbed inside carefully, almost daintily. She buckled her seat belt and then sat there, eyes straight ahead, rigid and almost completely still. She'd consciously or unconsciously clutched her purse against her body with her right hand.

"You can have the bottle if you want it. Hasn't been opened yet." She offered the water to her.

The woman shook her head. "No, thanks."

Wary, careful, Gwen thought. Still scared, but smart.

"Where you headed?"

The woman didn't reply, still staring ahead, but finally her head turned toward her, eyes suspicious.

"Why?"

Gwen laughed. "So I know where to drop you off!"

Some of the tension left the woman's shoulders, and she gave a weak smile. "Oh, yes, of course. Sorry. Anywhere, for now. I need a telephone."

"We're almost to El Paso. That work for you?"

The woman nodded, staring at the road again.

She shook her head, baffled, and pulled back onto the road, not bothering to check her mirror or give a signal. Five minutes out here and nothing had passed them.

She let the silence stretch out for several minutes. She could see the woman in her peripheral vision, tense and still next to her. It's fine, she thought. I don't want to make small talk, either. Still, she couldn't help the almost overwhelming curiosity gnawing at her. Where had this woman come from? Nothing was out here—no houses, no towns, no businesses, nothing at all. She'd have passed the woman's car if she'd had a flat tire or engine problem, and she hadn't seen anything like that all morning. It was possible she'd come from a different road, a side road to this one, but Gwen didn't think so. The only other explanations were far-fetched. Either she'd come from one of those broken-down farms she'd passed—and one glance at her was enough to suggest otherwise—or someone had dropped her off there on the side of the road. Either way, it was strange. And that expression, the one she'd seen when she first drove past her, had been telling. If she herself had been walking along this road, with no water and no car, she'd have been desperate to flag down the first car or truck she'd seen, alone or not. This woman hadn't even tried. And she'd been scared—more than scared. She'd watched her as if expecting something or someone else.

Finally, too curious to stop herself, she asked, "You have a name?"

The woman continued to stare straight ahead, her shoulders, if anything, tensing even further. Finally, she nodded, her eyes flicking sideways to meet hers. "Yes. Abby."

"Nice to meet you, Abby. I'm Gwen."

Abby didn't reply. She sat there, still rigid, eyes still rooted to the road in front of them. This response didn't bother Gwen. She'd expected this exact behavior, so it simply confirmed what she'd already known. The longer she sat here with this woman, the more she knew about her. Abby wanted nothing to do with her, and she was giving nothing away. She was frightened, terrified of something, someone. She simply wanted to get somewhere safe, away from whatever or whoever it was. She'd lied about her name, but again, Gwen had expected that. Something was clearly up with this chick. But what?

## CHAPTER TWO

Just shy of the city limits, the diner was the kind of place built specifically for people passing by—an inordinately large parking lot for what amounted to a double-wide trailer with lots of glitzy chrome. If it had been nighttime, Gwen was certain those neon lights she saw would be blaring and visible for miles. Still, it was a strange establishment this far from any major highway or interstate. This time of day, neither lunch nor breakfast, only two other cars sat in the lot besides hers, likely the staff's.

"This do it for you?" Gwen asked, pulling in to a spot.

Abby, who had remained virtually motionless for the last thirty minutes, relaxed a little. Her eyes met Gwen's briefly, and she nodded. "Yes. Thank you."

She reached for the door handle, and Gwen, almost against her will, touched her shoulder to stop her. Abby flinched and Gwen held up her hands. "Sorry. Listen—I just wanted to know if you need any help."

Abby met her gaze, held it, and then shook her head. "No. I'm okay. Thanks." This was the greatest number of words she'd said so far, and Gwen realized she had a slight accent—Southern, maybe West Texas or moneyed Dallas. Cultured, classy.

"Do you need any money? For the phone call?" She heard herself make this offer with a shock of disbelief.

Abby continued to stare at her, clearly wary, suspicious. "No. I'll be okay. Really. Thanks again."

She didn't stop to hear Gwen's reply. She got out of the car and almost slammed the door closed behind her. Gwen watched her walk away and then inside the diner, disappearing behind the glare of the large windows.

"Leave it alone, Ramsey," Gwen told herself, putting the car in reverse. She pulled back and stopped, staring at the diner. Her fingers itched to throw it in gear and get the hell out of here. She was so close now. New Mexico wasn't far enough, but it was a start, and it would be better than staying here. And anyway, who was this woman to her? What difference did it make if she helped her or not? She clearly had problems—anyone could see that. Getting involved was silly.

But she couldn't help remembering that first sight of her—that terror in her eyes. Who or what was Abby afraid of? Was she running from something? Was someone after her? Could Gwen live with herself if this woman got hurt, all because she was in a hurry?

"Goddamn it," she said, and reparked the car.

It was dim and blissfully cool inside, despite the enormous windows. The glass must have been treated with some kind of reflective surfacing, as the sunlight was markedly dampened inside. The usual long counter had empty, orange seats, as did the three booths to the left along the windowed wall. The lone waitress was dressed in a bright but dirty pink uniform, a little orange cap sitting jauntily on her bleached platinum hair.

"Sit wherever you like, hon," she said. She was, of course, chewing gum.

"I'm looking for—" Gwen said, finally spotting the phone booth at the back. Abby was inside, her back to the room. "Okay, thanks. I'll take a coffee, please."

"Sure thing. Menus are on the table."

Gwen took a seat in a booth, facing the phone, watching as Abby made her call. It was obvious, even from out here, that things weren't going well. Abby kept hanging up the phone, picking it up, and redialing. She wasn't putting any money in, which meant a collect call, so either she wasn't getting through or whomever she was calling wasn't accepting the charges. She kept trying, however, long after the waitress had brought the coffee and Gwen had finished her first cup. After the fifth or sixth try she'd witnessed, she saw Abby hang up and simply stand there, her shoulders sagging. She kept her hand on the phone, as if in deep thought, perhaps deciding whom to call next. She finally let it go and turned around, opening the little glass door. She spotted Gwen and stopped completely, eyes narrowing.

Gwen gestured across from her. "Have a seat. Let me buy you lunch."

Abby opened her mouth as if to protest and then, seeing the waitress watching them, nodded and joined Gwen in the booth. She sat there staring at Gwen for a long moment, her green eyes puzzled and wary.

Gwen tried to look reassuring. "Okay, Abby. I'm going to make this really easy on you. I'm going to buy you lunch because I want to help you. You don't have to tell me anything, we don't even have to talk, but you're going to let me buy you something to eat. After that, I'll take you someplace—anyplace. Better than this, anyway, where you can get a ride or something. I'll even get you a bus ticket, if you need one."

Abby said nothing.

The waitress appeared at the side of the table, a little notebook in hand. "What'll you have?"

Gwen glanced up at her. "Egg-white omelet, mushrooms, onions, no butter. Plain wheat toast."

Abby was silent a few seconds longer, and then, still holding Gwen's gaze, she said, "Double cheeseburger, onions, pickles, lettuce, and tomato. A full order of fries and onion rings. Ranch dressing. Large Coke. A slice, no, *two* slices of pie—cherry. Both with ice cream."

Gwen couldn't help but smile at the order, but she said nothing, waiting for the waitress to walk away. Soon Abby rested her arms on the table, eyes slit, brows creased.

"Why are you helping me?" she asked.

Gwen shrugged. "Maybe I'm a Good Samaritan."

Abby shook her head. "No. I don't think so."

Gwen laughed. "Why not? Don't I look like one?"

Abby gave her first genuine smile. "No. Sorry, but you don't."

"What do I look like, then?"

Abby surveyed her up and down, her eyes resting on Gwen's exposed forearms, clearly taking in the extent of her tattoos, which left very little natural skin exposed. Gwen had lost a great deal of weight recently on her last job, and her wrists and hands seemed scrawny, even to her. Abby's gaze shifted upward, taking in her visible clothing. Gwen was wearing an old, black band T-shirt, fraying at the sleeves and neck. Finally, Abby stared at her face again. Gwen had several piercings, both ears all the way up the edges, her nose and eyebrow, and she always wore a lot of black eyeliner. Her head was shaved on one side, the other side a bobbed mess of loose black curls that reached past her ears and the back of her neck.

Abby peered outside at the car and then at Gwen. "I don't know what you look like. I know one thing, though—that's not your car."

Gwen was surprised. She was right. "What makes you think that?"

Abby lifted one shoulder. "What difference does that make? It's not, is it?"

Gwen hesitated, and then, realizing she had no reason to lie, shook her head. "No. It's not."

"Did you steal it?"

Gwen laughed. "So that's what you think I am? A car thief?"

Abby hesitated and then shrugged. "No...I didn't say that. I don't know what you are. But you're not a Good Samaritan. So again—why help me?"

Gwen didn't know the answer. Almost every instinct had told her to keep driving, to mind her own business. She had her own problems and places to be. Well, places *not* to be, at any rate. Yet she'd turned around to pick her up. She'd had an easy out twenty minutes ago, too. She'd seen Abby safely here. It wasn't much of a place, but it had a phone, food, drink. She could have kept going. But here she was. So why *was* she doing this?

Gwen sighed. "I've been in a tight spot myself. More than

once. I would have done almost anything to get out of certain situations in the past, but I couldn't. I didn't have anyone to help me, anyone to call. Let's just say I know what it's like and leave it at that."

"What makes you think I need your help?"

Gwen laughed and counted off on her fingers. "I'm driving. I see a) a woman, dressed like," she gestured at Abby, "and b) walking along the side of the road, miles and miles from anywhere with c) no water in million-degree weather. A classic damsel in distress. What else could I do?"

"That still doesn't explain this," Abby replied, gesturing at the menu. "Why do this?"

Gwen bent her head closer, motioning for Annie to do the same. "Maybe this is for me. I wanted to buy a pretty woman something to eat."

Abby flushed, and Gwen sat back, laughing. The waitress appeared again, setting down Abby's Coke and refilling Gwen's coffee.

"Food's almost ready," she said, walking away.

Gwen touched her hand. "I'm sorry, Abby. I didn't mean to embarrass you. Have to get my kicks somehow. I'm just fucking with you." She grinned. "Sort of."

Abby was still flustered, her complexion an unflattering, mottled pink. She was one of those pale sorts whose skin gave away every emotion. Even her eyes were pale—an almost colorless green. Her brows and hair were almost white, that light platinum blond so many people tried to mimic, their waitress among them.

"Hey," Gwen said, tapping the table lightly. "Why don't we forget about motivations? You don't have to believe me, but I really want to help. Call it whatever you like, but that's all there is to it."

Abby frowned and then nodded. "Okay. I believe you. I think."

Gwen laughed again. "You *think*. Okay. That's good enough for me."

The food was delivered then, Gwen's modest lunch and Abby's mountainous feast. Abby dug in, eating as if the food might be taken away. The sight of her ravenous hunger made Gwen forget her own meal. Abby was completely absorbed in hers, stuffing in as much as she could with each bite. The enormous hamburger, which appeared to be too big for her hands and mouth, disappeared in perhaps five bites. She almost swallowed the onion rings and fries, doused liberally in the thick, white ranch dressing, whole. Next came the dessert, each slice of pie shoveled into her mouth in huge bites, the ice cream still so fresh it hadn't had time to melt. Gwen was holding her own utensils, lightly, not doing anything but watch this bizarre display, so astonished she almost forgot to breathe. Finally, Abby finished eating, pushing away her plates, all empty, all sparkling clean, her expression calm, unembarrassed.

She noticed Gwen's open-mouth stare and frowned. "What? Aren't you hungry? Do I have food on my face or something?" She wiped at her lips with her napkin.

Gwen shook her head as if clearing it, chuckling. "Not exactly, but you do have half a cow over there on the side of your cheek. Holy shit! I've never seen anyone eat like that. Where did you put it all? You have a wooden leg or something?" She glanced under the table at Gwen's slim, exposed legs.

Abby smiled again. "I didn't know there was a dollar limit on your charity. It's been a long time since I—" Her mouth snapped closed, and her expression grew suddenly wary again. "Never mind."

Gwen noted the slip but pretended she hadn't heard it. "Do you need something else? We could ask them to butcher a pig for you. Beyond that, they might have to call in delivery."

The smile returned, and Abby threw her napkin at Gwen. "Fuck you."

"Christ! It was like watching the lions at the zoo."

Abby giggled a little, and then, as if remembering something, she sobered almost at once.

"Can we get out of here? I mean, if you're not going to eat that?"

Again, Gwen noted the change but didn't remark on it. She frowned down at her meal, now unappealing and cold. "No. I'm done. Let's get rolling."

They slid out of the booth in unison and walked over to the old-fashioned cash register. The waitress met them there, seeming surprised.

"Finished already?" she asked, her glance sliding over to their booth and the piles of empty plates. Abby had eaten everything in less than five minutes.

"Yep—we gotta get heading," Gwen replied.

"You two ladies…" The waitress paused, taking them both in and seemingly unsure of how to finish. "Going far?"

"Phoenix," Gwen said.

"Something for…work?" the waitress said, clearly flummoxed.

"Family reunion," Abby said.

This explanation seemed to puzzle the woman even further, and Gwen had to bite the inside of her mouth to keep from braying with laughter. She gave the waitress an extra-generous tip and almost raced out the door, bursting into laughter the second they were both outside, back in the broiling heat.

Abby was smiling at her, clearly pleased with herself, and Gwen slapped her shoulder, lightly.

"That was good," she said, wiping her eyes. "'Family reunion.' I'll have to remember that one."

"Shall we?" Abby said, gesturing at the car.

Still chuckling, Gwen unlocked Abby's door before going around to the driver's side. Abby had unlocked it for her, and she climbed in, rolling down the window again at once.

"Airport? Bus station?" she asked.

"The bus station would be perfect. You don't have to buy the ticket, though. My friend will wire me the money once I get in touch with her. That's who I was trying to call earlier."

Gwen shrugged. "It's really not a big deal. I could save you a step, and you could send me the money later. I'll give you an address." She didn't have one right now, but Abby didn't need to know that.

Abby shook her head. "No—really. My friend will be happy to help."

"Okay—if you're sure," Gwen said, knowing already that she'd buy the ticket anyway. No way would she leave Abby stranded in a bus station. She'd been stuck in one herself a time or two, and that was no place to leave anyone, let alone a pretty woman, on her own. "Shit," Gwen said. "I forgot to ask where the station is. Let me go inside and ask that waitress." She moved to open the door, but Abby gripped her arm.

"Oh, don't bother. I know how to get there."

"You do?"

Abby hesitated and then nodded. "I used to live here in El Paso. I can tell you where to go."

Gwen nodded, turning the ignition and pulling back onto the road. They drove in silence for a few more minutes, the city gradually building up on either side of the road—houses, stores, a couple of schools. They were entering from the east, relatively far from the interstate, and this part of the city seemed nicer than Gwen remembered from her trips through town farther south—suburban, clean. Patriotic bunting hung on the light poles, ready for the Fourth of July next week. The road here looked as if they'd been recently swept and cleaned, perhaps in preparation for the inevitable parade.

A mile or so beyond this, she saw flashing lights and a long line of cars blocking their one-lane road. She slowed to stop behind the last car, cursing and craning her neck and head outside of the car to try to see what was happening. A dozen or so cars had stopped in front of them, but she could see very little.

"I don't think it's an accident," she reported, squinting her eyes. "I see some policemen and a wooden barrier across the road. I think they're talking to the driver at the front. Maybe a pipe burst or something." She watched briefly. "Nope! They let him through. It must be some kind of sting operation. Maybe immigration or drunk driving or something."

"Gwen?"

"Hmmm?" She was still trying to see, her head still outside against the window.

"Gwen? Look at me."

"What?"

Gwen's heart clenched, and she went cold. Abby was holding a gun, low in her lap, pointed at her.

"Gwen—don't panic. Just turn around, right now, and I won't hurt you."

## Chapter Three

Gwen swallowed, her heart pounding so hard it seemed to pulse in her ears. She broke out in a light sweat, and her breathing felt labored and tight in her chest.

"Wh-what's that for?" she asked, almost whispering.

Abby shook her head. "No time to explain. Turn around. Now. I don't want to have to hurt you."

Gwen licked her lips, glancing back at the car in front of her, which had pulled up a bit. She heard a honk behind her and jumped. Abby didn't flinch. She kept the gun steady, her eyes rooted on Gwen's face.

"Don't you think the police will notice?" Gwen asked. "I mean, it will be really obvious if I turn around now."

Abby shook her head. "It doesn't matter. We'll have to risk it."

Gwen was trembling now, but her heart rate had slowed a little, and it was already easier to breathe. She took a deep lungful of air and let it out, putting her hands on the steering wheel. She had two options. She could call Abby's bluff and start honking to get someone's attention, maybe even drive toward the roadblock. If Abby wasn't bluffing, it might surprise her enough to forget about pulling the trigger. She almost shook her head. No—it wasn't worth the risk.

The car behind her honked again to get her to move, and she did a little, cranking the wheel as hard as she could to the left to turn around. The car was fairly large—an old sedan—so she couldn't quite make the turn on this narrow road. She was forced to back up a little but managed to swing into the lane going in reverse. Her heart was racing again, and she could hear the squawk of a bullhorn dimly behind them. Someone was yelling at them through it, but she couldn't make out the words.

Abby had turned almost entirely around and slapped the back of the seat, hard. "Drive! Drive!"

Gwen peeled away, tires squealing, some small part of her brain aware of the stunned shock on the face of the driver of the car that had honked at her. Then she was driving, fast, racing back the way they came. Flashing lights began to follow her, so she pushed the gas pedal all the way to the floor. The old car surged ahead, throwing her back in her seat, and she saw Abby slip and almost slide over the top of their bench seat.

"They're coming! Faster!" Abby screamed.

Almost as if she'd willed it to happen, the car caught its stride, and Gwen watched the speedometer slide farther and farther up—80, 90, then 100 miles an hour, leveling off shy of 110 before the car started to shimmy in protest. The landscape whipped by outside, the houses and schools and small business at the outer edges of the city already falling behind.

Abby dropped back in her seat as the road dipped a little, throwing both of them up in the air for a moment as the car hopped. The bump back down was hard, and Gwen's mouth filled with blood as she bit her tongue.

"There!" Abby said, pointing at a road to the left. "Turn there!"

Gwen barely had time to hit the brakes, once again wrenching the wheel as hard as she could. For a second, she was sure the car would tip and felt a strange lifting on the right as they sailed onto the side road, the vehicle squealing and grinding with the smell of burning rubber. Gwen had to wrestle the car the last few feet over some dried grass before she pulled onto the side road.

"They'll see the tire marks," she said as she managed to straighten the car, once again speeding up.

"That's okay—we still have a few extra seconds. Look for somewhere to hide—something we can drive behind."

Gwen immediately saw what she meant. They were in a warehouse district. All the buildings here were enormous, almost like airplane hangars, windowless with blank white or yellow siding.

"There," Abby said, pointing at a small parking lot in front of the warehouse and a driveway on the far side, obviously intended for semi-trucks.

"Kind of close, isn't it?"

"They'll catch up any second." She sounded almost breathless.

Gwen turned into the little parking lot in front of the warehouse and drove around the side and to the back as quickly as she could. A raised loading dock stood here, blissfully empty—no trucks, no people. She pulled to a stop next to it, her knuckles white on the steering wheel.

Seconds later, they heard the police sirens rush by on the road in front of the warehouse, one after another, so fast the sound was dragged off almost as soon as they heard it. Several of them passed, and then there was silence except for their breathing and the ticking engine.

She turned toward Abby to grab her gun, but Abby was quicker, the gun already pointed at her.

"Goddamn it!" Gwen shouted. "What in the actual fuck?"

Abby's eyes were hard, the pupils so dilated they were almost black. Still, the gun was steady, unwavering, and pointed directly at her chest.

"I'm sorry, Gwen. I tried to get you to leave me alone. You had your chance at the diner. You should have left me there."

"Well, I'm doing that now," she said, reaching for the door handle. "You can have the car. I'll just get out now."

"No." Abby's voice was even and unemotional. "Don't move."

"What? Why not? I'll get out and walk away. I won't tell anyone where you are."

Abby shook her head. "Sorry. I can't take that risk. And anyway, they've seen this car now. I'll need something else."

"So go out and get something yourself!"

Abby frowned. "On foot? You must be kidding me. They'll pick me up right away."

"That's how I found you. What was your plan then?"

She didn't immediately respond. "I didn't really have one. I do now."

"And how is that my concern?"

Abby gestured slightly with her gun. "Because I say it is."

Gwen continued to glare at her, an almost overwhelming rage replacing her fright. She was slipping into that dark, angry place that had gotten her in so much trouble before—the kind of trouble that got her fired from so many jobs over the years. Soon, she would lose control, gun or no gun. Once that darkness took over, she wouldn't be able to stop it.

She closed her eyes and clenched her fists, tightening and untightening them, and taking deep breaths. She tried to remember some of the exercises Dr. Leichman had taught her. She was supposed to fix her mind on something else—something benign, something completely removed from the situation she was in. She chose her usual anchor and started repeating it to herself under her breath.

"Golden retriever puppies. Golden retriever puppies. Golden retriever puppies..." Already, she started to relax and her blood began to cool.

"What are you doing?" Abby asked.

Gwen opened her eyes, pleased to see that Abby's façade had slipped a little. She looked alarmed, almost scared.

"I'm trying not to beat the living shit out of you."

Abby moved back a little, almost a flinch. Gwen was glad to see this, and her anger cooled into a low simmer.

She held her hands up. "What do you want from me, Abby? Why can't you just let me go? Taking a hostage isn't going to help you."

Abby's head tilted slightly. "How will they know you're my hostage? They might think I have an accomplice."

Gwen tightened her jaw, almost biting her sore tongue to keep from shouting. "They haven't seen me yet. They don't know who I am or even if you're alone. Let me go, and we can call it quits. I won't say anything, even if I'm picked up. I swear it."

Abby's shoulders rose. "Like I said, I can't risk it. All I need is a car. You help me get one, and I'll drop you off somewhere." She gave her a sly smile. "A bus station, maybe."

"You asshole," Gwen said, almost laughing. She sat back in her seat, eyes closed, trying to think. Her anger was mostly gone, but her mind was still whirling, befuddled. She tried to calm herself, tried to focus, but the events of the last ten minutes had unsettled her too much. She couldn't think of a way out.

She sighed. "Fine. I'll help you. But we need to do this now."

Abby's eyebrows shot up. "Now? Can't we wait until dark?"

"It has to be now. Pretty soon they'll get a helicopter out here, and then dogs, and this whole place will be crawling with people looking for you. We won't have anywhere to hide." She paused. "I think I remember seeing a couple of trucks in front of a building back the way we came. We'll have to sneak over there, from behind, but I should be able to get one started, as long as they're as old as I think they are."

Abby's lips lifted in a slight grin. "I thought you said you weren't a car thief."

Gwen couldn't help but grin back. "I'm not."

"But you know how to steal cars?"

Gwen nodded. "I'll need my shit in the trunk to get the door open."

Abby's eyes grew wary again, but she nodded. "Okay, but let me check it out first."

"I don't have a gun, if that's what you're worried about," Gwen said. At least not one she'll see, she thought.

"Fine. Let's get going, then."

"Not before we wipe it down in here. They might think they know who was in here, but we don't have to give it to them so easy."

They spent the next few minutes trying to erase every fingerprint in the car. They cleaned every surface—the dashboard, the inside handles and window levers, the seat belts, and the bottle of water. Satisfied, she stopped, and Abby watched her for further directions.

Gwen pointed. "Grab that map—we'll need it. Don't forget to

do the outside handle and the area around the window on your way out."

They both got out of the car, and Gwen saw her chance. Abby was on the far side, and Gwen could run away now. Abby might try to shoot at her, but with a handgun like that, her accuracy wouldn't be very good. Even if she only managed ten or twenty feet before the bullets started, her chances were good. A smart, experienced criminal would have slid out after her instead of getting out on her side, kept her gun on her. Abby wasn't stupid, so far as Gwen could tell, so that meant she hadn't done something like this before. She was clearly practiced with her gun, but not in that way.

The chance passed almost as soon as she recognized it, and she sighed, joining Abby at the back of the car. She popped the trunk. She had left a sizeable leather messenger bag inside. Abby pulled it out, closed the trunk again, and then rooted around in it, glancing up at Gwen now and again as she did.

"What is all that stuff?" Abby said, handing her the bag.

"Some clothes. Tools."

"For stealing cars?"

Gwen nodded. "And other things."

They both flinched at the sound of sirens. They weren't far away.

Abby gestured with her gun. "Let's go."

Gwen walked in front, the strap to her bag slung across her chest. A little secret compartment at the bottom of the bag held her own gun. She'd been searched before, and no one ever found it—you had to know where to look. She hoped she wouldn't have to use it, but knowing it was there comforted her. She began to feel like herself again.

After taking a quick peek out front, they walked along the back of four large warehouses. Two of them had fences, but they managed to skirt the back of the fences with little trouble, finally reaching the fourth, which was designed very much like the one where they'd left the car. They made their way up the slanted driveway to the front, sticking close to the side of the building to survey the scene. Three trucks some fifty feet away were parked right next to each other. The safest bet would be to open the far one. The other truck would block the driver's side door and would be hidden from the road for the most part, especially if they stayed low to the ground.

"It's an old Chevy—1988, '89 maybe," she told Abby. "I should be able to get it started, no problem. Let's go."

Almost crawling on all fours, they moved away from the safety of their hiding spot, finally reaching the space between the trucks after a long, breathless scurry. They sat there on their heels, breathing heavily before Gwen opened her satchel. She gave them each a pair of latex gloves and pulled out her set of lock picks. She was practiced at this, but her nerves were slowing her a bit, and it took her several minutes to finally trip the lock. While she worked, Abby kept her gun leveled at her back. Gwen couldn't see behind her, but she knew it was there.

The door finally open, she hissed at Abby, "Slide in to the far side, and stay down."

Abby looked scared, the whites of her eyes visible all around the green. She hesitated for a moment and nodded. Gwen followed her inside, closing the door after them. The bench seat was fairly high, but she still had to contort herself to reach under the steering column to keep her head from view. Abby had chosen to squish herself into the footwell on the passenger's side, propping her back against the passenger door, gun pointed her way.

Gwen struggled to wrench the plastic panel off the column but eventually had to use a hammer and a flat-head screwdriver to pry it off before it finally popped out. Three covered bundles of wires fell out. She found the one connected to the steering wheel and pulled off the cap that held that bundle of wires together. She got her wire strippers out, exposed about an inch and half of the battery wires, and twisted them together. The radio blared on, and they both jumped, the wail of country music filling the truck's cabin. Gwen flipped it off and chuckled nervously.

"Step one."

Abby nodded, looking tense and scared.

"Next part's kind of dangerous," Gwen explained. "You might want to cover your eyes."

Abby didn't, still staring at her, wary now.

"Your funeral," Gwen said. "If I fuck this up, just make sure you push me away from the wires, okay? No need to catch on fire."

She stripped the starter wires and held her face as far away as she could.

"Ready?"

Abby nodded.

She touched them together, throwing off a few sparks, and the truck roared to life. She used her foot to rev the engine a couple of times, and then it settled into a comfortable, even rumble.

"Okay," she said, scooting back on the seat. She motioned for Abby to do the same. "Let's get out of here." She let go of the starter wires and threw the truck in reverse. This was the part she'd feared the most. She'd been almost certain she could get it started, but getting back on the road put them in police crosshairs again. She wasn't sure she was up for another car chase.

They were in luck. Wherever the police were now, she couldn't see them, and she pulled back onto the road, driving back to the highway they'd turned off. They sat at the stop sign for a long time, engine rumbling comfortably.

"So where to, Boss?" she finally asked.

Abby pointed left, away from the city. "We'll have to backtrack a little, I guess, try to get north some other way."

"Don't you think they'll have road blocks? I mean, no matter where we go?"

Abby nodded. "Yes. But maybe there's another, smaller road somewhere. I don't know. Maybe something they didn't bother with. They can't cover them all."

"We won't have much time. They'll probably figure out we stole this truck pretty soon. Within the day, at best."

Abby nodded, her expression grave. "Then we'll have to get out of here before then."

Gwen lifted her shoulders and pulled back onto the highway, driving south and west, away from the city. She knew not to continue what was clearly a pointless conversation. Abby could think whatever she wanted, but Gwen knew better. If the police had one road blocked, they'd have them all. Abby was trapped now, no matter how much she hoped differently.

And Gwen was trapped with her.

## CHAPTER FOUR

While it was blissfully cool in here, almost cold, the room was disgusting. If someone were in the mood to be generous, the motel might have been described as grungy, but it hovered near filthy. Musty with old cigarette smoke, the odor reminded Gwen of a bar on a Sunday morning. The beds didn't seem to have any bugs, but Gwen couldn't be sure the carpet didn't have fleas. Once or twice, she thought she saw something moving on the floor—a scurrying, furtive something that disappeared when she looked directly at it. The bedspreads had cigarette burns, and dust covered every surface. The carpet was stained a mysterious brown in several places, including one entire corner of the little room. Gwen wondered how many people had bled there. You got what you paid for in a place that took cash and didn't ask questions.

"You take me to such lovely places," she said to Abby.

Abby didn't reply, still standing at the window, peering outside through the partially closed curtain. She had angled herself in such a way that she could watch outside and still see Gwen with her peripheral vision. She was clearly smart enough not to turn her back to her. Still, Gwen thought she might be able to rush her if she moved quickly enough.

The afternoon had been long and hot. They'd traded the truck for a smaller, even older car almost immediately. Abby had hoped that getting a new car would throw the police off the scent. Gwen didn't bother explaining that keeping the truck longer might have been the smarter move. If an everyday person realized their car had been stolen, they were much more likely to call the police quicker than a business, like the warehouse where they'd gotten the truck. No one had been there, after all, so who knew how long it would take before someone called it in. Most likely, someone had already reported the little car missing. Abby had made her switch license plates a while ago, but someone would eventually figure it out.

Despite driving for hours, they were almost back where they'd started. Every single road into the city they'd tried had been blocked. They'd even attempted to go south instead of north, Abby hoping they could head east for a while and then north some other way, but those roads had been blocked, too. El Paso was effectively surrounded.

This kind of surveillance couldn't last very long. Eventually some of these blockades would have to be called off, and then all of them, but that didn't mean Gwen knew which ones would be taken down first or when. Even if she did, she wasn't sure she'd tell Abby. She shivered and pulled her jacket out of her leather bag, slipping it on. That was the thing about air-conditioning. It was almost always either dysfunctional or too much.

"Christ, Abby, give it a rest," she finally said, her patience so thin she almost shouted.

Abby frowned at her, letting the curtain drop closed. "I'm just looking."

"Why? What good does it do?"

"We might have a minute or two to leave if the cops decide to check this place out."

"You're fooling yourself. If they stop here, you're as good as caught. That piece-of-shit car couldn't do 50 miles an hour on a good day, even if we managed to get in and drive away." She gestured at the other bed. "Anyway, you're defeating the purpose of stopping. Take a load off so we can make some kind of plan."

Abby hesitated and then approached the second bed, grimacing at it before sitting down, perching on the absolute edge of the dirty duvet.

"You have any ideas?" she asked.

"We need some kind of farm road—something that wouldn't be on a ninety-nine-cent map from the gas station."

"How are we supposed to find that?"

Gwen held up her hands. "Exactly—we can't."

Abby's frown deepened. "So why bring it up?"

"I'm telling you the reality here. Maybe we could ask someone, pay someone for that information, but this isn't my town. It's yours. Don't you know someone you could ask?"

Abby started to shake her head and then stopped, her brows lowering. "Well, maybe. I guess it wouldn't hurt to try."

"Can you call them?"

"Is there a phone book?"

"Yes. With the Bible."

Abby scooted over, apparently forgetting the filth, and pulled out the thick set of White Pages from the little drawer between the beds.

"I'm gonna take a shower. I stink," Gwen said, standing up and grabbing her leather bag.

"Leave that," Abby said, gesturing with her gun.

Gwen looked down at the bag as if surprised to see it in her hand, and set it down without arguing. It had been worth a try.

The bathroom was grim, much worse than the bedroom. Clots of dark hair surrounded the drain in the tub, wiry tufts of it on the floor. The bathmat was moldy, dark instead of what might have once been yellow, and the towels weren't much better. Gwen's gorge rose a little, and she swallowed against it, disgusted with herself for being so squeamish. She'd seen worse.

The two washrags and towels were so threadbare and starched, they might have been made from bedsheets. She found two tiny bars of soap—both of them wrapped with labels from other hotels—and used one of them to give the bottom of the tub a quick scrub and rinsed it with one of the plastic cups.

She could hear the murmur of Abby's voice in the bedroom, so she stood up and put her ear to the door. The door was so flimsy she could have punched a hole through it, so she was able to hear the tail end of the conversation clearly.

"No. I haven't talked to him since his last visit," Abby said. A long pause. "I'm not sure it's safe to call him. I wasn't even sure I should call you. I'd have to try to catch him in person." Another pause. "Okay. I'll think about it. What do you think I should do about her?"

Gwen put her ear flush with the door.

"I can't do that. I won't," Abby finally said. Another long pause. "You can't ask me to do that, so stop suggesting it. Maybe I can…leave her here." Silence. "Stop saying that. I won't, do you hear me? I won't do it!"

Gwen flung the door open and ran toward Abby. Abby had her back to the door, so Gwen had a couple of extra, crucial seconds, long enough to launch herself at her and tackle her. She pinned Abby to the floor between the beds, her knees on Abby's elbows. Abby had managed to continue holding the gun, and Gwen smashed at the back of her right hand with a fist until she screamed and let go. She continued to try to buck Gwen off her back until Gwen put the gun to the back of her head. She stilled.

Gwen picked up the phone with her other hand.

"Hello? Hello?" a woman was saying.

Gwen hung up on her. She took a few deep breaths to calm down. Killing her was not the right move.

"Listen to me, Abby, and listen carefully." She kept her voice low and uninflected. "I'm going to stand up and sit down on the bed. Once I do that, I want you to stand and then sit across from me on the other bed. Don't try anything—just do as I say. Do you understand?"

Abby was still a moment longer, and then she nodded.

"Good."

Gwen got up and sat down, keeping the gun on Abby as she clambered up onto her hands and knees and then rose. She sat across from Gwen, her face pale and her eyes brimming with tears.

Gwen continued to stare at her, so angry her body thrummed with suppressed rage. "The only reason, and I mean *only* reason you're alive right now, is because of what I heard." She lifted her chin at the phone. "That woman told you to kill me, right?"

Abby was crying now, quietly, tears sliding down her cheeks. She nodded.

"But you refused?"

She nodded again.

"Why?"

Abby seemed taken aback. "What do you mean?"

"Why did you refuse to kill me?"

"Because I'm not a murderer."

"But she is? The woman on the phone?"

Abby hesitated and then nodded once more.

"So if you're not a murderer, what are you? Why is half the state of Texas out looking for you?"

Abby opened her mouth to reply and then closed it, licking her lips. "Turn on the TV. You'll see soon enough."

Gwen frowned, seeing, for the first time, the little clunky set sitting in the corner of the room. She gestured at it with the gun. "You turn it on. Stand over there by the set so I can keep an eye on you."

After a pause, Abby obeyed, keeping her hands slightly raised and away from her sides. She approached the set and then knelt next to it to switch the little knob. It took a few seconds for the TV to warm up, showing snow, and Abby turned the little knob for the channels until something finally appeared on the screen. A commercial was on, and Abby almost switched channels before the programming resumed. A male and female anchor dominated the screen, their faces grim.

The man spoke first. "Welcome back. We interrupt your regularly scheduled programming to bring you this special report. The El Paso County Sheriff's Office is working with the Texas Department of Public Safety to apprehend an at-large convict. Anne Pierce escaped from the Cornudas Federal Correctional Institution this morning."

Several pictures of Abby—Anne—appeared on screen. Other pictures of her followed her mug shot at various times, smiling and laughing, the other people in those photos blocked or cut out. The screen then went to half screen, one side a speaking reporter, the other Abby/Anne's mugshot. A bright-yellow phone number for the sheriff's department dominated the bottom of the screen. The woman spoke next.

"Details regarding her escape have not been shared with us at this time, but there is some speculation about inside collusion with various members of the prison staff."

The man's face replaced the female reporter's. "Anne Pierce was the ringleader of a criminal organization convicted of bank fraud here in El Paso. At the time of their trial, it was revealed that they had defrauded the El Paso Credit Union of millions of dollars."

The woman again: "As the bank manager of one branch of the credit union, Anne created several false accounts for her co-conspirators and authorized loans for hundreds of thousands of dollars in their accounts. The money was then transferred offshore and never repaid. An audit by the IRS and a sting with the FBI finally caught up with most of the criminals, including Ms. Pierce, though it was believed then and now that others were involved that have yet to be caught. Police officials suspect they might have aided in today's breakout."

The man: "Anne Pierce is believed to be armed, and after a theft at the prison by a female staff member last week, the sheriff's department believes that she has obtained street clothing that might make it difficult to recognize her. Anne is five foot two, about a hundred pounds, blond, with light-colored green eyes."

The woman: "Police officials believe she will head here, to El Paso, and an incident at a police barricade early this afternoon suggests that she might have arrived already. Be on the lookout for the woman you see here on the right of your screen, and call the number at the bottom of the screen immediately. Do not, I repeat, do not attempt to approach or detain her on you own. Simply call this number if you spot her. Information leading to her apprehension will result in a substantial reward."

"You can turn it off now," Gwen said, gesturing with the gun.

Anne had watched with her back to Gwen, and she knelt and

turned it off. She stood up again and faced Gwen, her cheeks stained with tears. She was clearly terrified, and Gwen remembered that same look in her eyes when she first saw her standing on the side of the road this morning. Had that actually been today? It seemed like ages, now. She remembered something else, then. Some miles before the gas station, she had noticed one of those signs warning drivers not to pick up hitchhikers—something about a prison or federal penitentiary. She'd forgotten all about it until now.

Gwen pointed at the other bed. "Sit down, Anne."

She came back slowly, her hands slightly up and away from herself again, and sat down across from Gwen.

"It's Annie," she said.

"Clever," Gwen said. It was smart, when taking a false name, to assume one as close to your own as possible. She'd done it herself many times.

"Bank fraud, huh?"

Annie nodded.

"Millions of dollars, they said?"

She nodded again.

"How much time did you get?"

"Thirty to life."

"Christ! I would have tried to escape, too. But I'd have had a car waiting, at least. Were you on foot the whole time?"

"No. I had a ride at first, but…" She sighed and shook her head. "The woman they paid to get me out got cold feet and left me there on the side of the road. Anyway, it doesn't matter."

Annie had physically collapsed in on herself. Her shoulders were slouched so far down that her arms, crossed tightly over her chest, were almost resting on her lap. She was the picture of misery.

"So what was your plan after that?" Gwen asked. "Why come here? Why not head east, toward Dallas or someplace far away?"

Annie's eyes, which had been frightened and tearful, suddenly looked hard again. Her posture changed, and she sat up straighter, her arms relaxing at her sides. She didn't reply.

"Ah," said Gwen, laughing. "You have something here, don't you? Some of that money, maybe?"

Again, she didn't respond.

Gwen frowned at her. "Listen—right now, you've given me no motivation to help you. You've held me up long enough. What's to stop me from calling you in right now? That reporter said there would be a 'substantial reward.' Can you top that or not?"

Annie still didn't reply.

Gwen shrugged and reached for the phone, and Annie lashed out, grabbing her wrist to stop her.

"Wait." She licked her lips. "Yes. There is money. About a million and half. It might have already been found, but I don't think so. My...business partner, the one I called earlier, has been watching it—the place where I left it. It's in an old office building downtown."

Most of this, Gwen knew, was bullshit, but she already was sure Annie was a relatively good liar, so it might be fairly close to the truth, too. She was probably hiding some details and almost certainly lying about the money.

"So your business partner might have taken it, then?"

She shook her head. "No. I have someone watching her, too."

"Layer and layers," Gwen said, leaning back on one hand. "I can tell you right now, Annie, it will be a miracle if that money is still there with all these other people involved."

"I know."

"What makes you trust them after all this time? The news said it had been what, three years since the conviction? So like four since you worked with them?"

"They helped me escape today."

"But the person they hired left you on the side of the road."

"That wasn't—" Annie shook her head. "That was different."

Gwen stared at her for a long, silent pause. Annie seemed hopeful now, her eyes pleading, but she was still clearly anxious. Her fists were clenched at her sides, almost punching into the bed, and she appeared rigid and tight. Her clothes, so fresh and crisp this morning, were almost worn, every piece wrinkled and damp. Her hair was mussed, and her makeup, professional and nice this morning, was smeared. All of this, and she was still pretty. Ramsey, you idiot, Gwen told herself, sighing.

"Okay," she said, setting the gun down on the bed beside her. "I'm going to help you. But I want half—half of whatever is left."

"I can't—" Annie said.

"Half. That's my only offer."

Annie hesitated and then nodded. "Okay. Half. But it might be half of nothing."

Gwen held up her hands. "I get it, fine. Half of nothing is still half."

"What will you do if there's no money? Will you turn me in?"

Gwen shrugged. "I don't think so."

"I want your answer now." Abby's voice was low, angry. "Either you turn me in right now or not at all. We're either in this together, or I'm going back to prison. I can't take this anymore."

Gwen frowned, her temper rising again. "If you want it that way, then yes, I'll swear it—I won't turn you in. But I want you to swear now, too, Annie. Swear to me that when we get the money, you won't turn on me. You'll give me half, and we'll part ways."

She held out a hand and Annie shook it. She knew, and she knew Annie knew, that they were both lying, but maybe they could relax a little if they pretended they were allies for a while. Holding a gun on someone was tiring.

She grabbed the strap of her leather bag and pulled it closer. Then she rooted around inside, pushing aside the tools, and lifted the bottom to reveal her own gun. She pulled it out, showed it to Annie, and held out Annie's gun for her.

"There," she said as Annie took it. "Now we both have one, and we can put them away. I'll put mine in my jacket pocket, and you put yours back in your purse. Deal?"

"Sure," Annie said. Both of them waited for the other one to move first.

Finally, Gwen laughed. "Are we going to sit here like two

assholes with our dicks in our hands, or are we going to start making a plan?"

Still, Annie hesitated, so Gwen moved first, slipping her gun into her pocket. She'd had the right pocket specially altered to fit this piece. She kept her hand on it for a second and then held them both up, palms facing Annie.

"There. You have a gun and I don't. Are you going to shoot me now?"

Annie's eyes were stony, still almost angry, and she genuinely seemed to consider the question. Finally, they flickered away from Gwen's, and she reached over and grabbed her purse, stuffing the gun inside. Gwen was fairly certain she could get her gun out faster than Annie could, which had been her plan all along. But she decided to ride this out a little longer—keep pretending. After all, if the money was real, she could certainly use it.

She stood up and unfolded the map, laying it opened on the bed. "Let's take a look at this again. We already know at least some of the roads into town are blocked, and all the roads out of town are. We've checked all of the ones with circles here. Do you see anything else?"

Annie stood and peered down at the map. "No—I don't. That's the whole problem. That's why we stopped here."

"Where's the money?"

Annie paused and then touched the map. "Here—it's downtown."

Gwen bent down, studying the map before standing up again. "What about this neighborhood, here? If we turn early enough, we should be able to avoid the barricade where we were stopped first. We'll have to wind around a bit, but look—we'd end up like five blocks behind the police. What do you think?"

Annie examined the route for a full minute before nodding. "You're right."

Gwen smiled and slapped her back, making her flinch. "See! If we work together, we might get through this. We'll still be stuck here in town, but at least we'll have the money, right?"

Annie nodded, but her expression was dark, uncertain. Earlier, Gwen had known that she was lying about something regarding the money, but she was starting to think there might not be any at all, or, even if there was some—a much smaller amount than Annie had mentioned. Annie was also likely to turn on her the moment they had it. So what are you doing? she asked herself.

She had no idea.

## CHAPTER FIVE

Gwen stopped at a Goodwill they'd passed a few times for new clothes. Annie's rumpled suit was too conspicuous. Already, Gwen was afraid they would stand out walking around downtown this time of day after business hours. Annie, however, had insisted on going there now rather than waiting until tomorrow, so Gwen was forcing the issue on the clothes.

"Think of it like a makeover scene in a movie," Gwen told her as she parked the car. "A transformation, if you will."

"A disguise," Annie said coolly.

Gwen lifted a shoulder. "If you like. I thought a makeover would sound more fun."

"So what kinds of clothes should I get?"

"Uh-uh. You're not getting anything. I'm going in without you. Your face has been on the news for hours now. Someone might recognize you."

"You're leaving me here?"

"Yes. It's not the best plan, since it'll seem pretty strange if you're sitting out here in this heat. If I'd thought about it earlier, I'd have come without you."

Annie still looked uncertain, and Gwen held out the keys. "Here—you can keep these, just in case."

Annie stared at them without doing anything, her eyes flickering back and forth between the keys and Gwen's face. Finally, she took them. Gwen turned to leave, and Annie grabbed her arm, squeezing it painfully.

"Are you—are you going to tell someone about me? In there?"

Gwen pried her hand away and had to force herself not to fling it away. "I already told you—I'm not going to turn you in. You have to trust me, just like I have to trust you not to drive away." She tried to give her a smile, and Annie appeared to buy her reassurance as she relaxed a little back into her seat.

"Here," Gwen said, reaching into her inner pocket. She pulled out a pack of cigarettes and a lighter. "Take these."

Annie took them, brows lowered. "What for? I don't smoke."

"Neither do I. They're for blending in. Pretend. Light one, and blow on it once in a while to keep it lit. It gives you an excuse to wait out here. Keep your sunglasses on, and try to keep your chin down, like this, so no one sees your face." She demonstrated what she meant. "And try to clean your face a little bit. You've been sweating and crying all day."

"Okay."

"What are your sizes?"

"Two, extra small. Petite, if possible." Her cheeks were slightly pink as she spoke.

Gwen grinned at her. "All right. What about your shoe size?"

"Five."

"Jesus Christ," Gwen said. "You're like a gnome."

She started to leave again, but Annie touched her arm, lightly this time. "What kind of clothes are you planning to get?"

Gwen laughed. "You'll see."

She walked the aisles of the store as quickly as possible, looking for a shirt and pants. She didn't see jeans as small as she needed, so she ended up hitting the children's section. The glare outside was such that she couldn't really see the parking lot, so she didn't know if Annie had decided to leave. Gwen was half hoping she would, but the other half of her was eager to get back to her as soon as possible.

She relaxed when she saw the car there, still parked where she'd left it. She could smell the cigarette smoke as she approached, but with the heat, it probably hadn't been necessary anyway. No one was out here, and very few cars were on the road. She saw Annie toss the butt out the window once she spotted her.

She got back inside and threw the bag of clothes into Annie's lap. "Get changed."

"What? Here?" Annie asked, clearly alarmed.

Gwen laughed. "Where else?"

"Back at the hotel."

Gwen shook her head. "It's already too late, Annie. I told you that earlier. Business districts close down at night. Even restaurants are closed once the office workers go home for the day. We might find an after-hours bar or two, but even if we do, we'll stand out like sore thumbs. If we wait until after dark, it'll be that much worse." She checked her watch. "We have maybe two hours before the sun sets, and we should try to get the money before then."

Annie was clutching the plastic bag to her chest, her eyes wary, but she finally nodded. "Okay. But won't someone see me in here? I thought we were trying not to stand out."

"No one here but us chickens."

Annie glanced around and nodded. "Fine." She met Gwen's eyes. "Are you going to watch?"

"What? No. Sorry," she said and covered her eyes with one hand, feeling instantly foolish.

The bag rustled for a while.

"What is this shit?" Annie finally asked.

Gwen laughed. "You said you wanted a disguise."

She heard her sigh, and more rustling, the bag and then the clothing. Annie's arm brushed her a few times as she struggled in and out of her clothes. She cursed several times under her breath as she changed, struggling in the small space.

"You can look now," she said finally.

Gwen had to blink a few times for her eyes to adjust to the light, and she smiled when she saw her. Annie was now wearing an overly large, black band T-shirt, dark jeans, and a pair of boys' cowboy boots. She'd taken her hair out of her neat coif, and it lay in almost white, tangled, damp ringlets past her shoulders. Her face, now free of makeup, coupled with clothing, made her appear much, much younger. She'd be carded for a beer if she tried to buy one.

"Are we supposed to be twins or something?" Annie asked.

Gwen laughed. "You're the one that said we're related. We're still going to the family reunion in Phoenix after this, right?"

Annie smiled for the first time in hours. "Right."

"Anyway, it works. You're unrecognizable."

Annie nodded, plucking at her shirt. "It's true. I've never worn stuff like this." She gave another smile, this one spreading to her eyes. "Thanks. I wouldn't have thought of it."

Gwen didn't respond, her heart suddenly tight. She turned her attention to the car to hide her embarrassed pleasure, keying it on and pulling out of the lot. She didn't talk to Annie for several blocks, waiting for the strange, almost buzzing excitement in her chest to die down.

"Turn there," Annie said, pointing left.

Her arm brushed Gwen's as she pointed, and the feeling she had been suppressing intensified. Stop it, Ramsey, she told herself.

She turned into the neighborhood, following Annie's directions at the end of every block. They had to stair-step their way through neighborhood roads lined with large homes with brown lawns. Children were playing in the streets, and they were forced to slow down several times to let them get out of the way. They passed a nice little park with a well-maintained playground and green, manicured grass. Some teenagers were sitting on a picnic table smoking, but the smaller children around them largely ignored the teens, intent on their games. Many of the children were throwing popping fireworks on the ground, others squealing in dramatic anger or joy when they landed too close to bare feet. She glanced at Annie and thought she saw something wistful in her eyes as she stared out at the kids. Longing, maybe, Gwen thought, or something like it, anyway.

"Wait at the next stop sign for a sec," Annie said a few minutes later. "We should be able to see the main road from there."

Gwen stopped the car at the intersection. The two of them

peered to the right, craning their necks, but even from here, she could tell the road was empty.

Annie turned her way, smiling broadly. "It worked."

Gwen was less certain, but she returned the smile. "Told ya."

Annie rolled her eyes. "Just drive, genius."

Gwen turned left once they made it to the main road, away from the police barricade some ten blocks behind them. She was surprised that more cars weren't sitting here on this road, waiting to get through, especially now at rush hour. Maybe they were waving people through a little faster now, rather than stopping them, probably a little less careful with cars driving away from town than toward it. After all, there were secondary roadblocks on the highways outside of town.

Annie directed her downtown, and as they neared the business district, Gwen wasn't surprised to see emptier and emptier streets. Hardly anyone besides a few homeless people were walking around down here this time of day, exactly as she'd expected.

"There's a parking lot about a block from here," Annie said, pointing at a sign with a large "P" that pointed to the left. "I think it's free this time of day."

"How are we going to get the money back to the car?" Gwen asked. Annie didn't reply, and Gwen didn't push for a response. She turned toward the lot, saw it, and parked in the spot nearest the road. She turned the car off, and it clicked and rattled for a minute or two as it cooled down.

Finally, she looked at her. "It's time, Annie."

"Time for what?"

Gwen gestured outside. "Time to cut the bullshit and tell me what we're really doing here. Let me guess—there's no money. Right?"

Annie, her eyes dark and frightened, shook her head. "Not as much as I said, no. Ten thousand dollars."

Gwen shook her head, disgusted. She'd known something like this would be the case, but she'd almost started to believe otherwise, especially after they'd gone through so much crap to get here.

"That's it? Ten thousand bucks? Nothing else?"

Annie hesitated. "No. A new ID, too. Then, once I get set up somewhere, I call them—my business associates—and they'll give me my share of the money. One point five million, like I told you."

Gwen laughed, surprised to realize that none of this upset her. After all, she'd suspected this would happen all along, and anyway, what difference did it make? Had she actually planned to take stolen money? Was she really that low?

"What's funny?" Annie asked.

"Oh, nothing. The world is tripping me up, as usual. If I hadn't picked you up, I'd be halfway to California by now. Instead, I'm here," she gestured around them, "in a crappy parking lot in Texas."

"What's wrong with Texas?" Annie asked, eyes narrowed.

Gwen laughed and held up her hands. "Nothing, nothing. Sorry—I always forget how touchy Texans are about their state."

Annie grinned, somewhat sheepishly. Still staring, she asked, "So are you still going to help me? After all this?"

Gwen watched her for a long, quiet moment. After all, she didn't have any reason to help this woman. Five thousand dollars wasn't worth this kind of risk. If they were caught together, she'd be in a shitload of trouble, far worse than she already was. So why bother? She could leave Annie here and make it to New Mexico, maybe even Arizona, by tonight.

"I'll help you," she heard herself say.

Annie's head snapped her way. "What? Why?"

Gwen didn't answer right away. She didn't know how to put it into words. She touched the back of Annie's hand. "I want to. Isn't that enough?"

Annie didn't immediately respond. Instead, she seemed to search Gwen's face, almost as if trying to read her thoughts. Finally, her expression cleared. "Maybe you are a Good Samaritan, after all."

"So much so that I'm helping a bank robber escape prison."

Annie smiled. "Okay. Maybe not."

Gwen continued to return her smile until her stomach starting doing the funny flipping trill again. She had to look away, and she slapped her thighs. "So are we doing this thing, or not? I want my five thousand, and no offense to Texas, I want to get the fuck out of here."

"Okay. Let's do this."

"Let me grab my things."

Once out of the car, they walked away from it at a fast clip, almost as if trying to escape. Gwen was glad to leave the car behind and half hoped they wouldn't have to pick it up again. Not many cars were parked in the area this time of day, but several of those she did see were far nicer than that piece of junk.

"There," Annie said after a couple of blocks, pointing. "The package is in that building."

Across the street, a three-story office building was under construction, scaffolding out front, windows on the ground floor boarded over.

"How are we supposed to get in?"

"In the back. There's a door that's never locked."

"Never locked three years ago," Gwen said.

Annie shook her head. "No. Someone put a package there a week ago."

"One of your business partners?"

Annie nodded.

Gwen didn't like any of this. Too many people were involved, people she didn't know. This kind of thing took trust, and even Annie seemed skeptical. They'd spent all afternoon trying both to leave and enter El Paso, so obviously she had some doubts. Once Annie had realized she wouldn't be able to get here very easily, she'd been willing to desert whatever was in the package, but the roadblocks had stopped them from leaving or coming here.

"Okay, let's go," Gwen said.

They walked past the building to the alley in back, turned down it, and picked up the pace, dodging trash and assorted construction materials. Several other office buildings shared the alley, but Gwen thought they'd be safe back here this time of day.

"It's here," Annie said, pointing at a door. She seemed to hesitate and then pulled on the handle. For a second, it seemed this was all a ruse—the door refused to budge. Then, after throwing

Gwen an embarrassed glance, Annie depressed the button on top of the handle, and the door opened.

This was a big step. If Gwen went inside, she was breaking the law. After all, until recently, she'd been held hostage. If they'd been picked up, she could have claimed she'd been a hostage all along. Going inside with her was different—criminal. Annie waited, eyes worried, and Gwen shook her head, motioning for her to keep going. It was too late to turn around now.

They stepped inside, and once Annie pulled the door closed, pitch-darkness enclosed her. Annie cursed next to her.

"Hang on a sec," Gwen said, and opened her bag. She dug around inside, feeling her way through the various tools, and pulled out a flashlight before turning it on.

Annie jumped a little and grinned. "You're like Mary Poppins with that bag."

"After this, we can go fly a kite." She glanced around. "So where are we supposed to go?"

"Upstairs. It's in a little desk up there."

Even with the flashlight, it was hard to navigate the crowded space. They had to walk very close together, arms touching, and very slowly through loose nails on the floor, piles of boards and bricks, as well as assorted shards of broken glass. It took them several minutes to find the staircase, and when they did, they both stopped to stare. The stairs had been ripped out in places, leaving gaps, and even in places with steps, exposed nails pointed upward.

"Jesus," Gwen said.

"You don't have to come," Annie said. "I can take the flashlight and be right back."

"And wait here in the dark? Are you kidding?"

Annie lifted an eyebrow. "Afraid of ghosts?"

"Spiders."

Annie turned to the stairs again. "So how are we going to do this?"

Gwen glanced around, spotting a plastic sheet thrown over a pallet of tile. She pulled it off, motioned for Annie to grab the other side, and they folded it into a small square. They did the same with a blue plastic tarp lying on the ground and put the first on the bottom step, the blue one on the second, and so on. The gaps were fairly narrow, so that by balancing with their hands on the wall to their right, they could stretch their legs across the gaps. The climb seemed so interminable that when they finally reached the top, Gwen wanted to lie down and go to sleep.

The second floor was large and open, with exposed structural beams and dusty, unfinished wooden floors. Two of the large front windows had been soaped over instead of boarded up, making it much lighter up here. Gwen turned off her flashlight, afraid someone might see it from the street, and they stood there letting their eyes adjust to the gloomy murk.

As Annie had mentioned, a wooden desk, clearly out of place, sat in the middle of the large, open space. Annie walked over to it, Gwen following her a moment later. Annie pulled out four drawers one by one, all of them empty. Cursing, she knelt, peering into the leg well, and then she reached inside and peeled something away from underneath, standing up with a stuffed manila envelope. She unclasped the little brad and then took everything out, setting it on the desk: a bundle of hundred-dollar bills and several documents—a passport, a birth certificate, and a driver's license.

"What's your new name?" Gwen asked.

Annie read it and made a face. "Bertha Agnes Perry."

"Jesus—who chose that?"

"Not me."

"So should I call you Bertha now?" Gwen elbowed her.

Annie swatted her arm. "No. Hopefully, it's only temporary. If it isn't, I'll have to use my new middle name."

Not anxious to go back down those stairs, Gwen left her absorbed in the documents, walking around the empty space, stretching her shoulders and rotating her neck. The day had been long and tense. She'd already been awake for over twelve hours, and it wasn't over yet. She regretted skipping her omelet at that diner now—she hadn't eaten in a long time.

Almost as if thinking about it made her hungrier, her stomach gave a low growl, and Annie's head turned her way, sharp and quick.

"Was that your stomach?"

Gwen nodded.

Annie started stuffing things back into the envelope. "I'm hungry, too. Let's get out of here."

"How can you possibly be hungry after that lunch?"

Annie was about to respond, but she suddenly flinched, staring at something behind Gwen. Gwen spun that way, automatically reaching for her gun, but she saw what it was at once.

Flashing police lights outside.

## CHAPTER SIX

She and Annie raced over to one of the soaped windows, and with the sleeve of her jacket, Gwen cleared a little circle. Down on the street, two blocks away, several police vehicles were parked around the little car they'd left in the lot.

"Oh, shit," Gwen said. With so many uniforms swarming around down there, it was hard to see what was happening, but Gwen could tell they'd managed to open the passenger door. She touched Annie's shoulder. "Did you leave anything in there?"

Annie flinched. "My old clothes."

"Fuck!" She slammed her hand on the windowsill. If they had a K-9 unit, the dogs would lead them right here. A moment later, she realized their fingerprints were all over that car. "Goddamn it," she whispered, her stomach dropping. They had been stupidly careless.

Annie started pacing, her hands in her hair, muttering to herself. Gwen approached her, hands out at her sides, empty palms up. Closer, she could hear her.

"Can't go back, can't go back, can't go back," she said, sounding like she was stuck on a loop.

"Annie? Annie, stay with me, here. Don't lose it."

Annie's eyes flew open, and her hands dropped from her hair. "What are we going to do? What on earth are we going to do?" Her voice was high, quavering, almost hysterical.

Gwen had to quell the urge to shake her, and she clenched her fists at her sides. "Annie, stop it. Stop it right now, or you're going to get us caught before we even have a chance to try. Take a deep breath and calm the fuck down."

Annie reacted as if slapped, her head snapping backward. Her face reddened and her eyes darkened. "That's easy for you to say! You're not looking at life in prison!"

Gwen had to bite back an angry retort. Again, she clenched her fists, fingernails biting into her palms. "You don't know me, Annie. You know absolutely nothing about me. Maybe I don't want to be caught, either. Ever think of that?"

Annie's eyes darted from side to side. She licked her lips. "No, I guess not. I don't know anything about you, except that you can steal cars."

"Exactly."

Some of the tension left Annie's shoulders. She was studying Gwen's face, seeming almost concerned now. "So what should we do?"

Gwen sighed in relief. She was being reasonable again. She walked back to the window, peering out, and then gestured for Annie to join her.

"See? They're all still at the car. They're going to put the net down on this neighborhood if they haven't already, but most of them are just standing over there yakking away. Any minute, the dogs will show up, and then we'll be in deep shit. But until then, we have the advantage since they don't know where we are. I say we get the hell out of here and as far away as possible on foot. Some patrolmen might be walking around already, but we should be able to dodge them if we're smart about it."

Annie took a deep breath and nodded. "Okay. Let's go."

It was a little easier getting down the stairs than up, but it wasn't quick, either, nerve-wracking in a different way. Gwen braced herself, waiting for the door to open and their exit to be cut off. By the time they were back on the ground floor, her legs were shuddering with tension and fatigue, and Annie was almost staggering. She got the flashlight out again, and the light shook with her hand.

"Let's sit down for a second," Gwen said, steering her over to a pile of wood. It was telling that Annie didn't challenge her. She simply dropped onto the wood as if her legs had given out. Gwen sat down next to her, thigh flush with Annie's on the small available surface. Annie gripped her hand, squeezing it so hard Gwen almost cried out.

"Do you think we can do it? Can we get away?"

Gwen squeezed back. "It's worth a shot. If I didn't think we might, I wouldn't try. I'll be in enough shit as it is, now—aiding and abetting, breaking and entering, grand-theft auto, evading police…"

They were silent.

"I'm sorry, Gwen," Annie finally said, her voice quiet, pained.

"Don't be. It's my fault as much as yours."

Annie still looked guilty, shoulders sagging, eyes directed at the floor. Gwen touched her chin, making her meet her eyes.

"I mean it. It's not your fault. I knew what I was doing."

Annie's eyes filled with tears, and she turned away, blinking rapidly. She slid off the wood and stood up, stretching.

"I'll make it up to you."

Gwen stood up. "With the money?" She couldn't help her note of mockery.

Annie's expression was serious, her lips a thin line. "Whatever it takes."

It was starting to grow dark now, but the heat of the day was still intense, blasting them like a furnace when they opened the back door. Gwen poked her head out, peering up and down the alley, then motioned for Annie to follow her. Without talking, they both crouched, dashing from trash heap to garbage can to debris as they ran the length of the alley, away from the police and their old car.

Ten feet from the street, Gwen motioned for Annie to wait and crept up to the edge of the nearest building, peering in both directions. She gestured for Annie to join her, and the two of them started walking down the street, again in a direction away from their car. They were entirely exposed here on the sidewalk, and Gwen could almost feel her skin shrinking in alarm, terrified someone would see them, call out to them.

"We're sitting ducks here," she said, almost whispering.

"I know—I'm trying to think. I used to work down here. We have to get away from this district a little. All the delis and restaurants down here are closed for the day." She paused, frowning. "But we're not too far from the edge of this part of town now. There's a little neighborhood not far from here, with bars and things, but I have to remember how to get there. It's different on foot."

They kept walking, passing banks and insurance companies, primarily, all closed for the day. A few cars passed, each one tempting Gwen to bolt. Any of them could be an unmarked police car.

Five minutes later, they approached a bigger, busier intersection. Again, Gwen motioned for Annie to stop, still blocked by the building, and threw a quick glance up and down this busier road. More cars and people were here, but none of them, as far as she could tell, were police.

She turned back to Annie and lifted her hands. "Where to?"

Annie pointed to their right. "I know a place that way about four blocks. A bar. At least it used to be there. It's closer than that neighborhood I mentioned earlier." Her eyes lowered. "I've only been there a few times."

She seemed strangely nervous, or maybe guilty, but Gwen chalked that up to her uncertainty. Three years was a long time— restaurants and bars closed and reopened as something new all the time. They might get there and find an empty building, or any manner of store or business. A bar, however, would be a good place to hide for a few minutes, and at least they'd be off the street. Gwen had no idea how long it would take for the dogs to find them, or if the police were even using dogs to track them. If they were, she didn't think it would be very fast, as the dogs would be on leads with their handlers, but they needed to hurry. If the dogs and police didn't stop and check the building they'd gone into, they would be faster. She and Annie might have as long as half an hour, if they were lucky.

"It was here," Annie finally said, pointing down an alley.

Gwen frowned, staring that direction and not seeing anything but trashcans. "What do you mean? At the other end of the alley?"

"No—it's right there. That black door. It's…secret."

"Like a speakeasy or something?"

Annie hesitated, not meeting Gwen's eyes. "Not exactly."

She could tell Annie was hiding something, and Gwen was losing the last threads of her patience. "What the hell is it, then?"

Annie's face colored, and she finally met Gwen's eyes. "It's a gay bar."

Gwen flinched in surprise. "Oh."

Annie was flustered now, her face a dark, mottled red. "I wasn't a regular or anything. I wasn't…I mean, I only came here a few times. With a friend."

Gwen laughed. "Sure, sure, whatever you say. So how do we get in? With some kind of password or something?"

"You knock and ask for Marge when they open the hatch. I think she used to own the place."

"Will anyone know you in there?"

After a pause, Annie shook her head. "I don't think so. It's been a long time."

Gwen stifled a laugh. "Okay. Lead the way."

Annie knocked on the door, and after a long, breathless pause the little hatch at eye-level opened. A pair of dark eyes stared out at them, and no one said anything.

"I'm looking for Marge," Annie said.

"She's not here anymore," a man said from behind the door.

Annie's eyebrows shot up.

He laughed. "Sorry, kid. Just giving you a hard time. Any friend of Marge is a friend of ours. You two have ID?"

"Yes," Gwen answered.

Something inside was unlatched, and then the door swung outward, making them back up a couple of steps.

"Get in here before the heat creeps in," the man said, motioning them in. He closed and locked the door behind them, sitting down again on a stool in front of the door. Gwen had reached for her wallet to get out her ID, but he didn't ask for it, and Annie motioned for her to follow her down a little hallway and into the bar.

The bar was dingy and dark, the walls painted a solid, deep black that made everything seem smaller, dirtier. The smell of smoke filled the air, but other than the bartender and a pair of men playing pool, they had the place to themselves. A few high-top tables stood near the pool table, and there were a couple of booths on the far wall, some arcade games, and the usual rainbow-colored neon beer advertisements above the bar. A tiny dance floor had been set up in front of an old jukebox next to a cigarette machine. It looked and smelled like almost every gay bar Gwen had ever been in, and despite the general dankness, it felt familiar. Having a locked front door between them and the police was also a bonus.

"Go sit in a booth," Gwen said, pointing. "I'll grab a couple of drinks. What do you want?"

"Beer's fine."

Gwen approached the bar, and the bartender, who had been watching a baseball game on the little TV above the bar, was clearly annoyed at the interruption. She had that same platinum-blond hair as the waitress had this morning—the kind of crisp, fried blond that killed your hair. Her face was darkly tanned, lined from the sun. She could have been the other waitress's sister.

"Jim ask for your ID?" the woman asked, a cigarette tucked in the corner of her mouth.

He hadn't checked them, but he'd asked, so Gwen nodded.

"What'll you have?"

"Two beers. Whatever's on draft."

Gwen had guessed correctly that there was only one offering, and the woman filled two glasses clearly meant for tall cocktails, not beer. The usual bum's rush, Gwen thought.

"Six dollars," the woman said, turning back to the TV.

Gwen had to bite her tongue—even for a bar like this, she was clearly up-charging. Still, she threw the money and a sizable tip on the bar without complaint and took the glasses over to the booth. She set one down in front of Annie before sitting down across from her. She slipped the strap of her leather bag over her shoulder and pushed it against the wall. Annie frowned at the small glass but didn't comment.

"Nice place," Gwen said, taking a sip. "Wonder if we'll get tetanus."

Annie grinned and took a drink, grimacing soon after. She offered the glass to Gwen, and she took it. Between the two glasses, she might get an actual pint. Annie glanced around and moved closer across the table, motioning for Gwen to do the same.

"I don't think anyone can hear us, but I can't be certain," she explained.

"Don't you think we're more conspicuous like this? Hunched over and whispering?"

Annie smiled a little wider. "Maybe—but we might seem... friendly."

Gwen smiled in return and took one of Annie's hands in hers. Annie started to draw it back, and then she left it there, clearly understanding what Gwen was doing. Gwen ran her thumb across the back of Annie's hand and saw her eyebrows lift slightly. The contrast between their skin was striking, absorbing—Annie's almost translucent with a hint of pink, hers a dusky gold, darker in here than outside.

She wrenched her eyes away and winked at Annie. "All part of the disguise."

Annie nodded. "Listen—I've been thinking." She paused, gaze shifting around the room again. The men at the pool table were wrapped up in their game, swearing and teasing each other, and the bartender was back to her baseball game. Still, Annie hunched closer, her face now inches from Gwen's.

"I've been thinking about the car, wondering how the police found it so quickly."

Gwen nodded. "I wondered the same thing. It was in that lot, what, half an hour? Forty minutes? Even if everyone in town was out looking for it, that's really fast. I mean, there must be a hundred of that same make and model on the road, and the plates were different, too. Someone would notice if their car was stolen, but it takes a while to realize your plates have been changed."

"Exactly. It was too quick."

Gwen wondered how she could word what she'd say next delicately. Annie, as if reading her thoughts, nodded.

"I know what you're thinking."

Gwen was surprised. "You do?"

"Someone betrayed me. One of my business partners set me up."

Gwen shrugged. "You did say someone was watching that building for you. Maybe they were waiting until you showed to call in."

Annie nodded but then shook her head. "But why? Why help me break out, only to call me in once I'm out? It doesn't make any sense."

"Who knew about the package in the desk? How many people, I mean?"

"Two. The woman I talked to on the phone—she was the one watching it—and the person who put it there."

"Which one is more likely to screw you over?"

Annie didn't hesitate. "The second—the man. I don't trust him as much. But he's not in town right now."

Gwen leaned back. "It must have been her."

Annie shook her head. "It couldn't be. Really, it couldn't. We planned the escape together for months. Why would she do that?"

"So she's the main reason you're out?"

Annie nodded. "I'd still be in prison without her."

"There's no one else? No one that knew?"

Annie started to shake her head and then stopped, frowning. "Well, there is one more person. As far as I know, he didn't know about the package, but he's...angry. He testified against me in court." She shrugged. "But that's pretty far-fetched, especially after all this time. He doesn't even live in town anymore."

"Maybe he hired a private detective," Gwen suggested. "Do you think he knows what's inside the envelope?"

Annie's eyebrows shot up, and she paled slightly. "Christ. I hope not."

"Either way, you might have to be careful using any of those IDs. He might leak the name to the police."

Annie paled further. Gwen squeezed her hand and got up. "Let me go get you a real drink."

She walked back to the bar, and the bartender turned at once, all smiles and warmth. The tip had done its job.

"Need something else, sugar?" The cigarette had burned down in the last few minutes, the ember almost to the woman's lips.

Gwen jerked a thumb back in Annie's direction. "My girlfriend's having a bad day. Think you could make something special to cheer her up? Something sweet—like you."

"Aren't you a flirt, now?" the woman said, giggling. She started picking up various bottles of alcohol and poured them all together. Gwen turned around to watch the men play pool, surprised to see that several other patrons had come in while she was distracted. She glanced at her watch. Almost eight. The night crowd was starting to arrive. She and Annie would want to leave sooner rather than later. More eyes meant more people that might have seen Annie's photo. She turned back as the bartender finished her liquid masterpiece and set it on the bar. Gwen could smell vermouth and something fruity.

"Anything else for you, hon? Another beer?"

"Whiskey, if you have it. Double. Neat."

She paid for the overpriced drinks, once again tipping wildly, and brought them back to the booth. Annie was fiddling with a book of matches, lighting them one at a time before dropping the spent sticks into the ashtray. She took the glass of whiskey before Gwen had a chance to stop her and threw it back in one gulp.

Seeing Gwen's face, she said, "Oh. I'm sorry. Was that red one for me?"

"It's okay," Gwen said, sitting down. She took a small sip of the cocktail, gagged, and pushed it away. "Tastes like cough syrup."

Annie grabbed the glass, drained it, and then smiled. "Tastes fine to me. Anything's good after three years."

"No toilet gin in the joint?"

Annie laughed. "Not that I saw. I was trying to be good— maybe get early release."

Gwen liked seeing her laugh. She liked the way the alcohol had brought a little color back to her face. This was, she thought, the first time she'd seen Annie almost relaxed, normal.

She wrenched her gaze away from her face, watching the growing crowd of men fill up the area around the bar. Most of them were very young. Some, she suspected, had gotten in based on the loose carding policy at the door. She'd benefitted from something similar when she was their age, making her first forays into places just like this. She felt Annie's eyes on her and looked back to find her staring, a smile lifting one side of her mouth.

"What?"

Annie shrugged. "You looked, I don't know, wistful, for a minute."

She took Annie's hand in hers again, not realizing she was doing it until she had. "I was remembering something."

Annie nodded, and her eyes grew wary again. "What are we going to do, Gwen? We can't sit in here all night."

"I don't think it's safe to go back to the hotel, either." She paused. "Don't you know anyone in town, someone you could call? What about that woman from earlier? What did she suggest? I mean, besides killing me."

Annie ignored the last part. "She suggested I contact an old friend of mine. A trucker. She thought maybe he could smuggle me out in his rig."

"What's stopping you? Afraid he won't help?"

"No—that's the problem. I know he will, but I don't want to get him in trouble. Tom and I go way back. Childhood friends. Anyway, I don't know if I should call him. I'm worried they might have tapped his phone. He was on my list of known associates."

"They couldn't tap his phone, could they? Is that even legal?"

"It was tapped before. They used it in court."

"Jesus. Still, I think those rights expire or something. They wouldn't have tapped it this whole time."

Annie shrugged. "Maybe. Still, I can't be sure either way. At the very least, they're probably watching his place."

"Could you meet him somewhere else? Like, does he go to a bar somewhere, or something? Somewhere you could run into him?"

Annie's face lit up. "What time is it?"

"Eight fifteen."

"And it's Tuesday, right?"

"Yep. Still Tuesday." The longest Tuesday in existence, she thought.

"Tom works the night shift. He'll get to work around ten. We might be able to catch him before he heads inside."

"What if he's out? I mean, like out driving somewhere."

Annie shook her head. "He won't be. He works Tuesdays through Saturdays, back and forth from different cities up through Wyoming."

"What if his schedule's changed? When's the last time you spoke?"

"Two weeks ago. He visits me at least once a month."

"It's worth a try."

"I hate to think of him getting into trouble, but if we can get out of town, he won't be in danger for more than an hour, tops."

"Let's go," Gwen said, sliding out. At the last second, she remembered to grab her leather bag, her heart tripping for a moment in relief. Leaving it would have caused a major problem.

"How are we going to get there? He parks his truck way across town," Annie said, standing up next to her. She slid her hands through her hair, those pale, loose curls catching on her fingers. Gwen had to look away, that pinched, tight feeling rising in her stomach again.

"What did you say?"

"I said how are we going to get there? Stealing a car would be…risky, wouldn't it? With all those police nearby?"

Gwen didn't respond, leading her by the hand through the now-crowded bar. Annie kept her head down, but no one really watched them too closely, everyone wrapped up in showing off, having a good time. The only person who seemed to focus on them briefly was the only other woman in here besides the bartender. She was an older butch, and she grinned at Gwen and lifted her chin in Annie's direction, as if praising her choice. Gwen grinned back at her and kept going, winding through the people that towered above them.

It was a relief to be outside again. The night had already taken some of the edge off the heat. That was the nice thing about dry climates—the sun went down, and it actually cooled off in the summer.

"So?" Annie asked. "How are we going to get there?"

Gwen was about to respond when she heard her answer coming from the street. She led Annie out of the alley, spotted a bus stop, and walked over to it. The bus was still a block away.

"But we don't know where it goes," Annie said, peering at it like she was.

"Away from here. That's good enough for me. We can take it a mile or two, get out, and grab a cab."

They were still holding hands by the time the bus finally stopped for them, and Gwen reluctantly let go in order to pay. If Annie had minded the handholding, she hadn't let on, and as they sat down together, Gwen wondered what that meant.

## CHAPTER SEVEN

O h, crap," Annie said. "I meant to pay. I keep forgetting I have money again."

"I doubt the bus driver could have broken a hundred. Also, keep it down about having money."

"What? Why?" Annie said, glancing behind them. "Oh."

A group of young men sat some ten seats back. Each took up an entire double seat, legs wide and shoulders slouching in a kind of aggressive casualness. The one closest to them had been staring at them since they climbed in. A couple of blocks passed, and Gwen thought they might be able to get through this ride without being bothered, but then she heard it: kissing sounds.

"Hey, ladies!" one of them called. "Why don't you come back here and sit with us?"

"Yeah," another said. "I got an empty lap."

Gwen felt Annie tense next to her and gripped her hand. "Don't say anything," she whispered.

"Hey, blondie!" one of them shouted, a little louder now. "What are you doing with that weird-looking bitch?"

"You'd have more fun with us!" another called.

"Maybe we should get off here," Annie said as the bus slowed down to let someone on.

Gwen shook her head. "No. Not far enough. If we ignore them, we should be okay. The bus driver will stop them from doing anything."

"He will?"

Gwen nodded, not really believing this. The driver might caution them, but he wouldn't be able to do much unless or until they tried something—neither was a good scenario. She changed the subject.

"Can you tell where the bus is going?"

Annie squinted out the window and nodded. "Yes. If we stay on this road, we're heading north."

"Is that a good thing?"

"Tom's job is this way, so we're going the right way—the right direction, anyway. The truck depot is somewhere on the north end of town, at any rate. I'll have to find the actual address somehow."

Almost as if saying it had jinxed them, at the next intersection, the bus made a right turn. Annie was peering outside to get her bearings, and she sagged a moment later. "Damn it. We're going the wrong way—east, I think. We need to go west and north."

Gwen pulled the little cord above the windows, and the bus started to slow. In the reflection in the glass, she saw the young men stand up with them but didn't turn around. She maneuvered herself between Annie and them and followed her to the exit door. Annie seemed oblivious to the drama taking place behind her. She got out of the bus and stared up and down the street, not paying attention.

Gwen, however, planted herself on the bottom step and stared up at the man in front of the others. He met her eyes, and she heard him mutter an ethnic slur about her under his breath. His smug grin disappeared when she pulled the gun out of her pocket a little. He backed up so fast he bumped into the guy behind him, and she left the bus right when they started swearing and swinging at each other. They would probably be kicked off a block or two down, so she and Annie needed to get off the street as soon as possible.

Annie was still peering around, then shook her head at Gwen. "I have no idea where we are. I didn't see the street sign when we turned, and I don't think I ever went down this way."

Spotting a little diner across the street, Gwen pointed. "Let's go in there and call a cab. Maybe they have a phone book we can use."

This time of the evening, after the dinner rush but before the post-bar crawl, the diner was almost empty. Someone in the back called for them to choose their own seats, and Gwen led Annie to a little two-person booth farthest from the windows, making her sit with her back to the street. The table hadn't been cleaned since the last patrons, a cigarette butt still smoldering in the ashtray and a couple of used coffee mugs sitting in wet, brown rings. Gwen pushed both to the edge of the table, disgusted.

"God, I'm starving," Annie said.

"Me, too. Do you think we have enough time to eat?"

"Tom's job shouldn't be more than ten or fifteen minutes from here. What time is it now?"

"Almost nine."

"Something quick, then."

The waiter—a pallid, scrawny, college-aged kid—appeared, his uniform and hair depressingly greasy. Still, Gwen knew she needed some food, hygiene be damned.

"Egg sandwich with cheese," she told him. "And coffee, please."

"The same, but with fries and a Coke. And a side of ranch, please," Annie said.

"Is there a phone here?" Gwen asked him.

The kid pointed with his pencil to a little hallway nearby.

"I'll go get the address and call a cab," Annie said, standing up. She hesitated. "Can I borrow thirty-five cents? I still don't have any change."

Gwen dug around in her pocket and fished one out.

"Thanks."

Gwen watched the street, waiting for the dickheads on the bus to appear, but they didn't show up outside or across the street. She relaxed a little, starting to feel more than a little foolish. It had been stupid to flash her gun at them like that—too memorable, too obvious. If they saw her picture on the news, they'd remember her. Like leaving the fingerprints in the car, she'd been careless, impulsive. She needed to stop being stupid, or they'd be caught—it was that simple. Part of her anger-management therapy had focused on her impulsive behavior. She was slipping.

She turned around and watched Annie flipping through the phone book. Annie opened her purse and took out a little notebook and pen, writing something down. Then she flipped around some more and picked up the phone. Despite her proximity, the ambient noise of the diner was loud enough to drown out her conversation, and Gwen felt uneasy. Annie could be calling anyone, talking to anyone, and she wouldn't know.

"Stop it," she said aloud, making herself turn back toward the street. She didn't have any reason to distrust Annie now, not after their near escape. They'd been through a lot together in the last few hours, and she felt like they'd turned a corner. And yet... Gwen couldn't stop thinking about that woman on the phone in the motel—the one that told Annie to kill her. If Annie was mixed up with people like that, who was to say she wouldn't turn on her when it suited her?

What did Gwen know about her, anyway? She was smart and pretty, yes, and her accent was sexy as hell—Gwen would never deny her attraction to her. She was halfway convinced that Annie was attracted to her, too. That lovey-dovey charade back at the bar had been a little too easy, a little too normal for her. And, of course, she'd taken her to a gay bar, for God's sake, so the likelihood was pretty high she was gay or bi, too. Still, Gwen didn't want to let any of those possibilities blind her to reality. This woman was a convicted felon and friends with killers. Annie hadn't denied her involvement in the crime, which, while nonviolent, apparently involved violent people.

Annie sat down, and her eyebrows shot up. "What?"

"Sorry—little jumpy."

"S'okay. I think I found the address. I was there one time, so I should recognize it. So many of those trucking companies have similar names, but they're all next to each other. We should be able to find the right one, even if I got the name wrong. The cab will be here in half an hour. That should give us enough time to eat and get over there before Tom shows up for his shift."

"Good idea."

The food was delivered, and Gwen dove into her sandwich at

once, the yolk dripping out and running down her fingers. She was done before it felt like she'd even started. She watched Annie sock away her much-larger meal, amused, once again, by how quickly and messily she ate. The waiter reappeared as Annie stuffed in the last fry.

"Anything else?" he asked, his tone as washed out as his uniform.

"Slice of cherry pie, if you have it. And the check."

He slouched away, head down, shoulders dropped, to put in the order.

"You really like your fries and pie," Gwen said.

"And ranch dressing," Annie said, grinning. "I could go swimming in the stuff. We didn't get it on the inside, not once. Not even with the sad pieces of lettuce they called salad." Her face sobered, her eyes distant. "Funny, the things you miss when you can't have them. Even bad pie is better than no pie. My sister—" Her mouth almost snapped closed.

"What about your sister?"

She focused on Gwen, her eyes welling with tears, and shook her head. "Sorry. I don't want to talk about her."

So, Gwen thought, the distrust was on both sides. Still, she didn't really blame her. She wouldn't have trusted herself, either, if they'd met under any circumstances, let alone like this. She didn't look like a trustworthy person, dressed like this or any other way. Hell, maybe she wasn't. Attraction or not, she'd betray Annie the moment she had to, so she couldn't expect anything different.

Annie ate the pie in three bites, but it took a manager to break the hundred-dollar bill she insisted on using to pay. Gwen was aware once again that they were being too noticeable, too recognizable and memorable to blend in. She would have to convince Annie to stop using her money or get it exchanged somehow. Otherwise, they'd leave a trail behind them even the laziest policeman could follow.

They stood outside in the now-chilly evening air, waiting for the cab. Annie's arms were crossed over her chest as she shivered, and Gwen was tempted to offer her jacket. Gallant as the gesture might be, that would put her at a disadvantage. She had nowhere else to store her gun, nowhere handy, anyway. She could put it back in her bag, but she wouldn't be able to get to it quickly if Annie should decide to pull one on her.

"Christ, it's cold," Annie said.

"Shouldn't be long, now."

"I hope so. I don't know what we'll do if we miss Tom before he goes in."

"So this Tom…" Gwen said, unable to stop herself. "Is he an old boyfriend?"

Annie laughed. "Tom? No. He's not. Just an old friend."

Some doubt must have shown on Gwen's face, as Annie smiled and touched her arm. "Really—we're friends. He's the one I went to that bar with. Before, I mean. I went with him for support."

Gwen met her eyes. "Yours or his?"

Despite the dim light leaking out from the diner, Annie's face colored, and she looked away, not responding.

You idiot, Gwen thought. Nice and subtle. She was about to apologize, but the cab appeared, pulling into the empty parking space in front of them. They got inside, Annie gave the driver the address, and they sat in what felt to Gwen like an awkward silence for the entire trip.

Maybe this was better. The camaraderie they'd built since leaving the motel could only be temporary. They had planned, after all, to get the money, skip town, and part ways. The first part of this scheme was moot, but once they finally made it past the police barricades, they'd probably never see each other again. In the meantime, they had no reason to be friendly—it complicated things.

Already, Gwen was going to have to figure out how to clean up this mess. By now, the police had her fingerprints, and if they managed to track their movements for the last couple of hours, they'd know she was with Annie and certainly not a hostage anymore. There was probably video surveillance of them at this point, from the bus, if nowhere else. It would take a lot of work to undo today's fuckup, if that was even possible.

Annie asked the cab to drop them off a block from the trucking company Tom worked at. She recognized the logo, so they were in the right place. As they approached on foot, Gwen was tempted to wave the cab back down and leave Annie here. After all, while the police very likely had her fingerprints, they wouldn't have a recent photograph, so she might be able to slip out of town without any problems. She was about to do just that, when Annie smiled at her. The chance passed without regret as the cab drove away.

"He's going to be so pissed at me," Annie said, still smiling.

"And that's funny?"

She nodded, almost eagerly. "Yes. You'll see why."

The building was enormous—several blocks, if Gwen had to guess—with thirty or forty trucks with trailers at the loading docks. Several empty truck cabs were parked in a large lot nearby. Annie led them toward a car lot, pointing at a set of industrial-sized garbage bins at the far end.

"Let's wait behind those. I don't know how many people start when he does, so who knows how many will be around."

"What's the plan? Are you going to walk up to him? What if someone's around when he shows up?"

Annie frowned. "I'll point him out, and you can bring him over here."

It was tight, but they found enough space behind the garbage bins to crouch, and Gwen had to breathe through her mouth to keep from gagging. The ground here was sticky with some kind of runoff and littered with bits of debris, various wrappers, and black, rotten chunks of something that stuck to her boots.

Annie was peering around the edge of the bin, and after about five minutes of eager anticipation, she started shifting from foot to foot. Gwen could tell from her profile that she was becoming anxious. What if he didn't show? They had no way to get back to town.

"Oh, thank God," she finally said.

"You see him?"

"His car's pulling in now, and I think he's alone. No one else is in the lot. Still, it would probably be safer for you to go out there and get him in case someone shows up."

"Do you think anyone's following him? The police, I mean?"

Annie turned frightened eyes on her. "Shit. I didn't think of that."

"We'll have to risk it," Gwen said, struggling up from her the balls of her feet. She inched around Annie and hurried to Tom's car. By the time she reached it, he was still inside fiddling with something on the passenger-side seat, not seeing her, so she had a second to observe him. He was younger than she'd expected—younger than Annie, it seemed, and handsome. He had a cleanly shaved face and square, Buddy Holly–type glasses. He glanced up and froze, hands on the steering wheel. Gwen lifted a hand and waved, smiling and trying to seem friendly. He climbed out of his car, his face dark and threatening. Standing up, he was incredibly tall—well over six foot and scarecrow thin.

"Uh, hi," Gwen said. Her voice almost squeaked.

"Who the fuck are you? Get the hell away from my car."

Gwen took an involuntary step back. "Uh, I'm here with your friend. Your...childhood friend."

"What? Who?"

"Jesus, Tom!" Annie yelled from across the lot. "She's here with me! Get over here!"

Tom started running that way at once, brushing past Gwen without another glance, and she could barely keep up. Annie had come around the side of the trash can, and they launched themselves at each other, Tom scooping Annie into his arms and twirling her around, crushed to his chest. Annie screeched, laughing and giggling when he set her back down.

"Holy shit, Annie! I saw you on the news all day and could barely believe it. What the hell are you doing here?"

Annie's expression sobered. "I need your help, Tom. We have to get out of town."

At the "we," Tom looked at Gwen, frowning. "Who the hell are you?"

Again, Gwen couldn't help but distance herself from him and took a step back, hands up.

"This is Gwen, Tom," Annie said. "Be nice. She helped me out today."

Tom's face cleared, and he stepped toward her, hand extended. "Sorry. Nice to meet you."

"Likewise." His hand enveloped hers like a blanket, and she had to crane her neck to meet his eyes.

"Hell, Annie," he said, moving back to her and hugging her under one arm. "I still can't believe it. I never thought I'd see you on the outside again."

"I never thought I'd get out."

"When did you plan this escape? You never mentioned it to me." He seemed almost hurt.

Annie shook her head. "I couldn't, Tom. You couldn't be involved. I wouldn't even be here now, but I didn't have any other choice. You're my last hope."

"Well, shit, Annie. Of course I'll help you. What do you need? Money? A place to crash? Anything."

"Like I said, we need to get out of town. The police are after us. I don't know how much longer we can hide."

"Do you need my car?" he asked, digging in his pocket. "I got the keys right here. Just let me know where you leave it."

Annie folded her hands around his fist. "No, Tom. It won't work. They have police barricades up all over town, and more of them outside of town. We were hoping you could...well smuggle us out. In your truck."

He reacted as if slapped, his head jerking back. He rubbed his mouth with his giant hand. "Oh."

Annie grabbed his arms, peering up into his face. "I know it's a lot to ask, but I didn't have any other ideas."

He stared down at her for a long time, his expression troubled and twisting on itself. He bit his lip and shook his head. "Gee, Annie. I don't know if I can do it."

Annie let go of him and took a step back, her features crumpling.

"It's not that I don't want to. I just don't know how we'd do it and get away with it. Everything gets checked and triple-checked before they close the door to the trailer. Something like ten guys are involved. I don't know how I'd get you in there. I don't think it's possible. Someone would spot you."

"I see." Annie's voice was quiet, choked.

"I'm sorry. Here—take my car keys, at least. I can always claim you stole it. Maybe you can find a way out of town after all."

Annie didn't take them, so Gwen held out her hand. Tom gave her a weak smile, and she grasped them. He stepped close to her and, almost under his breath, said, "Take care of her for me."

He turned back to Annie and gave her a tight hug. "Sorry about this, champ. You need any money?"

She shook her head, wiping her eyes. "No. But thanks. We'll be okay."

"Call me when you get somewhere safe."

"I will."

He started walking back across the lot toward the main door, but Gwen was watching Annie, who was obviously trying not to cry. She was overtired and upset but seemed more heartbroken than anything. She'd pinned her hopes on this.

Gwen thought of something. "Hey, Tom?"

He spun back.

"What about the cab? Does anyone check that?"

He slapped his forehead, groaning. "Jesus! Of course!" He ran back to them, pulling out another set of keys. "The little one on here's for the sleeper. No one checks that. Leave the keys on the driver's seat for me once you're in." He frowned. "You'll have to be careful, though. A few people are usually checking out their trucks, getting their stuff together, that kind of thing, but you should be able to sneak in if you're careful. It's kind of tight, but two little girls like you should fit in okay." He looked back and forth at them. "Close the little curtain between the seats. I'll be in and out a couple of times before we're on the road, so stay quiet if you hear me. I'll say your names when it's safe. You might try to get some sleep. There should still be some snacks and water in there, too, from last week. Nothing healthy or anything—jerky, chips, that kind of thing. Help yourself."

"You're a lifesaver, Tom," Annie said, hugging him.

"Wait till we get somewhere before you thank me. You could still be caught."

"Well, thanks for trying, anyway, no matter what happens."

"Jesus!" Tom said, after glancing at his watch. "I gotta go. My boss is gonna have a conniption fit already."

"How will we know what truck it is?" Gwen asked.

He laughed. "Annie knows. See you soon."

## CHAPTER EIGHT

They hid behind a little bush near the side of the building where the truck cabs were parked. To Gwen, they were identical—large, hulking machines in uniform whites or blacks.

"Which one is it?"

"We have to check the driver's door," Annie whispered.

That was easier said than done. As Tom had predicted, several men were climbing in and out of their cabs, doing inspections or dropping off bags of their belongings. She and Annie had to run, first from the bush to the front of the farthest truck, then from that one to the next and the next. At each one, Annie would pause, crane her head around the driver's side, then gesture for them to keep going. It was relatively dark outside, but a couple of times Gwen was certain a man inside his truck had seen them. He could have easily been spotted them if he'd glanced outside.

"It's this one," Annie finally said.

"How can you tell?"

"You'll see. But wait a sec—there's a guy inside the one next to this."

They were sitting on the balls of their feet as they waited, and the long day was starting to make Gwen quake with fatigue. Finally, Annie turned to her, put a finger on her lips, and gestured for her to follow. They inched around between the two trucks, still stooped, and Annie stopped by the door to the sleeper and pointed. There, under the little American flag on the driver's door, was a tiny rainbow flag. Gwen grinned back at her and waited for Annie to open the little sleeper door. Annie slid inside a moment later, and Gwen followed, closing the door behind her. She waited a few seconds, catching her breath, and listened, ear pressed to the door. If anyone saw her feet slipping inside, they would probably call out, but she heard no cries of alarm. She scooted back a little, engaged the lock, and then put her back to the door.

Annie had already partially closed the accordion-style plastic curtain between the seats and the bed, leaving it cracked open for the light. The truck sat directly under a streetlight, and it was surprisingly bright with the light reflecting off the windscreen. Annie was sitting with her knees tucked up, almost under her chin, bent awkwardly in half to give Gwen enough room to get in. They had plenty of room to sit upright, but the bed itself was short and narrow, not even as wide or long as a twin. Gwen could hardly picture Tom sleeping in here.

After double-checking that the door behind her was latched and locked, she mimicked Annie's pose, and the two of them sat facing each other. Gwen immediately felt cramped. With so little room, the toes of her boots touched Annie's.

"Jesus," Gwen said. "How the hell does he fit back here?"

"Can't imagine. He must have to bend in half."

A little shelf on the right had a footlocker. Gwen slipped the strap of her tool bag off her shoulder and stuffed it into a space next to it. Tom had mentioned snacks, so she opened the locker to peek inside.

"Chips, jerky, some bottled water. Want something?"

Annie shook her head, and Gwen pulled out some water. It was fairly cool, despite sitting in here for God knew how long, and she took a long pull before offering it to Annie.

"Thanks."

"Well, this is cozy," Gwen said.

"That's one word for it. I was thinking it was more like a coffin."

"Do you want to try to sleep? Who knows how long this'll take. I'm beat."

"How? I can barely breathe, let alone sleep."

Gwen hesitated. "We could lie down. It might be more comfortable that way, anyway."

"You mean next to each other?"

Gwen laughed. "Of course. What else?"

Annie's face tightened, her expression anxious, and Gwen waved a hand dismissively. "Sorry. It was just a thought."

Annie shook her head. "No. You're right. I don't think I can sleep, but lying down might be nice. I'd love to get out of these boots, too. They're a little tight."

Gwen wasn't sure if it was a good idea to take off their boots—it would make it harder to run if they had to, but it would be more comfortable. Lying down also presented another problem: her gun. It was still in her coat pocket and would be incredibly uncomfortable to lie on. After a moment's hesitation, she decided to risk it and shucked off her boots and jacket, cramming them on top of her tool bag. She set Annie's tiny ones next to hers when she handed them to her. Annie was still clutching her purse, but Gwen didn't mention it.

"There's a blanket," Annie said, pointing.

The mattress was already covered in a thin sheet, and a pillow lay on Annie's end of the bed. Gwen grabbed the blanket, and the two of them maneuvered awkwardly until they were lying down, facing each other. Annie had pushed herself as far away from her as possible, her back against the curtain that hung between the bed and the seats, but they were barely a few inches apart. Annie still seemed tense, rigid, clasping the purse next to her chest.

"Now, this *is* cozy," Gwen said, trying to ease the tension.

Annie gave her a weak smile, not meeting her eyes.

"Do you want the blanket?"

Annie nodded, still looking away.

Gwen sat up a little and flapped the folded blanket a few times to release it, tucking it down around their legs before lying down and settling it over them. It was a heavy flannel, and she felt almost instantly warmer. It was surprisingly cold in here.

"Better?"

Annie nodded, her eyes meeting hers briefly. "Better."

Gwen took the opportunity to examine Annie up close. She knew Annie could see her staring at her, but she continued anyway. Here, inches away, Gwen could see the beginnings of tiny lines at the corners of her eyes and around her mouth. She was older than Gwen had first assumed—maybe early to mid-thirties instead of in her twenties. She had one of those young faces. Being small like she was added to her youthfulness. Now, without makeup and with her hair still loose and wild, she could still have passed for almost any age between eighteen and forty.

Annie finally met her eyes, her expression almost angry. "What are you staring at?"

"You."

Annie flushed and opened her mouth a few times, fish-like, clearly at a loss for a reply.

Gwen laughed. "Can't I look at a pretty woman?"

"N-no!" Annie sputtered.

Gwen couldn't help but goad her. "Why not?"

"Because I said so!"

"Ah, I see." Gwen closed her eyes. "Is this better?"

"Yes," she said, but she sounded uncertain.

They were quiet long enough that Gwen found herself starting to drift off. She was facing the gap between the curtains, so the light outside was full on her face, but she was so tired it didn't bother her. It would likely be a long time before she was in a bed again—hours, at least, so a little catnap might be just the thing.

"Gwen?"

She opened her eyes. Annie had inched a little closer, and her body had lost some of its tension.

"Hmmm?"

"I'm sorry. I'm not used to—"

"It's okay. No need to apologize. I was teasing you."

"I know. I'm sorry I overreacted."

Gwen nodded and closed her eyes again, tugged toward sleep almost at once.

"Gwen?"

Annie looked, if possible, even closer than before. Gwen blinked a few times, stretched, and rubbed her face, trying to focus and wake up.

"Yes?"

"Where were you going today? When you picked me up? I mean, where were you headed?"

Gwen saw no reason to lie. "Los Angeles."

"Why?"

"A client fired me this morning."

"Oh. You were working here in Texas?"

"Sort of. The main office is in California, but I have to travel all the time. I was in Austin for a few months helping out."

"Is that where you're from? California?"

Gwen shook her head. "Colorado, originally. I still sort of live there, sometimes."

"Sounds complicated."

"It is."

"So you were fired from *a* job, but not fired altogether."

"Exactly. But my boss might fire me altogether when I get back to LA. This isn't my first fuckup."

"Sorry."

Gwen shrugged. "It's okay. It might be a good thing. I've been in this line of work too long. Starting to lose my edge."

"As a car thief," Annie said.

Gwen laughed. "No—that's incidental." She paused, realizing once again that she didn't need to lie. "Stealing cars isn't really part of the job. Officially, anyway. I'm a PI."

"Oh!" Annie said, eyebrows shooting up.

"Not what you expected?"

"No, but it makes sense, now."

They were quiet for a while, and once again, Gwen didn't bother to fight her sleepiness, her eyes dropping closed almost of their own accord. She heard Annie scooting around a little, and the blanket was twitched off her, so she made herself open her eyes. Annie had gotten up on her elbow.

"Something wrong?"

"A handle back here, for the curtain—it's poking my back."

Gwen sat up. The curtain had two plastic handles, one for each side. She reached behind Annie to try to move it a little, but it was firmly attached.

"You'll have to turn around," she said.

"What?"

"Like spoons," Gwen responded, grinning.

Annie shook her head. "No—that's okay. Maybe I can put something over the handle—pad it, or something."

"Suit yourself."

Gwen lay down and closed her eyes again. Annie scooched closer, their legs almost flush, and then she sighed, and Gwen felt her sit up entirely. She opened her eyes and watched Annie put her purse on top of their other belongings before she turned, twisted around, and lay down, moving back into Gwen. Gwen kept her arm up on her side a few seconds longer before letting it drop down over Annie, who tensed and then relaxed.

"See! Much better," Gwen said. "In a bed this small, spoons are the only way to go."

"Sounds like you have a lot of experience with small beds."

"My dorm bed wasn't much bigger than this."

"Your roommate must have loved that."

"I think she did—she was the one in bed with me."

Annie didn't respond, and Gwen could have kicked herself. It was one thing to flirt and flatter, but she hadn't actually come out until now. Still, Annie didn't move away or tense up again, so that was a good sign. Judging from her choice of bars in El Paso and her behavior there, Gwen was more than certain Annie was gay or bi—that act in there had been a little too practiced, too natural, as if she'd been on a date there before. She'd noticed other, less obvious signs all day today, and Gwen had fairly accurate gaydar. And even if Annie didn't swing her way, cuddling in this little bed together clearly didn't repulse her. In fact, at least for Gwen, it was pleasant—comforting, really.

They were both dozing when Tom climbed inside. He slammed the truck door and, speaking almost under his breath, said, "The trailer is finally loaded. I'm moving over to hook up. There'll be some final inspections, and then we'll be on the road—twenty, thirty minutes. I'll close the curtain the rest of the way when I get out. My boss will pop in to check the mileage and the brake lights."

Neither of them replied, and the truck rumbled to life a moment later. They were insulated from the engine a little by distance, but Gwen was surprised by how loud it seemed. The bed was shaking, and she was reminded of road trips to Phoenix as a child. Once, her family had stopped at a motel somewhere in New Mexico, and the bed she shared with her brother had something called Magic Fingers. They'd spent the evening begging their parents for dimes and giggling as the bed shook them hard enough to rattle their teeth.

The truck shifted into reverse, and Tom slowly backed up, a loud beeping alarm announcing the move. Eventually, they moved forward, then backed up once more. Tom closed the curtain, plunging them into darkness, but he left the truck on when he got out. Soon Gwen heard and felt as the trailer was attached. Something slammed into place, jarring them, and shouts came from behind the wall of the cabin outside. The men's voices, laughing and calling to each other, were too indistinct to catch any words, but she could occasionally make out Tom's voice in the hubbub.

The driver's door opened again, and a stranger was laughing as he climbed inside. Annie tensed under her arm, and both of them held their breath.

"—You old son of bitch! Let's see what we have here," the man was saying. Gwen heard the sound of a pen scribbling something. She heard something else—movement of some kind. "How's that?" the man shouted. He turned off the engine and climbed out again, slamming the door behind him.

Gwen let out her breath and heard Annie do the same. "I think we're going to be okay," she whispered. Annie didn't reply.

The wait seemed endless. Gwen could only imagine that they were doing some kind of inspection out there, as nothing seemed to happen for a long time. After what seemed like hours, the driver's door opened again, and the cabin shifted a little with, she hoped, Tom's weight. He closed the door, the truck thundered to life, and then they were moving, slowly at first, turning at one point, and then with more and more speed.

"Stay quiet a little longer back there," Tom said. "My boss said one of the other drivers hit a police barricade outside of town. Let's hope they're just doing visual inspections."

It wasn't long before she felt the truck slow again. "In line at the barricade now," Tom said. "Doesn't look too bad—maybe ten or fifteen cars and trucks in front of me."

Annie was trembling in her arms, and Gwen gave her a reassuring squeeze. Gwen closed her eyes, inhaling deeply and catching the hint of something flowery and sweet in Annie's hair. Despite the prison break this morning, she had apparently taken the time to wash it before she left.

The waiting was worse this time. The truck would move a few feet, stop, and then move again, and each time it did, Gwen wondered if this was the end. If the police did any kind of inspection beyond a very casual visual check of the main cabin, they'd be caught. If they had dogs, for example, or if they asked to check back here, they wouldn't be able to do a thing. Who would she call after she was arrested?

The investigations firm she worked for kept a lawyer on call— she'd had to contact him herself a few times—but she wasn't sure they'd let her use him for something like this. She had some money saved, so she could hire someone, but she had no idea how to go about it. Tom would be in trouble, too, and as for Annie, she would probably be back in prison by daybreak. All of this was starting to seem like the stupidest idea of all time. The fact that the woman Annie spoke to on the phone had suggested it did nothing to ease her mind.

The truck crept forward again, the brakes and transmission hissing in protest. This time, Gwen heard the window roll down.

"Hello there, Officers," Tom said. "How's it going?"

The truck shifted as someone climbed up on the step to look inside. She saw a flash of light on the other side of the curtain as it swept the cabin.

"Fine," a woman said. "Where are you headed?"

"Albuquerque first, then up into Colorado and Wyoming—Denver, Cheyenne, and a few other stops."

"Can I see your permits and inspection logs?"

"Sure."

Gwen heard some rustling and pages were turned.

"Here you go," the woman said, and stepped down again. "Have a good night. Drive safe."

"Thanks, Officer."

They were moving soon after, and again, Annie was shuddering in her arms. Gwen heard her sob.

"Shh," Gwen whispered. "We're okay now."

"I can't b-believe it," Annie said, her voice choked and almost indecipherable.

"It's going to be okay. We're safe."

Annie turned, hugging her tightly, and, after her initial surprise, Gwen hugged her back, running her hands in little circles on Annie's shoulders and making soothing sounds.

"You ladies okay back there?" Tom called.

"We're fine," Gwen said. Annie was still crying.

"I want to make some miles before I drop you off, if that's okay. It might be better for you to wait until right before my first stop in Albuquerque. I could leave you at a motel or something."

"Sounds perfect."

"You guys want some light?"

Gwen felt Annie shake her head under her chin. "No—we're good. Gonna try to catch some shut-eye. Long day."

"No problem. I'll wake you up in couple of hours when we're closer."

Gwen was afraid Annie would cry the whole time, but it wasn't long before the tension seemed to suddenly leave her body. A few minutes later, she was breathing deeply, almost as if someone had turned off a switch.

Gwen thought she'd be forced to stay up, her nerves still jangling with spent adrenaline, but she drifted off almost at once, the delicate scent of Annie's hair filling her, comforting her.

# CHAPTER NINE

Jesus, Annie, don't you have a coat?" Tom asked.

The rise in elevation and the trip north had turned a chilly night downright cold. Even in her jacket, Gwen was uncomfortably cold, and Annie, with her bare arms, was shivering hard.

"Didn't get the chance to pick one up," Annie said, her teeth clattering.

Tom climbed back into his truck and pulled out his jacket, handing it to her. It hung on her like a blanket, the effect making her seem even smaller, younger than before.

"And you're okay for money?" he asked again.

"Fine," she said. "I'll be okay, Tom."

He frowned and chewed his lip, clearly reluctant to leave. He'd parked on the street in front of a motel. They were off one of the first exits for Albuquerque, the motel the first in a series of run-down businesses near the ramp. When he'd woken them some twenty minutes ago, Gwen had asked to stop near a used-car dealership, and she saw one down the block from the motel, exactly the kind she'd wanted—older cars of various makes and models.

Annie hugged him, her arms circling his waist. He stared at Gwen as she did this, his eyes dark and distrustful. She understood this antagonism. He had no reason to trust her, likely thinking she was part of Annie's mess. Which, as she thought about it, she kind of was.

"What are you going to do, Annie?" he asked when she stepped back. "What's your plan?"

"I can't tell you that, Tom. If they catch up to you, it's better..." She lifted one shoulder.

He was clearly hurt but nodded. "Yeah. I get it."

"I'm sorry. I'll get in touch with you once things settle down a little."

"Okay, Annie, but make sure you call me if you need anything. I check my messages every day, and the police can't listen to those."

"Okay, Tom—I'll call if I have to."

"What should I tell her? When I call her?"

Annie threw Gwen a quick glance and shook her head. "Don't tell her anything. I don't want her mixed up in this. It's already bad enough that you're in it."

Tom sighed. "You know I don't care about all that, Annie, and she wouldn't either. I know you. You're a good person. She knows that, too." He frowned. "She asks about you all the time. You really should call."

Again, Annie glanced at Gwen and then shook her head at Tom. "I can't. I won't, Tom. I hope she understands why."

He shrugged. "Maybe she does, but that still doesn't mean you have to pretend she doesn't exist."

Annie squeezed his hand. "I'll phone her, okay? Once all this is over. I promise. You can tell her I will."

He gave her another hug and then held out his hand to Gwen. "Nice meeting you." He clearly didn't mean it.

"You, too."

"Take care of my girl, okay?"

"Will do."

"See ya, kiddo."

"Bye, Tom," Annie said.

"Get a coat, for God's sake. You look like you're wearing your daddy's jacket."

They watched as he climbed back into his truck and stared out the window at them in silence before starting it. Then he gave them a quick salute and slowly drove away, reentering the interstate at the on-ramp a few blocks away. Annie had tears in her eyes, and Gwen walked away to check out the motel while she collected herself.

The office was dark, but Gwen found an after-hours button next to a glass window, pushed it, and waited. Annie joined her long before anyone appeared, and Gwen could hear someone cursing inside and the sound of something breaking, followed by more cursing. An older man finally appeared from a door in the back of the lobby, looking disheveled and upset. They'd obviously gotten him out of bed.

He frowned and actually slowed his pace as he walked across the small lobby. He took his time collecting some paperwork before finally opening the little window. No one spoke for a moment, the man clearly above a simple greeting.

"We need a room," Annie finally said.

"Might be a problem there," he said.

"What? Why?"

"We're remodeling."

Gwen almost laughed. The place clearly hadn't been remodeled since it was built—sometime in the fifties, judging by the look of it.

"So what does that mean?" Annie asked. "You don't have any rooms?"

"Oh, we've got a room, but you two don't want it."

The guy was giving them a hard time, judging them entirely by appearances and circumstances. He hadn't seen them get out of the truck, but it was obvious they hadn't driven here themselves—there was no car behind them. It was the middle of the night, and they were on foot—that meant they were likely homeless or sex workers or both. Gwen couldn't exactly blame him for his rudeness, but she didn't have to like it.

"So what do you have?" Gwen asked, trying to keep the anger from her voice.

"One room with a king bed. That's all."

Gwen could see by the little sign on the window that it was the most expensive room they had, and she almost laughed at his guile. Only one car sat parked near the motel itself, so unless only two rooms were available at any given time, he was obviously lying and knew they knew he was.

"We'll take it," Annie said.

"Cash up front," the man said, harsh and clipped.

"Of course," Annie said. She was clearly reading him the same way, her impatience obvious. He gave them a price well over the one posted on the window, but Annie paid without complaint. He seemed surprised and then pretended he couldn't break her hundred-dollar bill. They both threatened to walk away and find another place, so he finally caved, giving them slightly less money in return than he owed them, sighing and complaining as if they were robbing him. Still, as he didn't ask for an ID or a credit card, Gwen thought they'd gotten a pretty good deal. The whole situation was promising, in a way, as in the unlikely circumstance their faces were on the news here, or if someone managed to track them here at a later date, he'd be less likely to report them because of the extra money he'd pocketed.

The room was almost as bad as the one they'd been in yesterday afternoon, but Gwen was far beyond caring about niceties now. Despite the three-hour nap in the truck, she felt, if anything, worse than before. Now that they were relatively safe, her exhaustion was finally taking over. She threw down her bag and flung herself on the bed, facedown.

Annie, however, seemed to have found her second wind, and she fluttered around the little room like a caged bird. Gwen was almost able to ignore her—she could feel the welcome drag of sleep trying to pull her down, but she sighed and flopped onto her back, slipping off her boots and scooting up to the pillows. Annie, oblivious to her activity, was still pacing. Gwen watched her a while longer, wondering if she'd eventually notice her gaze, but she was in her own little world, her eyes focused inward, her expression worried and scared.

"Take a load off, lady. You're making me nervous."

Annie flinched and stopped, staring at her as if she'd forgotten she was there. She glanced around before perching on the one chair in the corner of the room.

"What's the matter?" Gwen asked. "Why are you so freaked out? We're out of Texas—that's the main thing."

"No—not really. It's the first thing. And Tom was right. I don't know what happens next. I guess I never really believed I'd make it this far. I wanted to try—I had to try, but I didn't think I'd get out."

Gwen scooted up a little more on the bed, her prone position too comfortable for her to focus. She rolled her neck a few times, trying to loosen some of the stiffness in her shoulders, and slapped her cheeks lightly to wake herself up.

"What was your plan? Earlier? I thought you said you had one. Something about getting the rest of your money."

"But that's what I mean!" Annie said, almost leaping to her feet. "Someone set me up. Someone wants me to be caught again."

"So why help you get out of prison? Why bother with all that? Why not leave you in there?"

Annie stared at her. "So I won't talk—won't give them away. I…know things. Things that would get me a reduced sentence if the police had names, information."

Gwen rubbed her eyes. "Let me get this straight. You think the people that helped you break out are the same ones that called the police on you? That woman on the phone?"

Annie frowned and then nodded. "It has to be her. Or the other one—the one that hid the envelope. She told me he wasn't in El Paso, but she could be lying."

"Call me stupid, but I don't get it."

Annie sat down on the bed by Gwen's feet. "Think about it. The people who break me out, the ones that put that envelope there, they were watching, waiting for me to show up in that parking lot. They knew I was going there—she told me where to go to get it. No one else knew where it was but the two of them. They had to put it there, just in case, so the envelope was actually waiting for me, but all they had to do was make a simple phone call once they saw me get out of the car with you."

"Why not tell the police where you were? In the building with the envelope? Wouldn't that have been even easier? If the police had gone there first, we would have been caught for sure."

"That would have been going too far. By calling in the car, they could still cover their asses. If they'd told them which building I was in, it would give them up entirely."

"I still don't follow. Walk me through it, Annie. What's their motivation?"

"The money, of course! If I told the police about them, they'd lose all that money, whatever's left, anyway. And, of course, they'd be arrested."

Gwen's confusion must have been obvious, as Annie sighed. "Okay, listen. Four years ago, I was desperate for money. A lot of it—more than I could ever earn at my job at the bank. With my position, I could make something happen if I found people who could hide the money. Certain things led me to this woman. She said hiding the money was a sure thing."

"How could you believe her? Surely you must have known you'd eventually be caught."

Annie shrugged. "She said they'd never be able to trace it. I'm pretty sure I knew better, but I went along with the plan anyway. I had to have the money. It wasn't a question of want. I needed it, and desperation doesn't really begin to explain how much. Then, when I was caught, she made me a deal."

Gwen suddenly understood. "Ah. If you took the fall, they'd break you out. They'd hide the money and give you your share if you didn't reveal their names to the police."

Annie nodded. "Exactly. A few of the others were rounded up—they had to be, but the two...masterminds went scot-free. I got more prison time than the others, because I worked at the bank and admitted to planning the whole thing."

"With the idea they'd get you out in a couple of years."

Annie frowned. "It wasn't even supposed to take that long. Six months, they promised. They strung me along for a while until I threatened to give them up. Then they finally got their act together and planned the escape." She paused. "Even then, I knew they were trying to screw me."

"And now you think they're double-crossing you. If you're caught again, they can string you along for a few more years, pretend it'll be harder to get you out a second time. Meanwhile, your prison sentence will be even longer for breaking out."

"All the while, they're spending my money."

"Some of it's probably already spent. It's been years now."

Annie nodded.

"But why wouldn't you turn them in if you were caught again? That's the part I don't get."

"They're probably hoping I'll think someone else turned me in. One of the other bank managers I worked with, Edward, was fired when I was caught. He had nothing to do with any of it, but the bank blamed him for not catching me before the IRS and the FBI got involved. He's had it out for me ever since. He testified against me and has sent me nasty letters in prison. I finally had to put him on my no-contact list."

"But you don't think it's actually him?"

"How could it be? He didn't know anything about the breakout. And anyway, he moved to Kansas City a couple of years ago. I mean, I guess it's possible he's had some kind of contact in El Paso watching for news about me all this time, but that seems pretty far-fetched, even for him."

"Do they know he moved? These two 'masterminds,' as you call them?"

Annie's eyebrows shot up. "No. I don't think they do. Not unless they looked into it. I've never mentioned it, anyway."

Gwen shrugged. "Even if they did, they might have thought you didn't know."

"I wouldn't have, except Tom told me. He was keeping an eye on him after he harassed me."

Gwen pointed a finger at her. "There you go. They're counting on your not knowing."

"Jesus," Annie said, standing up again. "I'm totally fucked." She slapped a fist into her palm. "Goddamn it all. They really screwed me."

"They're playing a pretty dangerous game. They have to know you'll figure it out—unless they're complete idiots." She paused, wondering if she should ask. "Why not turn them in? Why not call someone right now and tell them all about it?"

Annie seemed briefly hopeful and then shook her head. "No. The police would never believe me. Not unless I turned myself in."

"They might."

Annie lifted one shoulder. "Maybe. But then what? I'd still be screwed. I'd have to live like this the rest of my life." She gestured vaguely at the terrible room. "I can't use that fake ID now, and I can't afford another one. At best I could get a crummy job that doesn't ask too many questions."

"And you'd lose all that money."

Annie shook her head. "It was never about the money. Not really. I needed it, but not for myself. It's too late now, anyway."

Her eyes filled up with tears, and without thinking about it, Gwen leapt up off the bed and pulled her into an embrace. She let Annie cry against her for a long moment before drawing back a little, hands on Annie's shoulders.

"Fuck them," she said.

Annie looked shocked for a second and then laughed. "Easy for you to say."

"No, really, fuck them. Double-crossing bastards. I don't expect anything from criminals, but it sounds like they really screwed you."

Annie shook her head, moving away. "I should have known better. Even now, I'm not surprised. I didn't actually think I could get away with it, not really, even before we moved all that money. I was so desperate."

"Why did you do it?"

Annie eyelashes were still sparkling with tears. "I had to, Gwen. The money was for my sister. She's mentally ill. She needed home care, and I couldn't afford it." Her eyes filled with tears again. "Now she's in an institution, and I can't do anything to get her out. They'd never release her to me, now." She paused, collecting herself. "I was hoping I could…make an anonymous trust for her, or something. Get her out of that hospital and pay someone to take care of her full time. Somewhere nice—somewhere pretty. She always loved the beach when we were kids. I was going to ask Tom to help me, once I got the money. He has power of attorney now. I wouldn't be able to visit, but I'd know she was taken care of. That would be enough. Even if I went to prison for the rest of my life, it would be enough to know she was safe."

"One point five million dollars would certainly help you do that for her."

"If it even exists anymore."

Gwen's skepticism must have shown in her face, as Annie turned away from her and cried silently. Gwen was tempted to put her hands on Annie's shoulders, turn her around, and tell her something comforting—a lie, but enough to get her to stop crying. She let the temptation pass, and soon Annie turned back, her face tear-stained but calm, and excused herself for a shower.

As she waited, Gwen walked outside to get them some cold drinks from the vending machine. She didn't drink soda herself, but the idea of something cold on her parched throat was inviting enough to tempt her to break her usual rules. She bought two of the least repugnant off-brand sodas and stood outside their door, thinking. After the turbulent feelings in the motel room, the cool mountain air was refreshing, invigorating. Despite what she'd said earlier, she didn't entirely agree with Annie. Something was missing, some part of this whole mess she hadn't quite understood, some angle they were overlooking. She stood there, an idea forming at the edge of her consciousness, but every time she tried to concentrate on it, it slipped farther away.

She stopped fighting it, knowing it would return with more clarity when she wasn't exhausted. She took one more deep breath of the thin air and opened the door with her free hand, sodas clutched in the other. As if summoning her, Annie came out of the bathroom at the same time, a towel cinched around her body with one hand, steam roiling behind her like a dreamscape. Gwen froze in place, the door to the room still open.

"Let's go to bed," Annie said, and dropped the towel.

# CHAPTER TEN

*P*ound, pound, pound, pound, pound. "Housekeeping!"
   "Jesus!" Gwen said, sitting bolt upright. The movement caused the blanket to drop onto her lap, and the cool air of the room hit her naked body. She pulled the blanket up to cover her chest.
   "We're still in here!" she shouted.
   She heard some muttering outside and the sound of the maid's cart being pushed away. She reached across Annie's body and pulled the little string for the lamp. Annie blinked, squinting. "What time is it?"
   Gwen glanced around the room, not surprised there was no clock. She'd managed to remove her watch before they finally dropped off to sleep, and she pulled it off the nightstand.
   "It's nine."
   Annie stretched, the blanket bunching under her breasts, and Gwen openly stared at them. Annie saw her and, obviously pretending modesty, pulled the blanket back over herself.
   "Perv."
   "Takes one to know one."
   Annie stuck out her tongue and giggled, and Gwen bent down, kissing her deeply. She pulled away and plopped down on her pillow again. Annie climbed over her, snuggling under her chin. They lay there in the darkened room, quiet for a long while. Entwined, they were a study in contrasts—Annie thin and soft and shockingly pale,

while she was toned and firm and golden brown in the dark room. Gwen was relieved they weren't awkward around each other now. Last night, before drifting off, she'd worried about just that, but Annie seemed to be taking things in stride. They'd been stressed out, tired, and the sex had been a distraction in the best way.

"Mmm," Annie said. "That was a nice kiss."

"Even with morning breath?"

She nodded. "Yes. Do it again."

Gwen obliged, putting a little more heat in this one, and Annie pulled her closer. One of her hands slid along Gwen's back, and she shuddered with a delicious pleasure. She made herself move away and climb out of the bed, naked and staring down at her. She shook a finger at Annie. "None of that, now. We have places to be."

"We do?"

"Yes. First, we need a car."

"No—first, we need more kissing. Then breakfast. Then a car."

"In that order?"

Annie flung the blanket off her entire body, revealing its softness, and Gwen climbed back into bed.

Freshly showered an hour later, they gathered their few belongings and vacated the crappy room, leaving the key in the door. The guy last night might not report them, but Gwen wasn't sure the person in the office this morning would be so accommodating. They walked away from the motel as quickly as they could and into a fast-food joint one building over. Gwen hadn't eaten at one of these places in so long, she wasn't sure she'd find anything she could eat, but the woman behind the counter was friendly and chipper, and didn't mind her request for an egg-white sandwich with no butter. Annie, as usual, ordered a huge amount: two sandwiches with eggs and cheese and meat, three orders of hash browns, an orange juice, and a Coke. Again, Gwen watched her eat with pleasure, finishing her own food long before Annie despite Annie's usual voracious speed.

Annie pushed the ketchup-splattered tray away from herself, sighing. "That's better."

"Worked up quite the appetite."

Annie gave her a grin and squeezed her hand. "Yes. We did." Her face fell, and she stared out the window, frowning.

"What's the matter?"

Annie made eye contact before looking away again. "I just—I don't usually…"

"Sleep with women? Could have fooled me."

Annie's eyebrows shot up, and she laughed. "No. That's not what I was going to say. I meant I don't usually sleep with strangers."

"You play hard to get?"

Annie shook her head. "No—not that. More like I only sleep with people I'm dating. Seriously dating."

Gwen laughed. "So what? Do you feel guilty?"

Annie was quiet for a few seconds and then shook her head. "No."

"Then what difference does it make? I had fun, you had fun, no problem."

Annie nodded but still looked grave, serious. "I guess."

Gwen leaned toward her. "If it makes you feel better, I don't usually sleep around, either. Well, not anymore. When I was younger, yes, but not now. We were both…vulnerable, worn out, and you're sexy as hell, even in that stupid getup I dressed you in. You don't have to feel bad about it. Okay?"

Annie stared at her, and some of the tension seemed to leave her face. They sat there quietly for a while, Gwen drinking her terrible coffee, Annie finishing her Coke. The sound of something crashing and breaking in the back of the restaurant startled them, and they grinned at each other.

Annie glanced around and brought her head closer to Gwen's. "So tell me how we're going to get a car. You said we might be able to buy one, cheap. How? Won't that give us away?"

A wave of relief swept through Gwen. The last thing she'd wanted to do was talk about last night. She lowered her voice. "Car dealerships like that one down the street usually insure all their cars against theft. That's money out of their pockets for cars they might not even sell. Most used-car dealerships shift their inventory pretty often to appeal to more buyers, so they're losing money that way, too, on the car leases."

Annie lifted her hands. "Okay. So how does that help us?"

"If I can talk to the right person over there, he'll probably let us…borrow a car for a cash fee. In return, he won't report it stolen for a few days, giving us a little time to get away and ditch it. We tell him where we left it later. He gets some money now, he'll get the car back later, and everyone's happy. Even if something happens to the car, he gets the insurance money. Either way, it's win-win."

"Have you done this before?"

Gwen laughed. "That car I had yesterday—the one I picked you up in—that's how I got it. Done it tons of times. It only works with little, off-brand places like the one over there, and you have to be careful who you talk to. Not everyone will go for it."

Annie frowned. "Seems risky. Isn't there some other way?"

Gwen nodded. "We could steal one again. Not from the dealership, but somewhere else. Long-term parking at an airport is usually a good bet. Gives you a little head start most of the time."

Annie didn't look pleased with this suggestion, either. She didn't say anything for a while, and Gwen excused herself to the restroom to give her time to think. By the time she came back, Annie had cleared their table and gotten them refills on their drinks.

"Let's try the dealership," she said before Gwen sat down again. "Use this." She handed her the envelope of cash.

Gwen smiled. "Okay. You'll wait here?"

Annie lifted a shoulder. "I guess. If you think that would be better."

"Yes. It would."

"Okay, but be careful. If it seems fishy, just leave."

Gwen turned to leave, but Annie grabbed her hand. "Gwen?"

"Yes?"

"Thanks for helping me. I wouldn't have gotten this far without you."

Gwen shrugged, more pleased by this remark than she would ever let on.

"I mean it, Gwen—you saved me. I owe you, big time."

Gwen wanted to tell her it had been her pleasure. Even at the beginning, when Annie had been pointing a gun at her, she hadn't been that upset. She knew Annie didn't want to hurt her, didn't want to force her to do anything. Then, after Gwen had gained the upper hand, she hadn't really wanted to leave her there in that first motel. She'd wanted to help her. She could admit that much to herself now. She'd pretended—to herself, to Annie—that it had been about the money, but even at the time, she hadn't believed the money existed. No, she only went along with all this to help her.

Now, in the bright, late-morning sunshine, with Annie's freshly clean, nearly white ringlets of hair brushing the side of her pretty face, Gwen was almost ready to simply call this what it was. And after last night...well, she never kidded herself. Less than twenty-four hours with this woman, and she was completely and utterly gone.

Annie was staring at her, obviously confused, and Gwen managed to give her a weak smile. "Sorry—just thinking. I'll be back in less than an hour. If you see me running this way, we might have a problem."

"Jesus. I hope not."

"I'm kidding. If it doesn't work, I'll be back even sooner. I doubt they'd call me in."

The dealership lot was cramped with old beaters, but she was happy to see only one employee here this time of day on a weekday. He was, she was even more pleased to see, the owner—his face plastered on the poster for the dealership above his desk. She got right to the point, explaining her proposition briefly and clearly. There could be no misunderstanding what she meant.

The man licked his lips, his eyes darting from side to side. "Are you a cop? You have to tell me if you're a cop."

"I'm not. I am not an authority of any kind. This is not entrapment. I'm simply a person that needs a car." She could tell he was nervous, so rather than give him a chance to keep thinking, she moved on to the next point. "Do you have cameras on the lot?"

He nodded. "A few."

"Do they cover the whole place?"

"No. We have a couple of blanks. But that wouldn't matter anyway. We don't keep the video more than a couple of days."

"Still, it would be safer to choose one of the cars the cameras don't cover. How often do you do inventory?"

"Every other day. Did it this morning."

"That doesn't give me a lot of time," she said.

This was, she knew, the real test. If he agreed to her proposition, he'd have to forge the inventory lists—say the car had been there when it was already gone.

He stared at her evenly for a long moment, tapping a pen against his teeth. Finally, he nodded. "Okay. But the best I can do is Monday. My salesman comes back from vacation then. He's the usual inventory guy, so he'll see it's missing right away."

Gwen understood. He was willing to take a little risk when it was easy, but he wasn't about to ask someone else to turn a blind eye. It was Wednesday now, so Monday was generously fair. "Perfect." She smiled. "Now let's talk about your fee."

She managed to bargain him down to three hundred, a hundred more than she'd paid the last time she'd done this, but she hadn't been in a hurry that time. This dealer also insisted that she take a much nicer car than the last one she'd borrowed, which she wasn't happy about. He clearly wanted the extra insurance should the car be lost or irreparably damaged. She preferred older junkers when she could get them—no one noticed them—but she wasn't in a position to argue. One benefit to this nice sedan, she realized immediately, was blissfully cool air-conditioning that functioned at once. It wasn't as warm here as it had been in Texas, but it was still a relief to be out of the dry, hot mountain air.

When she pulled up in the restaurant parking lot, Annie rushed out, clutching an enormous bag of food. Gwen rolled down the window and pointed at it. "What's that?"

"Provisions."

"You're going to stink up the whole car."

"Sue me," she said, and climbed inside and glanced around.

"Wow. Swank."

"Yeah. Not my first choice."

Annie ran her hands along the leather seat. "Still—it's a nice change."

Gwen pulled out of the lot and took the ramp to the interstate, heading north again.

"Where are we going?" Annie asked.

"North."

Annie laughed. "Yes, but where?"

Gwen glanced over at her. "I was thinking Colorado. I know a place in Denver we could hole up. Let things settle down a bit."

"Won't they check there? I mean, if they know who you are now? Wouldn't that be the first place the police will go?"

"No, actually. The apartment isn't listed under my name. It's totally safe."

They drove in silence for a few minutes. Out of the corner or her eye, Gwen saw Annie fidgeting next to her, her hands twisting nervously in her lap.

"You have another idea?" she asked.

"No. I guess I don't. And you're right—a few days in a safe place would be smart."

Gwen sighed. "Annie—I get it. You want this whole thing solved right away. But you have to realize that's not going to happen. It's going to take time, and we have to have a plan."

"For what? I mean, really, what can we do? We're totally screwed." Annie choked on these last words and started crying.

Gwen took the next exit for a rest area and pulled into a parking space. She unbuckled her belt and scooted over to Annie, pulling her into a tight hug. Annie immediately squeezed her back, shaking with sobs.

"Shh. It's going to be okay."

Annie drew back, her face dark and upset. "How? How the hell is it going to be okay? I don't want to spend the rest of my life running. I want this to be over."

"Do you want to turn yourself in?"

Annie hesitated and then shook her head. "No."

"So what do you want?"

"I want my goddamn money!" She almost screamed the words, and Gwen flinched in surprise. "I want my money, and I want the fuckers that set me up to pay. I want my sister taken care of, and I want my life back!"

Gwen let her cry for a while, hugging her with one arm, watching other travelers walk by their car. The families she saw, with their little kids and dogs, were only a few feet away from them, but they might as well have been on another planet. No one seemed to notice the little breakdown happening inside their car, for which Gwen was grateful, but she still felt conspicuous.

Finally, Annie seemed to calm down and wiped her face hard with her hands. Gwen moved away and reached into the back seat for her bag. She dug around inside and pulled out a little pack of tissues. Annie took one from her, her expression sheepish and embarrassed.

"I'm sorry. I kind of lost it."

"It's okay. You're allowed."

Annie raised her shoulders. "Maybe, but hysteria won't help, either."

"That's why we need a plan."

"You keep saying 'we.'"

Gwen laughed. "Yes, we."

"But why, Gwen? Why are you helping me? You could leave me right here. Drive to the nearest police station, and all you have to say is that I forced you to do it. I'll back you up if I'm caught. So why are you helping me?"

Gwen shook her head, exasperated. "You know."

"What? What do I know?"

Rather than respond, Gwen kissed her, putting the force of her feelings behind her lips. Annie gradually relaxed and responded, pulling her closer a moment later. When they drew away from each other, Annie's eyes, still sparkling with her tears, were large and surprised.

"Oh," she said.

"Exactly—oh."

To recover her composure, Gwen moved back to her own seat and pulled on her seat belt again. She gestured at the building with the restrooms outside their car. "Do you need to go?"

Annie was still staring at her, still looking startled, but she managed to shake her head.

"Okay, then," Gwen said, starting the car. "Let's get back on the road."

## CHAPTER ELEVEN

Gwen struggled with the key, her arms loaded with groceries. The apartment was on the third floor, a walk-up, and the last thing she'd wanted to do was make two trips. The paper bags in her right arm tilted precariously, and she sighed and set all of them down on the floor to properly work the lock. The moment she slid the key in, Annie opened the door for her, looking relieved.

"You were gone a long time."

"Yeah, well, I should have known better than to go out during the after-work rush. The traffic was crazy, and the store was a madhouse."

Annie bent down to grab half of the groceries. "Did anybody say anything about the car when you left it? What about the store? Did anyone recognize you?"

"No one gave me a second glance. I told you—it'll be fine."

They'd made it to Denver yesterday evening and had to sit through rush-hour traffic that stretched almost the entire distance from Colorado Springs. Both of them had been so tired when they reached the apartment, they'd gone straight to bed. Annie had woken her up early this morning, scared from a nightmare and still anxious, and when they'd finally fallen back to sleep, they'd slept until almost noon. They spent the early afternoon cleaning weeks of dust off the furniture and floors, and laundered the towels and sheets. Gwen had gone out to dump the car in a paid lot a few miles away, called the car dealer from a pay phone, and caught the bus back to this part of town to pick up groceries. Her errands had taken almost two hours.

The apartment was in Denver's Capitol Hill, a mixed socio-economic neighborhood of art students and young adults. This particular corner of Capitol Hill was considered one of the "gayborhoods" of Denver, but that was entirely by chance. As she'd told Annie, the place wasn't really hers. It belonged to her employer and functioned as a cheap alternative for a long-term hotel when one of the agents needed to stay in the city. The super kept the keys and gave them to anyone with an employee ID, no questions asked. He wouldn't report her to her boss—she'd stayed here before for jobs, no problem. He wasn't likely to think twice about her. Gwen often volunteered for jobs in Denver and had spent a lot of time in this apartment, and in Denver, in general.

"So what did you get?" Annie asked, peeking into one of the bags.

"Food. Real food. None of that garbage we've been eating for the last two days."

Annie pulled out a bundle of kale and frowned. "I knew I should have gone with you."

Gwen laughed and pointed at a bag on the counter. "Don't worry—I got you some of the junk food you requested, too. And three bottles of Coke." She shuddered. "How anyone can drink that stuff is beyond me."

Annie's eyes lit up, and she tore into a bag of cheese puffs, putting one in her mouth with clear pleasure. She was wearing one of Gwen's shirts, and the sleeves were rolled up on her arms. Gwen wasn't tall, by any means—slightly above average—but they had similar builds. If anything, Gwen was a little thinner. Still, as with Tom's coat, Annie looked ridiculous in her shirt. It was also the last of the spares Gwen kept in her travel bag. At some point, they'd need to shop for clothes again.

"Is anything better than a cheese puff?" Annie asked.

"I can think of a thousand."

Annie threw one at her, and Gwen laughed, dodging it. "Say— why don't you sit down and watch some TV? I'll make dinner."

Annie was surprised. "You can cook?"

"Yes." She hesitated. "I actually trained as a chef, before..."

"Before stealing cars for a living?"

"Basically."

"How did you get into it? Being a PI?"

"I was between jobs. It happens, when you're first working in kitchens. Restaurants come and go. I'm also kind of...temperamental, and some of my bosses didn't like me. I stormed out a few times and got in couple of fights. After my culinary training, I had like ten jobs in two years. I was being stupid. I quit one job without notice, only to have my new one lay me off two weeks later. Anyway, I had a bad reputation, so I wasn't getting anything, even part time, after that."

She paused, pulling out a bottle of chilled sparkling wine. She held it up for Annie, who nodded eagerly. She opened it and poured them two tall glasses in mismatched tumblers. She and Annie clinked glasses, and she took a small sip. The wine was soft and slightly tart, the bubbles kissing their way across her tongue.

"Ooh, that's good. What was I saying?"

Annie had downed her entire glass, and Gwen filled it for her again.

"You got laid off, and you couldn't get work."

"Right. So anyway, my friend Reggie had been doing some computer stuff for my current employer and was making okay money at it. He got me an interview, and pretty soon I had some cool gigs, got to travel, all sorts of things. I thought it'd be temporary—long enough for a few restaurants to forget my name. I did some footwork for a local branch of my company at first—stakeouts on cheating wives and the like. Eventually, I studied for the investigator's exam and passed, and started getting different kinds of work here and out of town."

"How long have you been doing it?"

Gwen considered for a moment and then shook her head. "Jesus. It's been twelve years. Christ."

"You don't sound like you like it much."

"Some parts are fine. I like the travel best—seeing new things, leaving before I'm sick of a place." She shrugged. "But other parts get really old. And sometimes things screw up, and it's not my fault, but I get blamed."

"Did that happen the other day? Back in Texas?"

Gwen laughed. "No. That one was my fault." She grinned. "I punched our client in the face."

Annie's eyebrows shot up. "Really?"

Gwen nodded. "Really. He pushed my buttons one too many times. I think I broke his nose, but I didn't stick around to check. I just walked out the door."

"Wow."

"Yeah. I don't think I'm employed anymore. That client was kind of a big deal—lots of money involved, lots of our agents. We'll be lucky if he doesn't sue."

"You haven't called in to the office?"

"No. No reason to. I know what my boss will say, and he can kiss my ass. I told him that client was a shithead, wasn't worth all the hassle, but he told me to put up with it. And I did—for almost six months. But like I said, the client went too far one too many times." She shook her head. "Doesn't matter now, anyway. I was kind of ready to move on. Have been, for a while."

Annie watched her prepare the salmon and asparagus, her eyes tracking Gwen around the tiny but functional galley-style kitchen. After the fish and vegetables were baking in the oven, Gwen took out the fresh loaf of bread she'd bought from her favorite local baker and sliced it in half, lengthwise, before spreading a liberal amount of garlic and butter on it. She set a timer and gestured for Annie to follow her into the little living room. A love seat and a single armchair were all that could fit in the small space. They sat together, and Gwen set the bottle of wine on the little coffee table for refills.

"In twenty minutes, I'll put the bread in, and we can eat in like thirty."

"Smells heavenly, already."

"Better than cheese puffs?"

Annie grinned. "Yes—better. Barely."

The apartment was a small, one-bedroom in an old, gorgeous building. The neighborhood hadn't entirely gentrified, so in a building like this, the renters were pretty mixed. Gwen had passed a young, attractive straight couple on the stairs wearing matching North Face jackets and had then seen several punk and goth twenty-somethings piling into their studio apartment on the next floor. The building had been built in the 1920s, so the construction was solid, the walls thick and soundproof, which was generally more than you could ask for in an older apartment. Another benefit was the large windows, which, on this summer evening, lit the apartment with a warm, yellow glow. Annie's hair shone like white, spun gold, shimmering on her shoulders, and Gwen had to fight the urge to run her fingers through it.

Annie's eyes were a soft, hazy green, and her lips curled in a gentle smile. "What are you staring at?"

Gwen smiled back. "You. You're gorgeous."

Annie pushed her arm. "You're not so bad yourself, lady."

"Even like this?" Gwen gestured vaguely at her ratty clothes and hair.

Annie's smile widened. "I like it. Kind of punk or something."

They both turned to the window, the sun finally starting to set outside. The view wasn't great—only the building next door, but the windows over there reflected the soft, golden pink of the sky.

"You seem to know your way around the city," Annie said.

"Spent a lot of time here. I actually went to college nearby. I also did culinary school a few blocks from here."

"That's right. I forgot you said you were from Colorado."

"Yes, but up north. A little town called Berthoud."

"Do you visit there a lot?"

Gwen shook her head. "Almost never. I see my brother once or twice a year, but he lives in Phoenix now, so I usually see him there."

"Your parents?"

"We don't talk."

"Are they…" Annie frowned. "I mean, did they grow up there?"

Gwen almost laughed. She knew this was Annie's way of asking where they were from and, by extension, Gwen herself.

People always wanted to know. Gwen was actually surprised she'd waited so long to ask.

"My dad's Korean, first generation. My mom's Guatemalan. They met in school in California and moved to Colorado for my dad's job."

"Oh."

Annie didn't push it further, and Gwen didn't offer more details, relieved to drop the subject. She hated talking about her family. But then she remembered that Annie hadn't mentioned her parents, either.

They drank their wine in relative silence, discussing the sunset, the food, nothing very serious or important. The timer went off, Gwen got up to put in the bread, and when she rejoined her in the living room, Annie's soft, relaxed expression was gone. She seemed tense again, anxious.

"Hey," Gwen said, sitting down. She squeezed Annie's knee. "Don't think about it for a little while. Let's try to enjoy ourselves tonight. We've earned it after the last two days."

Annie shook her head. "I can't. I wish I could. I keep thinking about my sister, all alone in that awful place." Her eyes filled with tears. "I can't stand the thought of her in there."

Gwen nodded, not wanting to say something stupid or pretend everything would be all right. It probably wouldn't, and there was no point saying so.

"What was your plan? I mean, if you got the money?"

Annie straightened up, eyes suddenly determined. "To bust her out of there."

"You can do that?"

She shook her head. "No—I can't, but Tom can. Like I told you, he has power of attorney. She's like a little sister to him, too. We arranged the legal stuff right before I was arrested."

The timer went off again, and they got up. Gwen did the last of the prep work for the salad as the fish rested for a few minutes, and Annie set the table. For the first time in days, Gwen was actually excited to eat. She refilled their glasses with the last of the bottle, and they both dug in. Despite being "good" food, Annie ate with as much relish and gusto as she had with all the crap they'd consumed in diners and fast-food joints. As usual, Gwen finished first, Annie moving on to seconds and thirds. Considering that she'd seen this bottomless appetite before with the kind of food they'd had on the road, it wasn't much of a compliment to her cooking, but she enjoyed watching her nonetheless. She suspected she would always enjoy watching Annie eat.

They sat there for a while, digesting and finishing their wine, and Gwen watched as Annie's face gradually reverted to that panicked, anxious edge again. Thinking and talking about her sister was clearly upsetting her, but she needed to do it, no matter how much it upset her. Maybe thinking of a new plan would help her. They had to do something, anyway.

"You said earlier that Tom can get your sister out of the hospital. Does that mean she can leave at any time?"

Annie sighed. "Not exactly. The state requires that she have full-time care until she can demonstrate basic competency, which she's never been able to do. She's been reckless and a danger to herself and others. She's not violent, but she's been known to wander out of the house and walk into traffic, climb onto tall buildings. She's gone swimming in public fountains, that kind of thing. She won't take her medication unless someone's there to give it to her." She lifted her hands. "Basically, if Tom can show he's hired a qualified caregiver, or lined up another place for her to go, he can sign her out, but not before."

"Doesn't she qualify for disability of some kind? Or a state funding?"

"Yes, but it's not enough money. Tom and I took turns with her for a while—him during the day, me at night, but it wasn't working very well. She still got out of the house a couple of times. She needs a professional. We had a guy coming for a while, but he only came for a few hours twice a week. I couldn't work full-time and was falling behind on rent and bills. Then she got into trouble again, and I was talked into putting her in the hospital. It was supposed to be temporary, while I lined up something else, but she's been in and out of there ever since."

"She gets out sometimes?"

"Hardly anyone is permanently institutionalized anymore. She's been released to an adult community program a few times—it's kind of like a halfway house for addicts and the mentally ill—but it almost never lasts for long. She acts up or does something to herself and goes right back into the hospital. Recently, it seemed like she might actually be able to stay there, move on to the next step. She was in their program for almost three months, which is really long for her. She was doing better, taking her meds, actually making plans. Tom visits a lot, and he said it was like talking to her when she was younger, before…Anyway, she was volunteering some afternoons at the animal shelter and thinking about getting a job there. Then something happened. Tom didn't give me any details, but she got sent back to the hospital two months ago."

Annie had tears at the corners of her eyes, and Gwen squeezed her hand. "It sounds terrible for all of you."

Annie wiped at her eyes. "It is. Tom says she's doing better, that this is just a temporary setback, but I don't know whether to believe him. It's not like I can check."

"Why not?"

Annie's eyebrows shot up. "Because they know who I am! I can't call, especially now."

Gwen leaned onto her forearms. "Of course you can, Annie. You're her sister, for God's sake. They have to give you information if you ask for it. Maybe you can even talk to her."

Annie shook her head. "No. I won't call. Not until I've figured this out."

Gwen didn't push it, but she might know someone who could check on her sister for them discreetly. She would wait to suggest it, though, until Annie brought her up again. She'd make some phone calls in the meantime.

They moved back to the living room, Gwen grabbing a second bottle of wine. She didn't particularly want the two of them to get drunk, but Annie was already looking a little more relaxed, and that wasn't a bad thing for one night. The sunset had almost faded from the sky, but the living room was relatively bright from the last of the day and the streetlights outside. The people in the apartment in the building across the alley from them were having a party, and that apartment was so brightly lit, the two of them could watch the entire thing. Everyone seemed impossibly young—too young to be drinking and smoking, but they were obviously enjoying themselves. The faint sound of music leaked through the two sets of windows, but Gwen liked to hear it. She'd been to lots of parties like that when she was their age and didn't begrudge anyone some innocent fun.

"We have to get that money," Annie suddenly said.

Gwen turned to her, surprised. In the dim light of the living room, Annie's face was cast in shadow, her angry expression heightened by the lack of light. She seemed murderous, deadly.

"Tell me about these people, Annie—the ones that screwed you. And use names, for Christ's sake. It's confusing enough as it is."

Annie turned, regarding her silently for a long time as if making up her mind about something. "I'm still not sure you should get involved in this. You have a chance to get out, if you do it now. I don't want you to get in trouble like I am. If you know too much, you'll be in more danger."

Gwen kissed her. "Stop saying that. I'm in this with you, Annie."

Again, Annie stared at her, clearly troubled. She was biting and twisting her lips anxiously. Finally, she sighed. "Okay, Gwen. But please don't hate me when we get caught. I-I couldn't stand that."

"I won't. Now spill."

Annie looked away again, watching the party. When she spoke, her voice was almost a whisper, and Gwen had to lean closer to hear her.

"It all started when I met Susan. She was the woman I called from the motel the other day. We met through a mutual acquaintance.

I had the idea for the fraud long before I met her. I knew how to make the phony loans, and I knew how to fake the recipients. I'd convinced myself that it was a victimless crime—the insurance would cover it. The problem was moving the money. I only knew how to move it legally. Basically, I could get the money, but then it could be traced. Someone would catch on in only a month or two, so unless I could hide it somehow, there was no real point. I thought about it a lot, but I didn't really try to do anything real or concrete. Not until I met Susan."

"How did you meet?"

"Through a mutual friend of a friend. It was stupid, really. I was at a friend's birthday party, and people were talking about their crappy jobs. My friend's husband, Greg, mentioned that he knew how to break into his workplace without getting caught. He was drunk, so he had an excuse. I wasn't—I think I was showing off. I mentioned that I could defraud the bank. I didn't realize someone would take me seriously."

She met Gwen's eyes. "I don't know if I ever really meant to try, Gwen. Do you understand? I don't think I would have gone through with it—it was a kind of fantasy, you know? A daydream. I liked pretending I could get away with it—picturing me and my sister on a beach somewhere, drinking mai tais and daiquiris and swimming with dolphins—kid crap like that. Anyway, I realized I couldn't move the money, so it wasn't even a realistic fantasy."

"I get it. Really, I do."

Annie frowned at her before nodding. "The morning after the party, Susan called me. She said that her friend Bill had overheard something, and she wanted to talk to me. She was vague, but I understood what she meant without going into detail. We met that same day, and she spelled it out for me. She knew how to hide the money and not get caught."

She was quiet, frowning. "Even then, I could have said no. I was desperate for the money, but most of me understood that we couldn't get away with it. Even later, when I did the paperwork for the first phony loan, I knew I should call it all off. Susan was forcing me to approve way too much money. It was going to draw too much attention too quickly. Still, I went along with it and kept going along with it for weeks."

"She must have been really persuasive."

Annie flinched and nodded, and Gwen's stomach dropped. "Oh—so it was like that, then?"

Annie looked at her, and even in the dim light, Gwen could see the tears sparkling in her eyes. "Yes. It was like that. I was a complete and utter idiot. She was stringing me along, but she gave me enough affection to doubt myself. Then she and Tom finally met. You saw him the other night—he doesn't trust anyone. It's funny, because if he likes you, he's a big, tall teddy bear, but until then, he's pretty cold. Tom didn't know anything about her or the fraud, but he hated her immediately, and he never warmed up. At first I was pissed at him, but he wouldn't change his mind. He kept telling me she was phony, no good. I finally started to realize how fucked up she was, and how deep she'd gotten me into this mess. I ended things between us long before I was caught, but the damage was already done. I'd stolen ten times as much money as I planned, and way too many people were involved. Even before the FBI showed, I was expecting them. Susan and Bill were smart enough to keep their names off any of the loans, so they were, of course, in the clear when all the shit hit the fan."

"What was in it for them?"

"Half of everyone's take."

"Half! Jesus."

Annie shrugged. "Like I said—stupid. All the people that posed for the phony loans were arrested at the same time I was, but Bill and Susan's names were never brought up at trial. Susan made the same deal with everyone that went to prison—don't rat, and she'd save their half of the money for them for when they got out. It was different for me, since I got so much time. That's why she promised to break me out if I kept my mouth closed. My cut was also the biggest after hers and Bill's."

"How much money, total, did you steal?"

"Ten point five."

"Wow. And those two have all of it now?"

Annie nodded. "Yes. Every cent."

"They haven't made any payouts? I mean, has anyone gotten out of prison yet?"

"No. The soonest is next year, from what I remember."

"Do you know where they moved the money?"

Annie lifted her shoulders. "Only what I read in the papers. The FBI tracked it to Europe, then Asia, before they lost it, but I can guess. The Caymans would be my bet. That's where I was going to put it if I could figure out how to cover my tracks on the way there."

"Do you think that's where they are now? Susan and Bill?"

Annie shook her head. "No. As far as I know, Susan's still in Dallas—that's where she was when I talked to her on the phone. She told me Bill was in Santa Fe."

"Why there? What are those two places to them?"

"They own houses there."

"They do?"

Annie nodded. "They're married."

"And you knew—"

"No. I didn't. Not until after I broke up with her. I think she told me to hurt me, but actually it made me feel better about the whole thing. It made me see that she'd been conning me the whole time, that I was better off without her. I don't even think she's really attracted to women. She was playing me. She's an asshole, and I fell for it."

Gwen thought for a while, the room now so dark that Annie and the furniture in the room were only vague silhouettes. The party was still raging on across the way, the music now loud enough to hear the lyrics, and the young people over there were, on the whole, visibly intoxicated, stumbling against each other flirtatiously and falling down a lot.

"I think that's the first step," Gwen finally said.

"What?"

"Finding the money. We have to know where it is before we try to get it."

Annie laughed. "And how the hell are we supposed to do that?"

Gwen flicked on one of the table lamps next to her, and they both winced against the dim light.

"Listen—you keep forgetting something, here."

"What?"

"You still have two things on your side." She held up her fingers. "One: Susan doesn't know that *you* know she betrayed you. She might suspect it, especially as you haven't called in since you talked to her in the motel, but she can't be certain. Two: you still have some leverage on her. You can still spill the beans to the police."

"But that's just it—I could never prove it! That's the main thing I keep coming back to, and part of the reason I never even tried. My lawyers kept trying to get me to fess up, to give names, but I knew nothing would come of it. They're too good. And anyway, why would anyone even believe me?"

"But Bill and Susan couldn't possibly be sure of that. You could talk at any time. And anyway, no one's perfect. There has to be some kind of trail, somewhere. If we can find something, anything, you've got them."

"And if not?"

"Then we need to find the money."

Annie laughed. "That's what I've been saying all along. But how? And even if we find it, how on earth can we get it?"

"Would a fake ID be enough?"

Annie laughed. "What—you mean pretend to be Susan? That's ridiculous."

"Why?"

Annie sputtered for a few seconds and then shook her head. "Having an ID wouldn't be enough. We'd need bank records, account numbers. And they wouldn't be stupid enough to put it in their own names. For all we know, they have hundreds of fake accounts to hide that kind of money. And I doubt they're all at the same bank."

"But some of them will be. If we can find some, we can find the others."

"Yes, but what then? We make a fake ID and get bank records for all of them?"

Gwen shrugged. "No—but enough of them. Enough to start a new life."

Annie shook her head, exasperated. "And how would we get the IDs, anyway?"

"I know a guy."

Annie laughed. "That still doesn't solve the main problem. We don't know where it is! We don't even have the bank-account numbers, for crying out loud. How on earth could we even find them?"

Gwen smiled, scooting close enough to Annie to kiss her. "Have you ever been on a stakeout?"

## CHAPTER TWELVE

The sun in Santa Fe Plaza was oppressive, hotter, it seemed, than it had been in El Paso last week. Despite the heat, the plaza was crowded with tourists. Many of them were laden with bags of souvenirs, dressed as if they were out for a day at the beach. The tourists here in Santa Fe tended to be older—retirees, mainly, many of them hippies or wannabes, dressed in funky linens and sporting turquoise or beaded hemp jewelry.

Gwen had checked out the area before coming here with Annie, and they were both dressed the part with wide-brimmed hats, white T-shirts, loud shorts, sandals, and oversized sunglasses. Gwen had never worn clothing like this and felt ridiculous. Even dressed this way, she'd gotten several weird glances and a few outright stares. Whether it was her skin, her tattoos, or something else, she didn't look the part. Annie, however, was a natural in her disguise, almost as if she belonged with these people. And for all Gwen knew, maybe she did.

She led Annie to a restaurant off the south side of the plaza, spotting her friend Tex on the patio out front. He'd found a table in the shade and waved at her when he saw them. They maneuvered around some other patrons to reach him, and he rose, all lanky six foot four of him, and pulled her into a long hug. When he drew back, he put his hands on her shoulders, peering down at her.

"What in the hell are you wearing?"

Gwen shrugged his hands off and made a quieting motion. "Shh. We're in disguise."

"Well, you look like a goddamn idiot. You might as well have worn a sign that said, 'Hey! See me? I don't belong here!' "

"I realize that now."

"Not that you would ever belong with this crowd. They might be a bunch of bleeding-heart liberals, but they tend to be, shall we say, a bit, uh, less colorful than they could be. Foreigners like you ain't exactly the usual. This one, on the other hand," Tex gestured at Annie, "is a natural. A natural beauty, too, I might add." He pulled off his cowboy hat, revealing his gray but luxurious hair, and gave her a slight bow before holding out his hand. "People call me Tex."

"Annie," she said, smiling and shaking it.

"Will you join me, ladies?" He indicated the table before slipping his hat back on. "I took the liberty and ordered us a pitcher of sangria. That's why I wanted to meet you here—best damn sangria in town, and that's saying something. Ain't no town like Santa Fe for good sangria."

The three of them sat, and Gwen drained a glass of water almost at once. It was nicer here in the shade, but the air was so hot it made her throat feel tight and almost painful. Tex and Annie were regarding each other, both of them slightly bemused. Tex finally shook his head, sighing.

"I hope you don't mind me saying, but you're a right looker, Annie." He turned to Gwen. "You sure can pick 'em, lady. You must have some kind of voodoo spell. Every lady friend you have is pretty as a picture."

Annie raised one eyebrow at her, and Gwen quickly changed the subject. "So, Tex, what do you have for us?"

He held his hands up. "Hold your horses, young lady. Let's have our drinks first. Are the two of you hungry? It ain't the best Mexican in town, but it's not bad, either."

"I'm fine," Gwen said. "We ate—"

"I could eat," Annie said. "What do you recommend?"

"Anything with green chili is pretty tasty—that's a New Mexico specialty. I like their queso dip, too."

The waitress appeared with their sangria, and Gwen waited as the two of them ordered, her impatience mounting. Last Friday, the morning after their conversation in the dark apartment in Denver, Gwen had called Tex, a colleague from work. Unlike her, and despite his name, he lived in one state—New Mexico. Most of his work was in Albuquerque, but he was from the Santa Fe area and had a place nearby. He was semiretired now, but she'd had a few jobs with him over the years. Calling him a close friend would be a bit of a stretch, but she trusted him, and they'd had a few afternoons like this—drinking sangria or tequila. By now, he would know what had happened down in Austin with her last client—everyone they worked with would—but he hadn't mentioned it. Instead, when she'd called and asked for his help, he'd given it, no questions asked.

She'd asked Tex to watch Bill and Susan's house just outside Santa Fe, and to track their movements if they came or left. Annie had said that of the two of them, Bill was supposed to be here, but Gwen wasn't so sure. She was almost certain that Susan had lied to Annie—that Bill had watched for them in El Paso and phoned the police. At the motel that first day, Annie had called Susan at her place in Dallas, and there was, as far as Gwen knew, no way for Susan to fake that. Someone had to have been in El Paso, so it must have been Bill, unless more people were involved than they thought.

She and Annie had spent the weekend in Denver, and despite Annie's occasional anxiety, it had been a nice break. The weather had been pleasant, and they'd walked around Cheesman Park, having picnics or reading together under a tree. They hadn't ventured beyond that area, spending their evenings quietly at the apartment. It had seemed, for a while, like a real life.

This morning, before they left for Santa Fe, Gwen had walked into a local branch of her bank and emptied her accounts. Doing this, she knew, would signal their movements to the police, but they couldn't use her credit cards anymore, and she'd been low on funds. Now, between the two of them, they had almost fifteen grand, and they would need it all to make this work.

She watched Annie and Tex become acquainted over a mountain

of food and a second pitcher of drinks. The two of them seemed to bond over horses, which, she learned, Annie used to own and ride. Tex had a small horse ranch outside of town, up in the mountains some twenty minutes away. Gwen had been there once overnight and had left with the worst hangover of her life, vowing to avoid mezcal forever.

Tex pushed his plate away and rubbed his stomach, smiling happily. "That was a fine meal, and it was nice to have a lovely lady to share it with. It's usually just me, myself, and I when I go out to eat now. Last girlfriend I had set sail for California, of all places. Thank you, Annie."

"My pleasure."

"I love to see a woman enjoy her food. Not like this one." He gestured at Gwen with a thumb. "She don't eat enough to keep a bird alive."

"Don't get me started," Annie said, grinning at her.

Gwen tried to laugh and sipped her drink. She hadn't finished her first glass. Tex rolled his eyes and leaned closer, gesturing for the two of them to do the same.

"Okay, Annie. Miss Impatience here can't seem to enjoy herself for twenty minutes." He frowned at Gwen. "I did as you asked, missy, but there ain't anything to report. The house is empty. I watched all weekend, and nothing. 'Not a creature was stirring' and all that."

"Really?" Annie asked. "What if they didn't come outside?"

Tex shook his head. "No. I would have heard them or seen a light on, something. No one is in that house, I promise. I even rang the bell this morning, but no joy. There ain't nowhere to hide up there. You'll see if you go there yourself—it's the only house on that stretch, and you can see inside with all them windows. I had to park behind some bushes on the other side of the road to stay hidden."

Annie seemed disappointed, but Gwen wasn't surprised. "What did I tell you?"

Annie lifted a shoulder. "I guess you were right. Bill must have been in El Paso. That proves it all, I guess. I was kind of hoping I was wrong."

"You weren't. They betrayed you."

Tex looked confused, and Gwen waved a hand dismissively. He didn't need to know the details. "Anyway, Tex, I don't know how to thank you. Can I pay you anything?"

He sneered. "Who do you think I am? I don't charge my friends."

"But you went through an awful lot of bother for us," Annie said. "Sitting there, watching that house, bored out of your mind."

Tex grinned and squeezed her hand. "It weren't too bad—I had a good book. And I'd do it again, just for you. You're as sweet as pie."

Gwen sighed and rolled her eyes. "At least let us pay for lunch."

"And take away my privilege as a gentleman? Not on your life."

Annie leaned across the table and kissed him on the cheek. "You're amazing. Thank you so much for helping us."

"Are you heading over there now?" he asked. "If you want, I can take the two of you, show you my spot."

Gwen and Annie shared a quick glance. "No, Tex. That won't be necessary."

He seemed a little hurt but nodded. "Okay. I get it. I guess this has something to do with what I read about you two in the newspaper."

"We were in the paper? The local paper?"

"It was a small spot in the national news, but I'd seen it on the TV before that." He frowned. "They were saying all sorts of stuff about the two of you, and I don't know what, if anything, is true."

Gwen squeezed the top of his hand. "And you don't need to, Tex. In fact, the less you know, the better."

He stared at her evenly before nodding. "Yeah. I guess you're right."

"You don't want to get mixed up in this," Annie added.

He reached across the table and took her hand in both of his. "Having met you, Annie, I don't believe a word of it. And even if some of it is true, I imagine you had good reason to do what you did."

Tears sprang to her eyes and she nodded. "I did."

He patted her hand again before letting go. "Anyway, you both seem eager to get going." He paused. "I wish you both luck. You stay in touch with me, ladies. I'm willing to help more if you need it."

The three got up to say good-bye, and Gwen's eyes prickled with tears as she, and then Annie, embraced him. He hadn't needed to do a thing for them, but he'd gone out of his way to help. Maybe he was a close friend, after all. She felt momentarily guilty, like she'd let him down, somehow. Maybe all this running around over the last twelve years wasn't the best way to live. She'd kept people at a distance, people like Tex, who might have meant more to her if she'd bothered to try. Staying in one place might mean she could try, if she could keep Annie in her life.

She and Annie walked back to the car in relative silence. The heat had a lot to do with this—it was hard to think when it was this hot—but Gwen suspected Annie was pondering some of the same things she was, and had been since they left Denver. What, if anything, were they hoping to get out of this? At best, they'd have the money, but then what? Annie's fantasy, where she rescued her sister, was a little far-fetched, but maybe it was possible with that kind of cash. But would Annie want her to come, too?

The car, when they reached it, was like an oven. Gwen had stolen a new one in Denver, from a downtown, long-term lot she'd hit once before. Most of the littler lots didn't bother with cameras and didn't staff at night, so it was only a matter of getting an older car she could open and jump. This car was solid black, inside and out, quite possibly the worst to have in weather like this.

Using the map they'd picked up, Annie directed her out of the older part of town and back to the interstate. A couple of miles down, they took an exit and started heading up into the mountains and single-lane highway that climbed and wound steeply upward. Bill and Susan had some kind of house up here, and, surprisingly, it had been listed under their names in the phonebook. Tex hadn't even had to track it down.

Five minutes later, they hadn't passed a single car on this road, and the tension gradually ratcheted up as they drove. If, by chance, Bill or Susan or both had come back this way since Tex checked this morning, they wouldn't know ahead of time. Tex had suggested they wouldn't find an easy place to hide, and now that she was on this road, she could understand why. On the left-hand side, the mountain rose up and up, with an occasional driveway that disappeared before she could even see the house it led to. On the right was nothing but a long drop-off into the valley below, often with no guardrail.

"Jesus," Annie said, staring out her side window. "That's a long way down."

"I think we're almost there. I saw some numbers on that last mailbox."

"So what's the plan? Are we gonna drive right up to the house?"

Gwen glanced at her and shrugged. "What do you think? Should we risk it?"

Annie shook her head. "No way. Let's watch, if we can, at least for a little while, just to be safe."

After the next hairpin curve, Gwen spotted a clump of bushes on the right, directly across the road from a mailbox. She slowed and drove behind them, guessing that Tex had hidden his car here over the weekend. She could see recent tire tracks on the dry, dusty ground, the mountain just wide enough here for some trees and bushes before it dropped off again about twenty feet away. They wouldn't be entirely hidden—the foliage was thin—but casual drivers on the road wouldn't likely see them unless they were looking their way. They rolled down their windows, letting in the dusty daytime air and the smell of sagebrush and pine.

Some branches were in her way, but Gwen could see the entire front of the house easily from this position, in part because it was up the hill on the other side of the road, about a hundred yards away. That's why Tex had been so certain no one was around. The front was almost entirely glass, with floor-to-ceiling windows on both stories. It was shaped a little like a point at the peak, resembling a large yacht or ship. The view up there obviously gave a complete panorama of the valley and the city below.

Gwen whistled. "Damn. That's a hell of a house."

Annie nodded. "I knew it must be big. I've seen their other place in Dallas."

"What do they do?"

Annie shook her head. "Nothing. It's family money—hers—as far as I know."

Gwen raised her eyebrows but didn't comment, and they turned to watch the house. No cars passed, and the only sound came from an occasional bird or a gust of hot wind. Nothing moved except the branches and bushes. They might have been the last people on earth.

Gwen let half an hour pass before turning to Annie. "What do you say? I think Tex was right—no one's home. Should we go check it out?"

Annie frowned slightly. "I don't know. It seems really risky. I'm sure they have a security system. We might be spotted on cameras or something."

Gwen nodded. "Yeah, we might, but as long as we don't trigger the alarm, we should be okay for a while. They might know we were here, but not right away. And who knows how often they check the tape?"

"I guess."

Gwen decided to force the issue. She reached into the backseat, grabbed her tool bag, and got out the car. They hadn't come all this way only to leave, but driving up to the house seemed more than foolhardy. If anyone showed up, they might have a chance to sneak out on foot before they were spotted. A car would be too obvious.

Annie was slow to follow, sitting in the car long after Gwen had gotten out. Finally, she opened her door and looked at Gwen over the car roof.

"Are we going to leave the windows open?"

Gwen gestured around them. "I don't think anyone will steal it. And it sure as shit isn't going to rain."

Annie slammed her door and came around the front. "What about animals?"

"Don't worry about them." She held out her hand. "You ready?"

Annie hesitated before taking it, finally smiling a little. "Yeah. I guess."

Gwen squeezed her fingers. "If it's too risky, we'll leave. If not, this might be a really good opportunity to get some information. That's what we're here for, right?"

"Right."

She obviously wasn't thrilled, and Gwen had to remind herself that Annie wasn't used to this kind of thing. Even her crime—bank fraud—had been a kind of reserved, almost behind-the-scenes affair. Gwen wasn't a master criminal, by any means, but she had been in circumstances almost exactly like this before. Breaking and entering, like borrowing cars, was a pretty normal Monday for her.

The driveway was tremendously steep and, to Gwen, the riskiest part of the whole plan, as they were completely exposed the entire length of it. Had someone driven up, they would have been spotted at once. She was relieved when they reached the top, both of them winded by the climb and altitude. She led Annie behind a tree to rest and leaned against it, eyes closed, breathing deeply.

As Annie caught her breath, Gwen peeked around the tree, spotting three cameras immediately. One was pointed directly at the driveway, the other at the front door, and the other on the garage. There were likely more that she couldn't see from here. These people might have twenty-four-hour observation security on the house, and guards or police might already be headed their way, but Gwen doubted it. More likely, the cameras fed into a taping system that overwrote itself every few days. The house, however, would definitely be wired into some kind of alarm system, which meant that if they did set it off, the police would come, and they'd be seen on the tapes, if not caught outright. Still, it was unusual to wire every single window on a house, especially on the second floor. Gwen was pretty sure that if they could get in up there, they'd be okay. The trick would be figuring out how to do that.

"I should have brought a ladder," she said.

"What?"

"Nothing—thinking out loud."

"Maybe there's a tool shed," Annie suggested. "I mean, if you think a ladder would actually help."

Gwen laughed. "You're a genius."

The two of them walked around the side of the house to the gated backyard. Not knowing if the fence was wired, they had to climb over it, but they did it easily by helping each other. The yard was oversized, like the house, with brown, dried grass and a few pine trees and cottonwoods. A pool dominated the center of the yard, strangely uncovered, and Gwen spotted a large utility shed in the corner, in addition to several more cameras pointed at various doors and windows. The shed's lock was a simple hinged one, which Gwen opened easily with one of her tools. The shed held various lawn-maintenance equipment and pool chemicals, and, hanging length-wise along one wall, a tall, expandable ladder.

"Bingo," Gwen said, and Annie helped her pull it down. It took both of them to carry the long, heavy thing comfortably.

"Which window should we go in?" Annie asked as they approached the house.

Gwen pointed at one on the second floor. A little balcony with a door was there, and a camera pointed directly down on it from an adjacent upper cornice.

Annie looked surprised. "Really? Isn't that one a little obvious? It's sure to be rigged to the alarm."

Gwen shook her head. "No—I don't think so. Not with that camera there. All these doors down here, for sure, but not that one. It's *too* obvious, if you know what I mean."

"What if you're wrong?"

"We should know pretty soon, one way or the other."

"You mean, like an alarm will go off?"

"Probably not—they're not usually so obvious. Most of them are silent, now. They don't want to scare away a burglar, after all. They want to catch him."

"So how will we know if we trigger the alarm?"

"The police will show up."

Annie's eyebrows shot up, and Gwen laughed, motioning for them to set down the heavy ladder. "Annie, we can't know either way. The days of visible alarm wires and blaring sirens are mostly over. We either luck out, or we don't—that's basically the gist. If we can find the alarm keypad fast enough, we might be able to tell that way, too, since it'll probably start flashing or something if it's alerted the police."

Annie stared up at the balcony for a while and finally nodded. "Okay, Gwen. I'll do whatever you think's right. You're the expert."

It took them a moment to figure out how to extend and lock the ladder, and even then, it barely reached the balcony upstairs. Gwen pushed on the ladder a few times to test the give, and it seemed solid enough. Still, she wasn't thrilled to climb all the way up there like this, but Annie looked scared, so she needed to bluff.

"Safe as houses. You want me to go first?"

Annie shook her head. "No way. I will go first, or I'll chicken out. That way, you can catch me if I fall."

Gwen pulled her into an embrace and kissed her deeply. She drew back, still holding her, and met her eyes. "You'll be fine. And I will catch you if you fall. I promise."

They heard the gate opening at the same time. Both let go of each other at once, whirling in that direction. Gwen instinctively dropped down, reaching wildly for her gun. But she wasn't wearing it—she'd left it in the car. Annie froze in place as a girl walked around the side of the house and stopped when she spotted them.

"Who are you?" she asked.

## CHAPTER THIRTEEN

The girl was perhaps nine or ten years old, with long, curly red hair loosely gathered into two side ponytails, and a splash of dark freckles on her fair skin. She was wearing flip-flops and shorts over a swimsuit, carrying a plastic grocery sack that revealed the corner of a towel.

Gwen stood up from her crouch and threw Annie a quick warning glance. "Well, hello, there."

The girl frowned. "What's the ladder for?"

"That's a funny story," Gwen said, trying to look friendly. "We forgot our key."

The girl's face creased in a deep frown. "You don't live here."

"Neither do you."

The girl rolled her eyes. "No kidding. But I have permission to be here."

"So do we!" Gwen said.

The girl frowned again, eyebrows furled. "Yeah? Who says?"

"Bill and Susan. They asked us to come over while they were out. We had a key, but we forgot to bring it."

The girl stared at them for a long time. "Why should I believe you?"

Gwen and Annie shared another glance, and Gwen put her hands up. "I don't know. But we could call them—they'd tell you."

Out of the corner of her eye, she saw Annie tense, but she didn't react, still smiling slightly at the girl, doing her best to appear non-threatening. The girl's eyes went back and forth between the two of them.

Finally, she shrugged. "Okay. If you call, and they say it's okay, I'll believe you."

"Can you get inside?" Gwen asked.

The girl nodded, setting down her plastic bag. She dug around inside and came out with a key. Regarding them warily, she walked to the back door before unlocking it. Annie and Gwen followed her in and watched as she typed in the code to disable the alarm. The girl pointed at the phone.

"There it is."

Annie went toward it, but the girl held up her hand. "Wait. Tell me what the number is."

"What?"

"Tell me the number so I know you're calling the right one."

Annie thought for a few seconds before responding. "214-555-6586."

Some of the girl's tension seemed to ease, and she nodded. "That's right. Susan made me memorize it in case something happened."

"Are you watching the house?" Gwen asked, surprised.

The girl lifted a shoulder. "Sort of. They let me use the pool if I water the plants inside. They have a guy that does the outside stuff, but I guess they didn't want him poking around in here. I'm also supposed to call if I see a broken window or something."

"Seems like a pretty good deal," Gwen said, glancing at Annie. She was delaying the phone call as much as she could, but Annie was clearly nervous.

The girl smiled for the first time. "It is. I love their pool. Normally they'd have it covered while they were gone, but I did such a good job with the plants last time, they said I could use it. I'm a good swimmer, so they don't have to worry about me drowning or anything. I get to use the pool, and I get five dollars a week for taking care of the plants."

"Wow," Gwen said, sounding impressed. "That's a lot of moola."

The girl giggled at the word, covering her mouth with her hand. "So my name is Gwen, and this is Annie. What's your name?"

"Jennifer. But I like Jen better."

"Okay, Jen. Nice to meet you. I think maybe you can help us."

"Oh? How?"

Gwen waited for a second, wondering if she was pushing this too far. This was a smart little girl, and she seemed to have a pretty good bullshit meter. Despite the relative trust they'd developed, Jen was still standing as far away as possible. Gwen knew she had to get the girl to forget, momentarily at least, about the phone call. She decided to risk it.

"The thing is, Susan asked us to come over here and get something for her. It's super important, or we wouldn't have tried to get in on our own without a key."

"What is it?"

"It's supposed to be in her office. It's a file, a business file. This is such a big house, we're not sure where to go."

"Oh, I can show you," Jen said. "Follow me."

She rushed out of the room, leading them to a staircase. Annie held back at the foot of the stairs, waiting until Jen was out of earshot.

"What are you doing?" she whispered.

"Improvising. Now come on."

She went up, Annie following a few seconds later. Jen was waiting at the top, shifting from foot to foot. She ran away down the long hallway once they'd caught up. Gwen and Annie followed at a more leisurely pace, Gwen glancing into the open rooms. They might find something in the office, but if not, she wanted to know where to look next. They passed a large TV room, a bedroom, and the next room was the office. Jen stood inside, clearly pleased with herself, and both Gwen and Annie paused in the doorway, taking it in.

"Holy shit," Annie whispered.

The place was a wreck. Papers were strewn across the room, on the floor and across the desk, piles of folders on almost every surface. A large computer monitor sat on desk, taking up most of the space beside the piles of file folders and loose papers.

"Wow," Gwen said.

"Right?" Jen asked. "It's a mess."

Gwen wondered, then, if something had happened—if someone else had been here before them. "Is it always like this?"

Jen nodded. "Just about. The rest of the house is always nice, but not in here."

Gwen felt a momentary relief and nodded. "Yeah. Some people are real slobs."

Jen giggled again. "So what are you looking for?"

Gwen glanced at Annie, finally out of ideas, but Annie was already smiling at Jen. "Bank records."

"What are those?"

"They should be pretty obvious. They'll have the name of a bank at the top and lots of numbers on them."

Jen peered around at the mess helplessly, realizing, perhaps, the extent of what was being asked of her, and frowned. "Jeez. I don't know anything about that."

"That's okay. I can find them." She glanced at Gwen.

"She's good at this kind of thing," Gwen said immediately. "Why don't you and I let her look, and you can show me the pool again."

"Okay," Jen said at once. She grabbed Gwen's hand and led her away, walking so fast she felt like her arm might slip out of its socket. She threw one last glance at Annie, who raised her thumb.

Outside again, the sun had reached its zenith, making the concrete around the pool feel like a stove top, even through the soles of her sandals. Jen immediately shucked off her shorts, slipped off her flip-flops, and raced toward the pool, diving in a surprisingly graceful arc at the last second. She came up a moment later, splashing and grinning wildly.

"That was great," Gwen said, clapping.

Jen swam over to the edge near her, still smiling. "I've been practicing all summer. I want to get on the swim team next year."

"Well, you will, for sure."

"I want to be in the Olympics when I'm older."

Gwen nodded, trying to seem sage and interested. "That's a really great goal. Takes a lot of work, I bet."

"And how. That's why I practice every day, even when it's cold out."

"That's a good plan."

"I was gone all weekend at my grandma's, so I have to get caught up. I'm going to swim for two hours today to make up for it."

Gwen again made herself appear suitably impressed, then watched for a little while as if interested. Eventually, when she could see that the girl was absorbed in her task, she took the opportunity to remove the ladder. They might get away with this, at least in the short term, so they didn't need to alert anyone sooner than necessary. The gardener would be over eventually this week, and he would certainly call someone if he saw a ladder out here. It was much harder to wrestle it back to the shed on her own, but she managed to hang it into the hooks where she'd found it, closing and locking the door on her way out.

By this time, Jen had climbed out and was watching her from a cross-legged position on the ground by the pool. Gwen gave her a quick smile, again trying to look reassuring and innocent. Some of that earlier suspicion showed again in the girl's eyes, and Gwen could have kicked herself for being so stupid. By bringing attention to the ladder, she'd reminded the girl of how they'd met.

"You were really going to climb in the window up there?" Jen asked, pointing.

Gwen nodded. "We had no choice. Susan really needs that file."

Jen was frowning again, eyes narrowed. "So how do I know you're not cat burglars?"

Gwen made herself laugh. "Do I look like a burglar to you?" She indicated her outfit. She and Annie were still wearing their tourist getups of shorts and sandals.

Jen shook her head. "No—you don't. But I guess I still don't know what you're doing here."

"We told you already."

Jen nodded. "Exactly. *You* told me. Why should I believe you?"

"I also told you we could call Susan and check."

Jen frowned. "Yes. And then you distracted me, didn't you?"

Gwen's pulse rate picked up. She didn't want to threaten this girl in any way, but it was starting to seem like that might be the only choice. She was running out of ideas. Suddenly, she thought of something and smiled.

"Okay. You got us. We're international cat burglars."

The girl's eyes lit up. "What? No way. You're fooling me."

Gwen shook her head. "Nope. Honestly. We came here to break in and steal secret files. They're worth lots of money."

The girl jumped up to her feet. "Are you serious?"

Gwen held up a hand. "Swear to God—we're here to steal files."

"But you know Susan and Bill's names!"

"That's because we cased the joint—checked it out ahead of time. Seriously—watch the news tonight. You'll probably see us on there. We're wanted by the police and the FBI."

As she'd expected, clearly none of this story frightened Jen. Instead, she seemed excited.

"Wow! How cool!" Then her face fell. "But wait. I don't want you to steal from Bill and Susan. They're my friends."

"But that's just it, Jen. We're not stealing from them. We're stealing from banks, and those are insured. We need some account numbers they have. They won't lose any money."

"For real?"

"For real."

Jen still seemed a little dubious, and Gwen laughed. "All right, answer me this. Why would I tell you anything, only to lie to you about this? We're not going to take anything that belongs to them. I promise."

The girl was frowning again, and Gwen decided to risk one more thing. She reached into her back pocket and pulled out her wallet. "Okay. I'll make you a deal."

Jen said nothing for a long time, her lips tight. Finally, as if she couldn't help her curiosity, she asked, "What kind of deal?"

Gwen slipped out two hundred-dollar bills and held them out

for Jen to see. "If I'm lying, you get to keep these. If not, I'll come get one of them from you in exactly two weeks." She rubbed the bills together when the girl didn't reach for them. "That's a lot of money for me to give away if I'm full of crap."

Slowly, as if expecting the bills to disappear, Jen took them from her gingerly. She examined the money and then smiled so widely, Gwen thought her face would crack in half.

"Wow, jeez! I've never even seen a hundred before. I get to keep one of these, either way?"

"That's right—a hundred of that is yours. The other hundred is mine in two weeks, so don't spend it!"

"Unless you're lying."

Gwen laughed. "Exactly. Unless I'm lying. Then you can do whatever you want with it. Deal?" She held out a hand.

Jen shook it. "Deal."

Annie came out the back door a moment later, smiling. She gave Gwen a long, knowing look and nodded slightly. She'd gotten what she needed.

"So I guess we're all done here," Gwen said.

"And you're sure you're not going to hurt Bill and Susan?" Jen asked.

Gwen saw Annie react but made herself laugh. "No. Like I said, they'll be fine. Everything we'll take belongs to someone else. They'll be fine."

Jen stared at her skeptically for a few seconds and then finally nodded, smiling. "Okay. I guess I'll know either way in two weeks."

"Exactly." She squeezed Jen's shoulder briefly. "You take care of yourself, now, and practice your swimming every day."

"I will."

Gwen turned to Annie, holding out her hand. If Jen thought this sign of affection strange, she didn't let on, only waving at the two of them once before diving into the pool again. Gwen and Annie went out the way they'd come in, this time opening and closing the gate.

"What was that all about?" Annie finally asked.

"It's fine. I handled it. She'll figure it out in a couple of weeks, so we have some time. How did it go on your end?"

"Better than I could have dreamed. I started by checking out the papers on the desk and stuff, but then I thought I'd look at the computer, too. It was all on there—hundreds of account numbers, some with a few thousand dollars, a few with a lot more. We lucked out. They didn't have any kind of security on any of it. They're incredibly careless."

"Or arrogant."

Annie nodded.

"Are the accounts all in the same place?"

"No. They're all over the place. The big ones are in the Caymans, like I thought. One with four million, one with two, and two with one—all with different names. The rest are all over the states, but much smaller, like ten or twenty thousand."

"You're not carrying anything. Did you write it all down somewhere?"

Annie laughed. "I emailed it to myself."

"Won't they be able to see that?"

Annie shrugged. "I erased my tracks, but maybe. Though only if they check on that computer."

"How much time do we have before they start moving the money?"

"I have no idea. None of the transfers were recent, not that I could see, so we could have lots. Still, they might get paranoid, especially once they know we have the bank-account numbers."

"So assuming they won't know before then, we have two weeks. If they come back sooner and talk to Jen, they could know at any time."

"Right. Or they might get hinky and move it now. There's no way to know."

They'd reached the car, and Gwen was glad they'd left the windows open. The black leather was scorching on her bare legs, but at least they could sit here without suffocating. She'd been debating something for a couple of days now, and she decided, finally, to ask.

"What do you think of calling Susan?"

Annie's eyebrows shot up. "What? Why would I do that?"

"To throw her off the scent for a while. Make her think you're still on her side—that you don't know anything."

Annie frowned. "She has to suspect by now."

"Yes, but she doesn't know for sure yet, right?"

"I guess."

Gwen let it rest at that, starting the car and turning it back around the way they'd come. She was fairly certain they wouldn't pass anyone on this road, but if they did, their faces would be clearly visible on this narrow road with the sunlight directly on them. Even with their sunglasses on again, if Bill or Susan was driving the other way, they'd be sure to recognize Annie.

She didn't relax again until they were back on the interstate, heading south. Annie had been quiet this entire time, but Gwen didn't push, letting her mull over her idea. It was true, it might not do any good to call Susan, but it might. Annie had said that Susan wasn't above killing people, and Gwen wasn't eager to have some hired killer on their tail on top of everyone else that was chasing them. If they could hoodwink her for a few more days, they might have a chance to get the money first.

"Okay. I'll do it," Annie finally said.

"What? Really?"

"Yes. You're right—it might buy us some more time. If not, it isn't as if I could make things worse than they already are."

"What if she tries to get you to come in?"

"I'll put her off—tell her I'm far away or something, hiding."

"What if she has caller ID? She'd know where you called from."

"I hadn't thought of that."

They were quiet, the afternoon sun starting to stretch into the evening, the shadows growing perceptibly longer. Gwen took an exit off the interstate into a secondary highway headed southeast.

"Where are we going?" Annie asked.

"Roswell."

"What? Why there?"

"Aliens."

Annie stared at her, not smiling, and Gwen laughed. "Sorry—stupid joke. I have another friend there. It would probably be better to call first, but we can get a hotel tonight, and I can contact her in the morning. She's done some computer stuff with my company, so she might be able to help us move the money, or know who to ask."

"Okay."

They were quiet again. For Gwen, the idea that they might succeed was starting to seem more and more real. Soon, she needed to ask what would happen when this ended. Her chest grew tight and almost hot with nerves. Would Annie have any room for her in her life once she had all that money?

"Gwen?"

"Yes?"

"Thanks again. I couldn't have done this without you."

Gwen smiled at her and grabbed her hand. Touching her, that simple contact, made her feel like everything would be okay. Even if they were deluding themselves, things couldn't be that bad if they had this connection.

## CHAPTER FOURTEEN

Trixie Dannon looked like the last person who would have any computer skills. Her bottle-red hair was curled and brushed out, as big as possible, held in place with a shellac of shiny, almost metallic hairspray. She had long, red, fake nails, supremely tanned skin, and was wearing a bright-pink miniskirt with a neon-green halter top. She stood about five feet in her heels and spoke with a Kentucky drawl. Gwen had suspected long ago that her appearance functioned as perhaps the best cover possible. People constantly underestimated her.

"Well, look what the cat dragged in!" Trixie said, launching to her feet. She ran across the little office and wrapped her arms around Gwen in a tight hug. Drawing back, she took Gwen in, her head moving up and down, then shook it. "Or should I say, look what the cat coughed up. You look like shit."

Gwen and Annie had spent the night outside Roswell in a fleabag. Despite their exhaustion, neither she nor Annie had slept very well, partly because of the terrible bed, and partly because of their busy day. They'd checked out early, twenty minutes ago, as soon as Gwen knew they could catch Trixie at work.

Gwen laughed. "Gee, thanks. We're not exactly staying at the Ritz."

"I'll say. You must've slept in those clothes. And who, may I ask, is your lady friend?"

"This is Annie. Annie, Trixie."

"Nice to meet you," Annie said, holding out her hand.

"Oh, you're cute," Trixie said, shaking it. "You're like a little doll. Gwen always did pick the good ones."

"Anyway," Gwen said, glaring at her, "we came to ask a favor."

"I assumed. You show up this early in the morning, looking like you do, and you must need something. Have a seat and tell me your problems. Anyone want coffee?"

Though she did some work for Gwen's employer, Trixie's day job was running a branch of the Roswell tourist office. The place was festooned with posters of aliens and UFOs, and flyers for every sort of tour associated with the famous conspiracy lay in piles all over the place. Several of the larger advertisements announced the festivities later this week that would take place during the celebration for the fiftieth anniversary of the supposed UFO crash.

"You managed to get a hotel room?" Trixie asked, handing them both a green alien mug with pitch-black coffee.

"Barely," Gwen said. "We had to drive all over to find one."

"And when we did, they charged us a ton for a smelly hellhole," Annie added.

"I don't doubt it." Trixie sat down on her side of the desk. "The big celebration starts this weekend, and people are already coming to town. Even the campgrounds are full. You lucked out finding anything, really, even now. I wish you'd called me. I have that guest room you could stay in."

"We might have to take you up on that tonight," Gwen said.

"You're welcome to it until Friday morning. The celebration kicks off on the fourth, and I'm renting it out to a big alien fan through the ninth for a bundle of money." She took a sip of her coffee, eyeing the two of them before resting her arms on her desk. "Okay. Lay it on me. I've seen you two on the news, so I know a little bit about it, but I want details."

Gwen glanced at Annie, not knowing how much to give away.

Annie set her coffee down and cleared her throat. "It's like this," she said. She described, in detail, the situation. Gwen was a little surprised at her candor. With Tex, she'd been friendly but reserved. For some reason, she seemed to trust Trixie. Maybe, Gwen thought, it had something to do with the fact that they were at the end of the line now. Holding anything back would be counterproductive.

"Wow," Trixie said when she'd finished. She held up her hands. "So let me get this straight—this woman, this Susan?"

"Yes?"

"She let you take the blame and get arrested, and you still believed her?"

Annie lifted her hands. "I kind of had to. What else could I do? I started having second thoughts right away, but it seemed like I was already in too deep. Then, when everything fell apart, she promised to get me out of prison and give me my share. I could only hope she was telling the truth."

Trixie shook her head dismissively. Gwen was sure Trixie would never have been taken in like that. She was nice enough not to point this out to Annie but was clearly baffled by her naïveté.

"So what do you want me to do?" Trixie asked.

Annie looked at Gwen helplessly.

"Well," Gwen said, "I guess we want your advice more than anything. We have the account numbers but nothing else. What do we do next?"

"Can you…" Annie said, rolling her hands.

"Can I get the money for you?" Trixie asked. She stared at Annie for a long, hard moment, then gave a single nod. "I might be able to help you get it, but I guess I have a question for you. What do you really want, Annie? Do you want the money, or do you want revenge?"

Annie flushed and reacted as if she'd been slapped, jerking back in her chair. "What do you mean?"

"You've got these bank-account numbers, right?"

Annie nodded.

"So that means you have all the evidence you need to put the two of them behind bars. It would be hard for them to deny that evidence when they've been so careless with it. Even if they moved the money now, it wouldn't matter—the proof is already there. With your testimony, they would probably go away for a long time, and like you said, it could help your sentence, too."

Annie's face had drained of color, and she seemed to have almost caved in on herself. Her arms were squeezed across her chest, and her shoulders were hunched up, her body far back in her chair.

"What if I want both?" she asked, almost whispering.

Trixie laughed. "Now you're talking. Tell me what you have in mind."

Annie's gaze darted to Gwen. "I guess, if I could make it happen, I'd get the money—some of it, anyway—*and* they'd be arrested."

"What about you? Would you be willing to go back to jail?"

Gwen's stomach dropped at the idea, and she watched Annie carefully, trying to keep the anxiety out of her eyes. She didn't want to influence her in any way.

Annie was quiet for a long time. "I guess if I had the money, then yes. It was for my sister, after all. If I know she's taken care of, then…"

Trixie laughed. "That's very noble of you, hon, but it might not come to that. It might be possible for you to have your cake and eat it, too."

Gwen's hopes rose. The last thing she wanted was for Annie to go back to prison. Even with a reduced sentence, she didn't know if she could take the thought of being apart from her for any length of time.

"So what do you suggest?" Gwen asked.

Trixie glanced back and forth at them and grinned. "Blackmail."

"What?" they asked in unison.

Trixie laughed again. "Blackmail. Get them on record, admitting what they've done—one or both of them. A recording would be best. You have the upper hand now, since you have the bank records. If you have them on tape, actually admitting what they did, it would go a lot further with the police. Let Susan and whatever his name is know you have proof—the bank accounts and the recording—and blackmail the hell out of them. Get them to transfer the money, however much you want, to your account, and I can help you hide it. Then, when you have the money safely tucked away, Gwen will make contact with the police and hand all the records over to them."

Annie's eyes were blazing with triumph. "Do you really think it would work?"

Trixie tilted her head back and forth. "Maybe, maybe not. The other option would be robbing them blind, but then they're still out there, and from what you said, these two are dangerous characters. You have some place you can hide for the rest of your life?"

Annie shook her head. "Not really. I was going to figure that out once I had the money."

"Well, that's the other option. I don't know how much I'll be able to move before they catch on, but if we start with the bigger amounts, you'd have enough to start over." She paused, frowning. "But it's definitely harder that way. It would mean hacking the bank accounts, which isn't easy. Much better if we can get them to give the money to you. I can hide it easy enough, and probably better than they did."

"Can you do it? Hack the banks?" Gwen asked.

"Maybe. But even if I could, it'll take some time. I'd have to make some phone calls, involve some other people, but I know it can be done. Of course, if we had passwords and key codes, it'd be a lot easier. Did you see anything like that on their computer?"

Annie shook her head. "No, but I wasn't really looking for them. I only looked for the account numbers."

"You said you were able to email them to yourself? So is their computer hooked up to do that?"

"They have AOL."

Trixie laughed. "Of course they do. Well, I guess if you're thinking of going that route, hacking them, it might be worth seeing if they've hidden anything else on that computer, or if they have any links to the passwords through the World Wide Web."

"How would we do that?" Gwen asked.

"You'd go back to the house and install a reader. I'd be able to see everything on their computer that way."

Annie stared down at the ground, clearly hesitant to make a decision. "I guess I need to think about it."

"No problem—and no pressure either way. It's going to get really busy in here later today, but I might find some time to poke around a little for you on my computer, make a couple of anonymous phone calls." She pointed at the computer. "Why don't you email that list to me, Annie, so I can get started." She bent down and picked up her purse, pulling out a set of keys. She slid one off the ring and handed it to Gwen. "That will unlock the house—you remember where it is, right? You two can hang out there till I get home. It's got a swamp cooler, so you won't boil to death. Just turn it on when you get there. Cools the whole place in like ten minutes."

"Thanks, Trixie."

"Don't mention it. Though could you be dears and pick up some tequila on your way over there? I ran out last night."

Gwen waited for Annie to finish emailing Trixie the list of bank accounts, and then the two of them left the office, both carrying flyers for local attractions in case anyone spotted them. Though she'd seen herself and Annie on the news a couple of times now, Gwen was fairly certain no one would recognize them on the street unless they drew attention to themselves somehow or someone was actually searching for them. Also, Gwen had noticed when they watched the news last night that they'd already been bumped down to a ten-second mention from the full minute they'd had the night before. Still, it didn't hurt to blend in a little.

Trixie's house was a nice, wide, bright-pink modular in a small neighborhood near downtown. The little front yard was crammed with colorful metal sculptures of aliens and farm animals, some life-sized, some comically over-large, like the seven-foot rooster near the front door. Gwen vaguely remembered from the last time she'd been here, some two years ago, that Trixie made and sold these things in her spare time, but she had clearly increased her earlier output, as there were far more of the sculptures than during her last visit. Trixie had a big metal workshop in her backyard almost as big as the house. A few of her sculptures were festooned with patriotic bunting, ostensibly for Independence Day, but with all the banners and signs they'd passed on the way here, the decorations could as easily stand in for the big alien celebration later this week. The sidewalks and parking lots throughout town had been full to the brim with visitors of every sort. They'd seen several people in various alien and science-fiction costumes, as well as every manner of tinfoil hat. The anniversary party was still a few days away, but some people were apparently making a vacation of it.

The little liquor store they'd stopped at on the way had been annoyingly crowded, despite the early hour, and they'd grabbed some things in a little grocery afterward. They were still driving the car Gwen had stolen in Denver, which she found no reason to trade in. No one would check the plates, especially here and now, with all these wackos visiting from out of town.

Trixie had left the blinds down, likely to keep the sun out, and Gwen immediately threw open a window and turned on the swamp cooler. They put the groceries and drinks away and carried their small overnight bag into the guest room. The cooler was working by then, and they sat down in the armchairs in front of it, letting the chilly wind blow on them. It was only ten in the morning, but the heat outside was crushing. Gwen let her eyelids drift closed, still tired from the previous day and a poor night's rest.

She dozed for a few minutes, then yawned, shook herself awake, and rubbed her face. "I could use a real shower."

"Mmm," Annie said. Her head was thrown back on the chair, her eyes closed tight.

"I'll make it quick."

Annie waved a hand weakly and vaguely as if to say she'd heard but couldn't respond. Sitting there almost boneless in her chair, she appeared as relaxed as Gwen had ever seen her. Two little red spots from the heat colored her pale cheeks, and her clothes, like Gwen's, were sweaty and threadbare. They'd changed from their fake tourist gear yesterday in the hotel, but everything they owned had come from a poorly stocked thrift store outside Denver. Gwen was tempted to kiss her cute little nose, but she left her there unmolested and headed to the bathroom.

Trixie had renovated since the last time Gwen had stayed here. The shower was much larger, with two heads and a little tiled seat. Gwen turned on the cold water, and after stripping off, she sat on the seat and let the water simply rain down on her hot skin. She must have dozed off again, as she woke up with a snap after almost slipping off the seat. She grabbed uselessly at the walls before regaining her balance, laughing nervously at herself. She hadn't done anything to actually wash herself, so she stood up and quickly washed her hair and body, using Trixie's food-scented soaps and shampoo.

She grabbed her towel to dry off, catching a strong whiff of her cake-batter-smelling skin, then stared down at her sweaty clothes with dismay. She didn't want to put them on again, so she wrapped herself in a towel to go see if anything clean was left in their bag.

Annie was coming down the hall from their bedroom, holding a towel and a new outfit. "I thought you'd drowned in there."

"Sorry. I think I fell asleep."

"Don't blame you. Last night was the pits. Why don't you go lie down for a while? We're not going anywhere today, are we?"

"I thought we might go buy some new clothes. Even something from a department store would be better than these rags."

Annie grimaced. "In this heat?"

Gwen sighed. "Yeah. I didn't think of that. I guess I should have waited to take a shower." She glanced at a clock on the wall. "Still, we have lots of time. Trixie won't be home till pretty late— four or five, I think, at the earliest. I'm not sure if we'll have another chance for a while."

Annie batted her eyelashes. "Darling?"

"Yes?"

"Could you go without me? The thought of braving a Walmart or K-Mart right now makes me want to kill myself."

Gwen laughed and kissed her. "Okay, hon. What color shirts do you want?"

"Anything but black."

Gwen returned about two hours later, struggling to carry all the bags. She'd gone a little overboard, but she was tired of looking like she was homeless. She'd hit three stores at the mall and Payless for shoes. Her boots worked well for most things, but in this kind of weather, it was like wearing heavy sweaters on her feet.

"My hero!" Annie threw her arms around her neck and kissed her soundly.

Gwen laughed and set the bags down. "I've come bearing gifts, milady. I had to guess your tastes, though, so no complaining."

Annie held up three fingers. "I swear I will not complain."

They spent the rest of the afternoon in relative quiet—doing laundry, napping, and playing cards. Like the previous weekend, Gwen found it incredibly easy to be around her—so much so that it was easy to forget everything else that was happening. Annie was still weighing her options about the money and Susan and Bill, and she didn't want to push her on it by talking about it too much, but she was also dying of curiosity. Occasionally, she caught Annie staring into space, clearly mulling things over, but never brought up the subject. Annie needed to decide on her own.

Around three, after trouncing her in poker, Annie suggested that she go lie down until Trixie came home. She wanted to make her a nice dinner as a thank-you, and Gwen was firmly forbidden from helping. Gwen fell asleep almost at once and slept soundly until Annie knocked on the door.

Annie stuck her head in a moment later and smiled when she saw Gwen. "Your hair's sticking up all over."

"Mmm. I bet."

"Take a shower and come join us. She just got here."

Gwen was surprised to see that several hours had passed. She'd expected Trixie home closer to four or five, and it was almost seven thirty. She'd napped for almost five hours, and judging by the way she felt, she hadn't moved a single time since she lay down. She stretched the stiffness out of her joints and grabbed some new clothes, heading for the shower.

When she joined them, she saw a large pitcher of margaritas on the kitchen island and a big bowl of salad. Something was cooking in the oven, filling the room with a mouthwatering scent.

"There she is," Trixie said, "and looking more like her old self again."

Annie had changed, too, and Gwen thought the casual T-shirt and cotton skirt looked nice and natural on her. She had no idea what kind of clothes Annie had worn in her everyday life before she'd been arrested, but it must have been something like this.

"Want one?" Annie asked, holding up the pitcher.

Gwen shook her head. "Not right now. I could use some caffeine, actually."

"You'll find some sun tea in the fridge," Trixie said, pointing. "It's sweet—just like my mama used to make."

Soon, the three of them carried their food and drinks over to the little dining-room table. Gwen had expected something heavy and fried, judging from Annie's usual restaurant choices, but she'd made what she called "margarita chicken"—a citrus and herb blend on moist breasts—and Spanish rice with vegetables. With a fresh salad dressed with red-onion vinaigrette, it was the perfect hot-weather meal. All three dug in and ate with barely a word.

"Well, gosh, Annie," Trixie said a while later, "that was lovely. Thank you. I can't remember the last time someone cooked for me."

"The pleasure's mine. I haven't been able to cook in a long time." Her face fell briefly, but she smiled again a second later. "And anyway, I wanted to thank you."

"For what?"

"For inviting us to stay, for helping us. You didn't have to do anything."

Trixie laughed. "Of course I didn't *have* to, Annie, but your girl Gwen here has saved my bacon enough times, I figured it was my turn. And anyway, I like her. Not like you like her, but well enough." She winked.

Annie laughed. "Okay. But thanks anyway."

"So what did you decide?"

Trixie's bluntness startled Gwen, and she waited for Annie's response. Annie was quiet for a while before shaking her head.

"I didn't really decide. I guess it's like you say—I want it both ways. But I want the money. I guess I'd like to see if we can get it without them knowing. I'll always have the bank records, and maybe later I'll turn them over to the police, anonymously, but I want the money more."

"So you want me to try to hack them?"

"Yes. I want to try that first. If you can't, then maybe we can move on to the next thing, but I'd like the money before that." Annie threw Gwen a quick glance, blushing slightly. "The truth is, I think I wanted revenge because I was so mad at her. She betrayed me. But really, it won't make me feel any better if she goes to prison. I don't want anyone to go through what I did."

Gwen was shocked. This morning and most of the last few days, Annie had been angry—furious, even. This was a complete reversal.

Trixie seemed to pick up on this difference as well. "Why the change of heart?"

Again, Annie glanced at Gwen and away, her expression strangely guilty. "Well, when I talked to her today—"

"What?" Gwen said, almost shouting.

Annie flushed. "When I called her this afternoon—"

"This afternoon?" Gwen leapt to her feet and raced to the front window, looking outside between the slats of the wooden blinds. She peered up and down the street, trying to remember if she'd seen all those cars earlier. So many were out there, parked on the street and in the driveways of the nearby houses, she had no way to know. She let go of the blind and turned around, fists clenched.

"Annie, what the hell? Why did you do that?"

## CHAPTER FIFTEEN

Annie was clearly shocked. Her mouth worked uselessly on itself before she managed to speak. "You told me to!"

"The hell I did!"

"You told me to call her, to throw her off the scent."

Gwen took a step toward her. "But not from here. How could you be so fucking stupid? They could be here any minute!"

"Just hold your horses there, buster," Trixie said. "Don't talk to her like that."

"Stay out of this, Trixie," Gwen said, almost shouting.

Trixie stood up, slamming her fists on the table. "The hell I will! You don't know what the fuck you're talking about. Shut up and sit your ass down."

Gwen's anger was roiling through her in hot waves, and she had a wild temptation to throw Trixie's nearest sculpture across the room. She made herself close her eyes and take a few deep breaths, forcing herself to relax. When she opened them again, Trixie was still glowering at her, and Annie looked frightened. That did it. She felt instantly terrible, and her tension and anger evaporated at once.

"Are you ready to act like a mature, normal member of the human race?" Trixie asked.

"Annie, I'm sorry—"

"Shut it," Trixie said, "and sit."

For a moment, Gwen was afraid to obey her—not because she feared what Trixie would do, but because of the damage she'd done.

The whole exchange had taken less than a minute, and already Annie was watching her like a stranger, her expression sad and bleak. Feeling like the world's biggest asshole, Gwen walked back across the room to the table and sat down again, unable to meet either woman's eyes. All that work she'd done in her anger-management classes had gone out the window the second she'd been frightened, and now she'd ruined everything. Again.

Trixie sat down and folded her hands in front of her on the table. "There now. That's better. I know you're a hothead, Gwen, but that kind of shit is unacceptable."

"I know. I'm sorry."

"You got a nice gal here, and you need to treat her better than that."

Gwen managed to make herself glance at Annie. She had tears in her eyes, and Gwen's guilt was like the stab of a knife.

"Annie, I'm so sorry."

"It's okay."

"No, it ain't," Trixie said, still glaring at Gwen. "You had no right to behave that way, missy, and Annie, you didn't deserve it. I had a husband that was always yelling at me, and it took me a long time to show his ass the door. Best decision I ever made. You two have some making up to do, but we don't have time for that right now." She paused. "For one thing, Gwen, you should know that I would never have a phone that could be traced that easily."

Gwen's stomach dropped. She'd been stupid to even consider that possibility.

"Oh."

"Oh is right, you idiot. And two, Annie, I was going to suggest that you call those people myself. I should have known you were smart enough to do it on your own."

Annie gave her a weak smile. "Really?"

Trixie patted her hand. "Really. Now what did y'all talk about?"

Annie licked her lips, her gaze darting from Gwen and then back to Trixie, staying on her. She sat up a little straighter. "I had to lie a lot."

"Where does she think you are?"

"I accidentally told her New Mexico, but not the town."

"Good—that's fine. What else?"

"She knew about Tom, about how he got us out of town. She called him, and I guess he told her everything he knew. He didn't know not to."

"Again, totally fine."

"I pretended that I was still on her side. I told her I was going to follow the plan she had for me—hide out for a while and then contact her again in a few weeks, when things cooled down."

"How did she respond?"

Annie lifted a shoulder. "Fine—almost normal. She seemed worried, upset, but *for* me. She kept saying she had been afraid I'd be caught, and she was so glad I made it out of Texas."

"Did you ask about the money?"

"Yes. She said it would be mine as soon as I got settled somewhere."

"Did she ask about Gwen?"

"Yes. I told her we went our separate ways once Tom dropped us off. I said I gave her half of the money from the envelope."

"How did she respond?"

"She wasn't happy about it, but she seemed to believe me, as far as I could tell. She told me to call if I needed some more ready cash."

"Anything else? You didn't have any sense that she was on to you?"

Annie shook her head. "None."

"So she's either the world's best liar and is playing the long game, or she really wants to help you."

Gwen had made herself stay quiet this entire conversation, but she finally started to object. Trixie held up a hand. "Sit there for a minute more, dumbass. I'm talking to Annie right now." She turned back to Annie. "So what do you think? Is she lying to you?"

Annie finally met Gwen's eyes, and once again, Gwen felt as if she were being knifed through the heart. Annie still seemed distrustful, wary, and she hated to see that reaction in her eyes. She'd put it there, with her stupid temper.

Annie frowned. "I guess a part of me still wants to believe her, but I can't. It would be easier, simpler, if she was telling the truth, but I don't buy it anymore."

"Did you ask her about the police showing up?" Gwen asked, unable to stay quiet. "When we went to get the envelope?"

"No—and she didn't bring it up, either. I think she avoided it on purpose, since the game would really be up then. I mean sure, she could have lied about it, but there wasn't really any reason for them to show up like that unless one of them called us in. She knows that, but I think she's hoping I don't." She paused. "And something else, too. It wasn't the words she was saying. It was her tone. A little too upset, if you know what I mean."

"You think she was faking it," Trixie said.

"Exactly. If I could have seen her face, I probably would have known for sure, but something about the way she was talking—it didn't seem real."

Trixie was quiet for a long time, and she held up a hand to silence Gwen again when she shifted in her seat. A touch of annoyance flashed through her, but she held her tongue, waiting.

Finally, Trixie smiled. "Okay, Annie. You did well. I can't think of any reason she'd know for certain one way or the other. It might have been better to tell her you were in another state, but that's pretty minor. I'm sure she's like you—she's doesn't know if you know, but she's probably hedging her bets. Do you think she'll start moving the money?"

"I have no idea, but it's probably pretty likely."

"So that means we need to get on it if we're going to do something. It's now or never, ladies, if we want to try to move it on our own."

Annie looked at Gwen again, her eyes searching, unreadable. Gwen thought she might be debating whether to include her in any of this now.

"Okay," Annie said. "I'm in. What do we need to do?"

Trixie stood up. "First, follow me to my secret lair."

Gwen had been there before and automatically moved toward the back door. Trixie had a storm shelter in the backyard that she'd converted to a kind of bunker for her computers. Several locks secured the metal doors, which opened in the middle. After a steep flight of steps, the three of them were down inside the computer hub. Despite several computer towers and large monitors on a small desk, and shelves of electronics and wires, the room was almost cold from the cooling system. It was also eerily quiet in spite of all the machines.

"The police came over one time to see if I was growing weed," Trixie said, laughing. "Apparently this little setup uses the same amount of energy as a grow lab. Luckily they didn't know what they were looking at when I showed them all this equipment, or I really would have been in some deep shit."

"I don't doubt it," Annie said.

"Gwen, grab that box there," Trixie said, pointing.

It was small but heavy, and Gwen had to use most of her strength to pick it up and move it to a small table in the center of the room. Trixie fiddled with the lock on the box before opening it. The box was lined with black foam, and three smallish black, plastic electronic boxes nestled inside in preformed cutout molds. Trixie examined them before pulling out one of the electronics.

"Okay, girls, this is how it works. When you go back to their house, you get to their computer, and you take the phone line from the computer out of the wall and plug it into this end here. Then you take the phone line on this end of the connector and plug it back into the wall. Dial in to AOL, and then give me a call."

"How can we call you if the computer's using the phone line?" Gwen asked.

"Oh, right." Trixie walked across the small room and picked up a cellular phone. It was smaller than the phones Gwen had seen before, almost pocket-sized. She took it from her and inspected it, making sure she understood how it worked.

"Neat, huh?" Trixie asked. "But you got to make sure it stays charged. Eats up juice like nobody's business. I'll give you a thing to plug into the cigarette lighter in your car so you can keep it powered up."

"Will it call from up in the mountains?" Annie asked. "I thought these things had terrible range, or whatever."

Trixie laughed. "Doesn't work like that, but you're right. You might have bad reception up there. If you do, make sure you hook up this connector right, dial in, and then hide it behind the desk the best you can. Then drive somewhere where you can call me and let me know I can start looking. I shouldn't need to have you guys there, but you can always go back if you have to."

Annie and Gwen shared a glance. The idea of breaking in two more times was unappealing, to say the least, but they didn't have any choice.

"What happens if there's nothing more on that computer?" Annie asked.

"We'll cross that bridge if we have to," Trixie said. "I have some friends that could help with a different way to do things, but I don't want to call them if we don't have to—too many cooks and all that. And anyway, you could always move on to blackmail next, instead."

As the two of them went over the details again, Gwen realized she wasn't satisfied with any of this. Annie might have moved on from her earlier anger at Susan, but Gwen hadn't. She also knew that even if they managed to get the money, that woman was still out there somewhere. Susan wasn't the kind to let things lie—even Gwen knew that, and she'd never met the bitch. Even if Annie managed to find some place that Susan could never trace, that was no way to live—looking over your shoulder for the rest of your life. No, Gwen thought. Susan had to be out of the picture forever, rotting in jail, or, if necessary, dead and buried.

"I'll start packing," Gwen said, moving toward the stairs.

"Wait, what?" Annie asked.

"We should go now. If we get back there tonight, we're less likely to run into anyone again."

"I guess so."

She sounded uncertain, but Gwen didn't try to explain further. She left the two of them down there together, almost running up the stairs. She went back to their bedroom and grabbed a couple of clean outfits, stuffing them into her old leather bag on top of her tools. Her gun was still inside the little hidden compartment on the bottom, and she checked it quickly for obstructions or dirt. Annie appeared as she was putting it away.

She frowned. "You didn't pack for me?"

Gwen hesitated, realizing that she had to come up with some kind of explanation. "You're not coming."

"Wait. What do you mean? Of course I'm coming!"

"It's too dangerous," Gwen said, pushing past her. Annie trailed her down the hallway back into the main room. The phone and the connecting box lay on the dining-room table, and Gwen picked them up and put them in her bag on top of the clothes.

Trixie, perhaps seeing something in their expressions, asked, "What's happening?"

"Gwen thinks she's going without me," Annie said.

"What?"

Gwen sighed, setting her bag down on the table. She needed to lie, and she needed to lie well, or her whole plan would be blown. "It's like this—two people cause twice the danger. If I go alone, I can slip inside and out again that much faster."

"You think I'd slow you down?" Annie asked. She sounded hurt, indignant.

"Not exactly. It's not just that. If I'm caught, I get a simple B and E charge, and I'm out on bail in a week. If you're caught, you go back to prison. The stakes are too high."

She started moving toward the front door, and Annie and Trixie ran to intercept her. They stopped in front of her, blocking the door.

"Stop being like this," Annie said. "I'm coming with you."

"You're being stupid," Trixie added. "You need her help, and you know it."

"And you're crazy if you think I'd let you go on your own," Annie said.

Gwen felt a flash of impatient anger. While her excuse was almost entirely a lie, it was also a little bit true, and she needed them to buy it. It *was* too dangerous for the two of them to go. If she went on her own, Annie would be safe here with Trixie. Also, she needed to have a means to ensure that Susan would never have power over Annie again, and she needed time on her own to think of a way to do that. Having Annie along would make her secondary plan impossible unless she let Annie in on it, and she absolutely didn't want to do that. Keeping her here would keep her safe from both the break-in and her other plan.

"Trixie," she said, trying to keep her voice calm. "Would you excuse us for a moment?"

Trixie looked as if she wanted to object, but she finally agreed, walking away. Gwen and Annie stared at each other in silence.

"Why are you doing this?" Annie said, her voice breaking with a sob. "Do you want to leave me?"

"That's the last thing I want." She didn't say that she wanted to spend the rest of her life with Annie—that she was terrified, in fact, that she wouldn't get to do that. She also didn't want to give away her plan. Instead, she pulled Annie into a long embrace, hoping she could show her this, if not tell her.

Eventually, Annie drew back, her eyes red and teary. "I wish you wouldn't leave. If one of us should go, it ought to be me."

Gwen shook her head. "I swear to God, I'm only trying to help you, Annie. If you knew how much you mean to me..."

"I'd what?"

Gwen was surprised to feel herself choke up, and she shook her head, unable to speak. Even getting that close to saying what she meant made her want to pull her into her arms and never let go. Annie watched her for a while, her expression softening.

"Okay, Gwen. If this is how you think it has to be, I won't try to stop you. I wish you'd stay and explain this to me better, but I can see that I'm not going to change your mind."

"I just want to keep you safe. You can understand that, can't you?"

"Don't you think I want the same thing? I don't want you risking your life for me."

Gwen grabbed her hands, squeezing them. "I'm not, and I won't. I'll be back before you know it."

Annie frowned but didn't object any further, and Gwen left her there to tell Trixie she was going. Trixie was clearly disgusted with her, but Gwen didn't have time to smooth things over. If she let this go on too long, she'd cave. She had to get out of here before she had second thoughts. She gave Annie a quick kiss good-bye and rushed out of the house, getting back into the sweltering car and driving away with only a quick wave to the two of them on the front stoop.

Three blocks away, she had to pull over to cry, shaking with nerves and sorrow. If she screwed this up, she might never see Annie again. Cursing her own weakness, she wiped her eyes and face hard and painfully. Annie was what mattered, and that's why she had to do this. She pulled back into the street and drove away.

# CHAPTER SIXTEEN

The mountain road was even creepier at night. She'd driven hard and fast from Roswell, pushing the speed limit more than she should, given that she was still driving a stolen car. It had been long enough that the plates were very likely in the system, so if someone pulled her over, she'd be caught. Still, she'd needed to make it to Santa Fe sooner than the others expected to give herself some time to snoop, and she'd gotten here almost an hour early.

The mobile phone beeped about a mile from the interstate, and when she slowed for a movement to examine it, she could see that she was now out of service range. She would have to drive all the way back here to call Trixie. She could picture the two of them in Trixie's house, Annie pacing the floor, Trixie sitting by the phone. She might have a little extra time before they really began to worry, but either way, she needed to move quickly. She parked the car behind the same group of bushes as last time and got out, surprised by the cold, almost bitter mountain air. Her denim jacket was entirely inadequate, and she suppressed deep shivers.

Her tool bag had a little flashlight inside, but she kept it off as she walked up the long, steep driveway. This too was more nerve-wracking than it had been last time, as she didn't know what to expect when she reached the top. Last time, she and Annie had been able to see that the house was empty, but she didn't have any way to tell now. It was too late at night for Susan or Bill to be up, if they were here, and in the nearly total darkness, she wouldn't be able to see any cars until it was too late.

She paused at the top of the driveway, ducking behind a large prickly pear. They were almost sure to have motion-sensor lights on every side of the house, so she would only have a minute or two to check the garage before needing to hide again if they were here. Her bag was hindering her movement a little, so she slung it off and set it down by the cactus. She dug around inside and found the connector box and her lock picks, sliding one into each of her jacket pockets before standing up. She rolled her shoulders, trying to loosen up a little, and then ran, as fast as she could, toward the garage. The lights turned on at once, startling in their brilliance, almost blinding her.

The windows into the garage were too high off the ground, and Gwen was forced to jump, foolishly, trying to look inside. She realized at once that it would be impossible. It was too dark to see anything. She made herself stop and take stock, listening. She could hear nothing, and no lights had turned on inside the house. She'd have to risk it.

She walked directly toward the front door, pausing to peer inside the large, front windows. It was too dark to see much beyond the first few feet of the entryway, but as far as she could tell, no one was here. She took out her lock picks and went to the door. She'd watched the little girl, Jen, when she entered the alarm code, so she saw no reason to try to sneak in any other way. She crouched in front of the lock, chose the right picks for this model, and started to work on it. Several long minutes later, she finally felt it start to give and stood up as the tumblers turned with the tools in her hands, the lock audibly clicking.

She put her hand on the knob, waiting again, ear pressed to the door. She was almost certain the house was empty. All of these outdoor lights had been on for at least five minutes now, and she wasn't trying to hide what she was doing. More than likely, monitors somewhere inside the house were hooked up to all these cameras, which meant anyone looking would have spotted her immediately. Actually, someone could be staring out one of these windows at her, and she wouldn't know. They could be standing on the other side of the door waiting for her. The police could be on their way, or the owners might decide to take matters into their own hands. This house was isolated enough to do whatever they wanted, and from what Annie had told her, she was sure Susan was capable of anything.

She took a deep breath and opened the door, pausing long enough to realize that no one was there before closing and locking it behind her. She went directly to the flashing alarm panel on the wall and entered the code. The flashing stopped and the system was off. She let out a long breath, realizing she'd been holding it. She was still a little rattled, and she jumped up and down a few times to shake off her nerves.

"You can do this," she told herself. "Get it together, Ramsey."

She started at the back of the house, near the door she and Annie had come in with Jen. She thought she'd remembered seeing an address book by the phone, and she spotted it again right away. She turned on her flashlight and opened the little book, not expecting to find what she was looking for, but hoping nonetheless. A little paper flag was sticking out at the edge in the D section, and she flipped there first. The entry read "Dallas House" but showed only a phone number, no address.

"Damn," she said, but she wasn't surprised. Who needed to put their own address in an address book? The phone number was probably for Jen, in case she forgot and needed to call them. Gwen flipped through the rest of the book as quickly as she could but didn't see anything helpful.

She glanced at her watch. Ten minutes wasted already. Annie and Trixie would expect her to be getting close now. Even if she was slowed down for some reason, she had, at most, an hour to call before they'd start to worry. She was almost certain that if she was gone too long, Annie would insist on coming for her, and she had to avoid that at all costs.

She began to make her way back upstairs to the office, almost jumping out of her skin on the stairs when the outside motion lights winked off again. She was plunged into a darkness so absolute she could hardly see her hand in front of her face. Realizing she had no choice, she turned her flashlight on again, hoping she would be out of sight should Susan and Bill suddenly come up the driveway. It was unlikely, but she also didn't want to give herself away that easily in case they did show up.

She felt safer in the office, deciding to risk the dim, desktop lamp. The office was at the back of the house, but she closed the door most of the way to block the light from the hallway just in case. She would have enough time to turn it off and hide if someone came in the front door or through the garage.

The room and its mess appeared to be the same as before, but Gwen couldn't be certain either way. It was possible that they had come and left again, but she didn't think so. Anyway, Annie had called Susan in Dallas this afternoon, and again, Gwen didn't know how that could be faked. It might be possible to reroute a phone number to another location, but she'd never heard of it, and Susan's phone number was a house phone. If anyone had been here, it would be Bill, but Gwen thought not. He would have stayed.

She leafed methodically through every pile of papers in the room, starting with the manila files on the desk and then working her way around clockwise from the door. Most of what she read was either bank or legal records. She spent a little extra time reading one brief but making very little sense of it. From what she could tell, Susan was suing someone, or someone was suing her, and the rest of the papers in that pile had something to do with the case. Only this address, the house in Santa Fe, was listed in the paperwork she examined. She got excited when she saw a Dallas address in the next pile, only to realize that it was the address of a bank.

Forty minutes later, she'd discovered exactly nothing, except that it seemed like Susan and Bill were involved in a great number of lawsuits. The second one she'd read had made it clearer that they were the ones being sued, over some kind of land dispute with their neighbors up here on the mountain. Another lawsuit suggested that they had defrauded a dry-cleaning business for $10,000. Another one seemed to be saying that Bill had pretended to be in a car accident for the insurance, but the insurance company was suing for a false claim. Basically, all she'd really learned was that they were con artists, and she'd already known that.

"Shit," she said, loud enough that the echo made her jump. She smiled at herself. What had she expected? She'd planned to get Susan's Dallas address, and then what? Go down there? A big part of her had wanted to do just that. But she would never have been able to go through with whatever that would mean. She wasn't a murderer and didn't want to become one. She'd half hoped she might be able to dig up something on Susan while she was here, but she didn't have enough time, and what was more, she didn't know what she was looking for. Trixie's idea was probably for the best. She should do what she'd told them she would do—no more bullshit. She could be back with Annie in a few hours. A wave of warm relief washed through her. Things with Annie were, she realized, still salvageable. She needed to do what she'd said—go back to her. She picked up the phone next to her and dialed Trixie's number.

"Hello?" Trixie said, almost breathless.

"I'm here."

"Thank Christ. What took you so long?"

"There was an accident on the highway. Anyway, I'm about to hook up the gadget here. The mobile phone doesn't work in this location."

"Do you think there's another phone line in the house?"

"No idea."

"Check and see if the phone you're using is plugged into the same phone jack as the computer."

Gwen followed the line from the phone to a splitter. One line went to the phone, the other to the computer, but they were definitely using the same jack. She told Trixie.

"Damn. Cheap bastards. Okay, so that little splitter makes things a little more complicated. It might interfere with my connector box. You should unplug the line from the computer and put that into the connecter. Then unplug the splitter and plug the connector into the jack."

"Won't that mean the phone won't work?"

"Exactly. That means you don't have any reason to bother trying to hide what we're doing. They'll know the moment they try to make a phone call that something's up. Damn! I wish that mobile phone was working."

"Me, too. It went out of range way the heck back there."

"It would be so much better if you could leave with the connector when I'm finished." Trixie was quiet for a few seconds. "You know what. I just thought of something. You're going to be on the web, so we could chat."

Gwen was only vaguely aware of what that meant. She hadn't had any reason to learn much about computers. "You mean like type-talking?"

Trixie laughed. "Exactly. Once you get logged in to AOL, I'll pull up a chat box and tell you what I need to do that way."

"Okay. Trixie, before I do that, could I talk to Annie real quick?"

"Sure." During a long pause, Gwen could hear a murmured conversation on the other end before Annie picked up.

"Yes? Hello?"

"Hi, hon."

"Hi, yourself. How are you doing?"

Her tone surprised Gwen. She'd expected Annie to sound relieved, glad to hear from her. Instead, she sounded almost cold, guarded, even, almost like she'd been when they'd first met.

"I'm okay," Gwen said. "I'm about to hook up the thingy to the computer."

"Good. I can't wait for this all to be over."

Gwen couldn't help but react with anger. "What's that supposed to mean?"

Annie sighed. "It doesn't mean anything but what it means, Gwen. It's after midnight. I'm tired. Don't jump down my throat."

Gwen's heart sank. She and Annie had been separated for less than four hours, and she already sounded like she'd moved on. Coming here on her own had been a big mistake. She should have stayed and tried to make up for her stupid outburst. She should have brought Annie along. Everything she'd done in the last six hours had been a mistake.

"Okay, sorry. I just wanted to hear your voice. I wish…"

"What?"

"I wish you were here. I know I said you'd be safer there, but I hate being apart."

Annie was quiet for a long time. "I hate it, too," she finally whispered.

Gwen's hopes rose, and she couldn't help but smile. "I'll make it up to you, Annie, I promise."

"Get back safe. Drive all night if you have to, but come back to me."

"I will."

"Okay. I'm putting Trixie back on the line."

After some more murmuring, Trixie picked up again. "You don't deserve that angel, Gwen. She's been here crying her eyes out since you left. Can't understand what she sees in you."

"I know it."

"All right. Let's get this show on the road. Hang up, hook up the connector, and dial in. I'll send you a chat through AIM in a couple of minutes."

"What's AIM?"

"Never mind. You'll see it."

Gwen hung up and did what she was told. Once she'd hooked up the connector, it took a while to turn on the computer, which, she realized, she should have done right away. Once it was on, it took her even longer to figure out how to make AOL work once she found it. The password was apparently preloaded, as all she needed to do was click "Sign On," but her inexperience with the mouse made all of this take longer than she'd expected.

A screeching sound greeted her once she'd clicked the right button, and she flinched at its volume. She'd seen people use this kind of thing before but never done it herself. Finally, something happened, and a new screen appeared. She looked at it curiously for a few seconds, using the arrows on the keyboard to move up and down. Suddenly a littler window popped up on the left side of the screen from "TrixieDixie." She hit "Accept" and waited. After a little sound, something appeared in the new box.

> *TrixieDixie: Hey, we're in.*

Gwen took a moment to review the keys and then hunted and pecked a response. A different sound accompanied her reply.

> *SueBill4Ever: OK. What do I do?*
> *TrixieDixie: Nothing right now. I'm going to take over your computer, but I'll keep this chat open. You'll hear a sound, and the little bar at the top of this will blink if I ask or tell you something.*
> *SueBill4Ever: Affirmative.*
> *TrixieDixie: LOL! You're a dork.*

Gwen didn't know what LOL meant, but she apparently didn't need to respond. She watched as the little arrow for the mouse began moving on its own on her screen. She assumed this meant that Trixie was controlling it on her end. The screen she'd been looking at disappeared, and Trixie was back to the Windows opening page. Gwen watched as she opened several of the folders on that screen, closing them as she went. She did some kind of search in Explorer, finally finding a folder labeled "Beach House." She tried to open it, and a little box appeared with a blinking colon. The chat box made a sound and flashed, and Gwen selected it again.

> *TrixieDixie: I'm thinking there's something in this folder. It's the only one I've found that needs a password. I'm going to transfer the file to my computer and see if I can run it against some encryption software. Hang tight. This might take a while.*
> *SueBill4Ever: OK.*

Ten minutes passed, then fifteen. Gwen was starting to get anxious and couldn't help but poke her head into the hallway, peering up and down into darkness. No sound and no light from anywhere else in the house. She was safe and had no reason to worry about being caught, but sitting here doing nothing was hard to take. Finally, almost the second when she was tempted to try to figure out how to use the chat thing on her own, it beeped and flashed again.

> *TrixieDixie: Okay, we might have a problem. Despite how incompetent these losers seem to be about computers and security software in general, they seem to have managed to do one thing right. My usual code-breaking software isn't working on this file. I have a friend I can call for a new one he's been working on, but that might take even longer. It would be best if you leave now, stay somewhere nearby tonight, and then, if I need you to do it, you can just go back.*

Gwen didn't respond right away. For some reason, she hadn't anticipated something like this. At no point had she thought she might need to stay the night. Coming here, she'd had one plan—to get Susan's address and possibly drive to Dallas. If she found something else on Susan, even better, but she hadn't. She'd ditched both ideas, so she'd thought she'd be back on her way to Roswell. Now, not only was she not returning to Annie, but she might have to do all this again.

> *TrixieDixie: Gwen? Are you there? Is something wrong?*
> *SueBill4Ever: No. Sorry. Just thinking. I wanted to come back there tonight.*
> *TrixieDixie: I know, and I'm sorry, too. Annie's pissed about it, if that makes you feel any better.*
> *SueBill4Ever: Not really. Can you tell her*

She couldn't finish what she'd starting typing, but she accidently sent it anyway.

> *TrixieDixie: ?*
> *SueBill4Ever: Just tell her.*

*TrixieDixie: She says me too. You two are too cute for words.
Now sign out of AOL, and take the connector with you.
Try to cover your tracks in case we don't need you to go
back. Give us a call when you get somewhere safe.*
*SueBill4Ever: OK.*

It took Gwen a couple of minutes to figure out how to sign out. After struggling to find AOL, she was tempted to turn the whole damn thing off and hope for the best, but she finally realized that the AOL screen had simply been sent to the bottom of the Windows screen somehow. She signed out and closed it, then had to figure out how to turn off the computer. She knew that the power button would do it, but she also remembered there was a safer way. She should have asked for a quick tutorial on all this before driving up here. Or, even better, she should have brought Annie along. She clearly knew how to do all this, and then they would have spent tonight together.

She was still cursing at it when she felt a slight breeze behind her and then heard the door slam into the wall. She spun the desk chair around, reaching automatically for her gun, realizing with a stab of dismay that she'd left it behind in her bag outside. Even if she'd had it, it was too late. A man stood in the doorway, holding a gun on her.

"Stand up and put your hands on the back of your head."

## CHAPTER SEVENTEEN

G wen obeyed, moving slowly.
"Turn around," he said.

"You're making a big mistake, here, Bill," Gwen said, trying to keep her voice calm. "You could make a lot of money—"

He took a step toward her, his face menacing and dark. "Shut up and turn around."

"Okay, okay." Gwen turned, thinking furiously. This was bad. Really bad. He could kill her any second. She needed to talk him out of it.

"Now put your hands behind your back—slowly."

"What's the point of all of this, Bill? You could have all the money for yourself. Why let Susan have any of it?"

She heard him step closer, and he pressed the gun painfully against the back of her head. "Shut. The. Fuck. Up. You say another word without my permission, and I'm blasting your brains out. I ask questions, you answer. Understand?"

"Yes."

"Good. I'm going to give you some handcuffs. Put them on."

"Behind my back?"

He pushed the gun hard enough to move her head. "Don't fuck with me, girlie."

He shoved the handcuffs into her left hand, and she struggled to get them on. The first wrist was easy, but the second was difficult to maneuver without looking. Finally, she managed. Bill tightened them down to her skin and then yanked her around and began patting her down. He found and threw her lock picks and flashlight across the room before pushing her back into the desk chair so hard she almost tipped over.

He was a short man but well-muscled, his yellow buttoned shirt tight on his arms and chest. There was something of the bulldog about his smashed face and thick shoulders. His hair was short and balding, his face almost scarlet with rage. Giant sweat stains were spreading from his armpits. He was breathing heavily, but the gun was steady at his side.

"Okay," he said. "Talk. What did you mean about the money?"

"We have it now," she lied. "Some of it, anyway. We'll have all of it eventually."

"The hell you do!" He took a step toward her, making her flinch back in the chair. She managed to recover her poise, forcing herself to sit up a little straighter.

"We do. We got the account numbers yesterday, and now we have the passwords to the accounts. Some of the money is already ours."

"You're lying."

Gwen made herself shrug, almost casually. "Easy enough to check. We started with the big accounts in the Caymans, but we'll get to the smaller ones, too."

Bill's face instantly drained of color, and he took a staggering step backward as if she'd kicked him.

"Bullshit," he said, but his voice betrayed him. He was starting to believe her.

Gwen shrugged again. "Like I said, easy enough to check."

Bill's eyes darted to the computer, and Gwen knew she had him. She planned to distract him enough to try something. Once he focused on the computer, she'd rush him, try to knock him down, and start running. It wasn't a great plan, but it was something.

"Okay," he said. "Stand right here." He pointed at a spot near the desk. She did as she was told, and he rolled the desk chair back in front of the computer and sat down. She was close enough that she might be able to tip him over with her foot if she kicked hard enough. If he looked at the computer, he couldn't watch her closely, and her feet would be below his line of sight.

He set his gun down on the right side of the keyboard, and she watched as he opened the "Beach House" file and entered a password. The gun was inches from his fingers, but it would still take him a second or two to grab it if she moved toward him. She'd have to move quickly. If he actually tipped over, she might have time to grab the gun before running into the hall. Luckily, he'd left the door open. She'd run back to the nearest bedroom and try to get outside that way. The drop wouldn't kill her, and if she landed right, she might have enough time to run into the mountains and hide. The fence at the back of the yard was, if she remembered, low enough to the ground at one edge for her to try to jump.

He reached for the phone, started to dial, and then cursed. "What the hell did you do to the phone?"

"It's not plugged in," she said.

Swearing again, he stood up, craning his head and shoulders over the far side of the desk. His back was to her, and she kicked out with one foot, connecting with his ass and pushing him forward. His head hit the wall with a heavy, hollow knock. He gave a startled cry of pain, and she turned around, groping for the gun. As her fingers found it, she saw him pushing himself up again and she kicked out, her boot connecting with the bottom of his jaw. His head snapped back and he screamed, the sound ending as he bit his tongue. She raced out the door, turned right, and ran.

"You bitch!" he roared, and she was dimly aware of the sounds of him throwing things, beastlike in his fury. She picked up her pace, pumping her legs as hard as they'd go. She darted into the next room, a bedroom, almost lost her balance, caught it again, and jumped behind the far side of the bed. She landed painfully on one shoulder to avoid her cuffed hands and then began wriggling across the floor to attempt to sneak under the bed. Her nose hit the baseboard a second later. The mattress was on a solid platform.

Just as she realized this, she heard the sound of his feet pounding down the hallway and had a second or two to prepare herself before the light turned on. He couldn't see her from the doorway, but with a cursory check on this end of the bed, he would. She closed her mouth, trying to breathe quietly through her nose, and stilled her body.

"Shit," he said, slamming something. She heard him continue down the hallway, his heavy tread taking him farther and farther away as she waited. He would be back after checking each of the rooms on this floor, so she had minutes, at most. Contorting her body, she was able to slide her hands under her legs and up in front of her. This was painful to both her shoulder and the handcuffed wrists, but she fought through it until she was able to lie on her back and look at her hands, panting slightly. Even if he was back before she could get them off, she could shoot the gun this way. He'd left the light on, so she could see easily, and her heart rose in triumph. These cuffs were the easiest to unlock.

In the upper right pocket of her denim coat, she found three small paperclips. She kept them there for exactly this kind of lock. She'd opened the lock on the storage shed this way the other day. With only one tumbler, it was simply a matter of making the pick to fit the lock. She eyed it for a moment and then straightened one length of a clip, bending the tip slightly with her teeth. She occasionally made the bend a little too short, and that's what happened this time. She threw the clip away and grabbed the next, making it a little longer. She slid it into the lock felt around, exploring. The length was better—almost perfect. Now it was simply a matter of finding the right spot inside to trip the lock. Forcing herself to calm, she closed her eyes and took a deep breath, stilling her shaking hands. It took seconds, and her wrists were finally free.

The pain she'd been suppressing surged through her as blood rushed back into her hands. She rubbed the sore, chafed marks, cursing when she realized that the cuffs had broken through her skin. She wasn't bleeding much, but the sting of the chafing made her suppress a hiss as she inspected her minor wounds. Her shoulder still ached from throwing herself on it, but she needed to work through all this and get moving. Now that she was free, the light wouldn't benefit her in any way. She might have the gun, but that didn't mean he didn't have a spare. It would be safer by far to get outside from this room.

She'd dropped the gun several feet behind her on the carpet when she'd fallen down, and she grabbed it. Gritting her teeth against the pain in her shoulder, she sat up, slowly inching her head up and over the bed. She listened but couldn't hear anything. Either Bill was somewhere far away in the house, or he was waiting, silently, for her to make a move. He'd managed to sneak up on her once, so this wasn't beyond him.

She paused there for a long while, staring into the hall from her position of safety, then finally made herself get up onto her knees, still worried about keeping herself low. Her shoulder shrieked in pain, and she had to bite her tongue to keep from calling out. It wasn't dislocated because she could still move it with some effort, but she was fairly certain she'd done something to it, twisted or strained it. It was a wonder he hadn't heard her hit the ground, but she supposed his rage and the thick carpet had helped her stay undetected.

She made herself stand upright and walk over to the windows. This wasn't the room with the balcony onto the backyard. By pushing her face against the window, she could see the balcony to the right, likely off the room beyond the office. With the balcony, she could dangle off the edge before dropping, taking something like ten feet off her fall. In this room, there was nothing out these windows, and all of them had screens.

Still, going back into the hallway would be incredibly stupid. He was surely out there somewhere, waiting for her. He must have realized by now that she'd hidden somewhere near the office. He'd had enough time to calm down and was being cautious. Even if he had a gun of his own, he knew she had one now, too. All he had to do was wait out there until she showed her face, and he could shoot her on the spot. No, she thought. Going out there again would be a mistake. It was far safer to risk the long drop. She might break an ankle, but she would, at least, have a chance to get away.

The windows were fastened on the inside, but the first one

she tried opened easily and slid up with very little sound. Still, she paused, listening. If he was anywhere within range, he would have noticed that sound, but after a few seconds, she heard no indication that he planned to do anything about it. She struggled with the screen, almost dropping it when it slid out on its runners, and pulled it inside the room with her. She stuck her head outside, peering down at the ground, which, in the dark, was difficult to see. Still, there were no obstructions as far as she could tell—just the hard concrete that surrounded the pool.

She paused again, listening. This was the dangerous part. Even beyond the high likelihood that she would hurt herself in the fall, she would be vulnerable before she let go of the windowsill. All he had to do was march in here and push her down, and she'd bash her brains out on the ground. But she had no choice.

She checked the safety and tucked the gun inside the back of her jeans. It was too big for her pocket. Hopefully she wouldn't land on it, or it wouldn't go flying with the impact. She lifted one leg and then her head and shoulders outside and sat there astride the sill, looking down. She'd never been afraid of heights, but staring into the darkness, not knowing what she'd hit or how she'd feel when she did, she couldn't help her fear.

Knowing the next part would hurt like hell because of her shoulder, she took a deep breath and held it to keep from groaning or crying out. She put her hands on the sill and slowly raised her second leg up and out, spinning around so she almost crouched on the sill. She grabbed it with both hands and started walking her legs down the wall, trying to keep her full weight off her shoulder as long as possible.

Finally, she had to let her legs drop, and she was dangling, the pain in her shoulder so glaring and almost hot she could hardly stand it. She tried to make herself relax. That would help her absorb the shock from the fall better, but the pain in her shoulder was drowning out common sense. All she could do was push off the wall a little with her feet and let go.

She almost managed to land well, but the shock of the impact rippled through her too quickly and threw her off balance. She remembered to wrench her body to the right, away from her painful shoulder, and hit the ground a second later, landing on her hand. She heard a small snapping sound as her wrist absorbed her weight, and then she was rolling on the ground, clutching it to her chest and trying not to scream. This blaze of agony made her forget the pain in her shoulder.

The piercing agony was monumental, but as she gradually returned to herself through the haze of pain, she had no idea how long she'd been lying there. That idea finally cut through some of the fog, and she made herself focus again. Her mouth was bloody from biting her tongue, and she felt like she had whiplash all over. She heard herself whimpering—a sound she'd never made in her entire life—and made herself stop. She sat up, almost screaming again from her various injuries, and managed to climb awkwardly to her feet without using her hands. Both of her arms were injured in some way now, but, she realized, her feet and legs were, miraculously, unscathed. That meant she could run.

She began in a kind of hobble, parts of her body reacting slowly and shouting out their various pains. She'd pulled some kind of muscle in her back, so that while her legs and ankles were reasonably uninjured, she couldn't move them very fast. The jarring of the ground also shot pains through her arms, and she clutched her broken wrist to her chest to keep from moving it or her upper body too much.

She had made it perhaps fifteen feet when he called out. "Stop right there."

She almost didn't listen. Gun or no gun, she'd been through too much to stop now. She hobbled a few more feet, tears of frustration and pain coursing down her cheeks.

"Stop, or I'll shoot you in the back. I got no problem doing that."

Something about the tone of his voice finally broke through her determination. He spoke with authority and a clear sense of certainty. He wasn't lying.

Sighing, she stopped, still cradling her broken wrist. She began to turn toward him, but he stopped her.

"Freeze right there. I know you have my gun—I can see it in your pants. Don't turn around, and don't make any sudden movements, or you'll be dead before you even try to reach for it."

He was silent for a while, apparently waiting for her to absorb this command, and she stood there trying to think of some way to get out of this situation. Nothing came to mind. Part of her failure was because of her pain and terror but the other part was the hard truth: there was nothing she could do. She could try for the gun, but with her broken wrist and twisted shoulder, she would never be fast enough. Hell, she wouldn't have been fast enough if she'd been sound. He had complete control now. She had to try to survive whatever he had planned for her.

"Okay," he finally said. "Stay right there, and don't move."

"You already said that, genius." The words were out of her mouth before she could stop herself.

"Shut up!" His voice was much closer.

A grin pulled at the corners of her mouth, and she was suddenly glad he couldn't see her face. Maybe it was better to goad him. If she was going to die, she wanted to go out on her own terms, under her own power. Who knew what would happen if he cuffed her again and took her somewhere? No, better to die now than let that happen. She didn't fear for herself, alone, after all. If he captured her, he would have the power to hurt and manipulate Annie, too. At this thought, some of her courage returned, and she squared her shoulders. She could hear him coming closer. He probably planned to take the gun from her, and that would be her chance.

She felt him begin to tug it out of the back of her pants and turned, fast, before ducking slightly. Using the momentum of her entire body, she brought her hands together in a kind of club and swung them up and out as she launched herself upright. She saw his startled reaction before she connected with his chin, snapping his head back. She turned to run but wasn't fast enough. He grabbed her jacket and pulled her back, almost off her feet. She struggled, pain forgotten, and he snarled behind her. She could feel him losing his grip—he had only one hand to use, after all—and thought she might be able to slip away and run again. But then, an instant before he hit the back of her head, she heard something whistling through the air. It connected with a blinding flash of pain, and the world went dark.

## CHAPTER EIGHTEEN

Gwen was in and out of consciousness for hours. The world would begin to come back into focus, she would stir to life, and then the pain hit again. They were in some kind of car, driving through the night. If Bill noticed her waking up, he hit her again, smacking her head against the window, or he punched the side of her face. Eventually she learned not to move so much when she roused, as it meant that more pain would follow.

He'd put some kind of white cloth bag over her head, so she had no idea where they were, but she could see that it was still dark out for much of the ride. She might have dozed or possibly simply passed out, but still they drove on. Eventually, more sunlight began to filter through the bag over her head, and he cursed. Finally, the car slowed and stopped, and he shook her shoulder, roughly.

"Wake up, bitch."

Shooting pain raced through her, and she had to bite down on her tongue to keep from screaming. She moaned and cringed away from him, waiting for him to punch her again.

"It's getting light, and I'm running out of gas," he said. "You got two choices here. I can take that thing off your head, and you can act like a good little girl for a few minutes, or you can go in the trunk. Which one do you want?"

Gwen's mouth was parched and her tongue swollen from various abuses. She had to work up some moisture to do more than croak her response. "Not the trunk."

The cloth was ripped off her head, pulling her hair for a second, and the light was suddenly blinding. She blinked, her vision still foggy for several more seconds. With the cloth off her head, she could smell him now, the dank, animal reek wafting from him and filling the car. His shirt was plastered to his body, drenched in his sweat.

"I'm giving you one chance, here," Bill said. "You fuck it up, and you're riding the rest of the way in the dark." He glowered at her, and she realized with a shock of pleasure that his face showed some damage. His lip was cut, and he sported two huge bruises— one on his chin and a knobby lump on his forehead. She almost laughed in his face.

"I'll be good," she said, trying to sound frightened, cowed.

"You better be."

He pulled back onto the road and starting driving again. Gwen took the opportunity to try to get her bearings. There were on a small, one-lane highway, somewhere in the desert prairie. It looked very much like the area around Roswell, but the highway she and Annie had used had been bigger and busier than this road. Given the amount of time that had passed, she and Bill should also be farther than that—already out of New Mexico, perhaps in Oklahoma. She watched for road signs, hoping for some indication of the area they were driving through, but saw nothing, not even mile markers. It was as if they'd driven into nowhere. Could be a farm road, she thought, but dismissed the idea almost at once. Even a farm road, if it was paved like this one, would have some kind of road markers, for authorities if nothing else.

The light and the effort to make sense of what she was seeing made her head ache worse than before. Her other pains were getting harder to ignore. Her broken wrist was duct-taped to her other hand behind her back, and her ankles were likewise trussed together. He'd belted her into the seat so that she had to sit at a strange angle to avoid crushing her aching hands. This position made the seat belt dig into her sore shoulder. The temptation to close her eyes and let all this pain fade away began to drag her eyelids closed. The hazy lure of sleep or unconsciousness promised an escape. She shook her head, hard, to rouse herself, and the movement must have caught the corner of his eye.

"What the hell are you doing over there? You look like a wet dog."

"Sleepy," she said, or tried to say. Her mouth wasn't cooperating.

"Well, wake up and sit up straighter. We're just coming to the highway now, and a gas station's here. Don't do anything but sit there."

She saw the station a few minutes later. The side and back windows of the store were darkly tinted, so she had no hope that someone would see her and do something about it—not unless she tried to yell or bang on the door, and Bill would quickly put a stop to that. Still, she might have an opportunity to get someone's attention when he was at the pump, or she might be able to open the door and get outside. It would make sense to try only if someone was there to see her and help her right away.

He was smart, pulling to the tanks farthest from the service station, her side of the car pointing toward the road and not the station. More cars were driving by on the highway that ran perpendicular to the road they'd been on, but she couldn't be sure they would see her in time. If anything, the attendant inside might spot her hopping around if she got out, but by then it could be too late. Bill might shoot her on the spot and take off, or he might wrestle her back inside and take his vengeance later. Either way, her odds weren't great. She did, however, learn one thing right away—they were in Texas again, according to the state lottery signs in the station.

"Back in goddamn Texas," she muttered.

"What was that?" Bill asked. "You giving me lip again?"

"Nothing."

"Good. See that it stays that way. I've got some dirty clothes in the trunk that would love to make your acquaintance." He peered outside at the pumps and then cursed. "Motherfucker. I have to go inside to pay."

Her hopes rose, and she had to turn her face away from him to hide her smile. He grabbed her shirt, yanking her toward him painfully. Gwen couldn't help the little whimper that escaped her lips. His eyes were red, his face mottled and tired. Up close, his BO took a back seat to the horrible smell of his breath.

"I know what you're thinking, bitch, and it ain't gonna work. You try to get out, and I'll shoot you like a dog—I don't care who sees me. You think I'm lying? Give it a whirl. You'll be dead before you know what happened to you." He grinned, the joy in his eyes dark and sick. "In fact, I'd love to kill you. So by all means, try to escape."

He let her go then, pushing her away from him with such violence that she slammed into her door. The back of her head smacked into the window, and the world starred and darkened for a moment. He was already out of the car before she came back to herself, and she watched as he disappeared inside to pay.

Now's your chance, she told herself, but did nothing. He was right. Trying to escape would be a suicide mission. Still, she tried to turn around to get her hands on the handle of the car door. She didn't know if he'd locked it, but she didn't think she remembered hearing the click, so all she had to do was open the door, undo her seat belt, and she could get out of here. She might be able to make it to the highway, get someone's attention, or at least be seen. Someone might stop and help her or call the police. Or, like he'd said, he'd come out of the gas station and shoot her before anyone noticed.

She'd told herself earlier that if she had to die, she wanted to do it on her own terms. The fact that he'd kept her alive must mean something. Most likely he intended to use her as leverage against Annie and would let her live until then. She wouldn't let that happen, but she also didn't want to die, and certainly not before she knew Annie was safe.

Her will to escape faded to nothing, and she stopped struggling, relaxing back into her seat. Annie was all that mattered. Judging by their location now, he was likely taking her to Susan. From what Annie had told her, Susan was the brains of the operation, and Bill the muscle. Susan would have plans for her. Gwen had to hope that Annie would know better than to negotiate with these people.

Bill reappeared, rushing back to the car. He opened his door again to check on her and then left it open while he filled the tank.

The morning heat and the fumes did nothing for her headache, and she gagged a little and swallowed hard to keep from being sick. She'd read that concussions caused nausea and could now confirm that was true. She'd be lucky if she didn't end up with some kind of brain damage.

Already, the world seemed strangely foggy and overly bright, and not from the weather. She needed medical attention for her head, if nothing else, and his frequent punches and smacks weren't helping. No, she'd play the good girl the rest of the trip and hold her tongue. Goading him wasn't helping her at all.

He climbed back in and slammed his door, sitting there for a while doing nothing. He stared out the front window, frowning, tapping the steering wheel. Then, as if he'd decided something, he put on his belt and started the car, wrenching the wheel hard enough for the tires to squeal. Instead of getting onto the highway, he turned back on the road they'd driven in on, the car surging ahead and racing back at high speed.

"Where are we going?" she asked.

"Quiet." His voice was low but impassive. The question hadn't bothered him. It clearly didn't matter to him.

A one-story brick building appeared on the left-hand side of the road about a mile back. Gwen had seen it earlier but hadn't thought much about it at the time. Bill turned into the lot in front of it, and Gwen saw now that whatever it had been, it was now abandoned—no windows or doors, splattered with bad graffiti. Bill drove around to the far side of the building, away from the empty road. Her stomach dropped with dread, and she stilled. He was going to kill her.

Bill turned the car off again. "We're going to be on some busy roads for a while, and I can't risk someone seeing you. In the trunk you go."

"But you said—"

"I lied. We can do this the easy way or the hard way. Which one do you want?"

She licked her lips. She had to find some way to dissuade him.

"Too slow," he said, and the last thing she saw was his fist drawing back.

❖

It was dark. Too dark. This wasn't the same kind of dark she'd seen when the bag had been over her head. This was something else. This dark was full, weighted, as if it crouched above her, waiting for her to wake up. It took her a moment to realize that nothing was over her eyes—nothing blocking her vision. Either she was sitting in total darkness, or she'd gone completely blind. There was no telling which.

She panicked at the sensation of a cloth in her mouth, momentarily afraid she couldn't breathe, but the sound of her whistling breath rattling in and out of her nose quelled some of her terror, and she tried to make herself calm down and assess the situation.

She had very little recent memory. She could remember him hitting her in the car and then coming to as he threw her roughly into the trunk. Seeing her awake, he'd disappeared again and then come back with something in his hand. He'd leaned down, and she'd felt a stinging sensation in her neck and nothing more. He must have drugged her. Who knew why he hadn't done that to begin with— it didn't matter, now. Her head felt stuffy, cloudy, the remnants of whatever he'd injected her with adding to her overall fogginess. It was hard to stay awake.

Now she was sitting upright, but it took her a few seconds to recognize this position and to understand where she was. She pulled each of her limbs, experimenting, wincing at the pain in her wrist and shoulders. Her arms and legs were strapped to the arms and legs of a chair, her waist and chest cinched to the back.

She tipped slightly to the right, but the chair didn't move. It was either bolted to the floor or tied down somehow. The arms felt thin under her fingers—polished wood, like a dining-room chair. By contorting her middle finger, she could just touch the strap around one of her wrists. It was leather and thick, wider than a belt. Without seeing it, she couldn't tell or see how it was fastened.

She tapped her foot on the ground, listening for an echo. The sound reverberated very near her, explaining the looming sense of something in front of her. A wall or large structure or object was likely a few feet away. The floor felt solid, smooth but almost sandy—probably concrete.

She froze at the sound of something slightly behind her and to her right—a rattling of some kind. She held her breath, straining her ears, and heard it again. This time it sounded more like a horse or dog harness, and, underneath that, she could hear something else: breathing. Something was here with her in the dark.

She flushed with terror and jerked in her chair, straining against the straps across her as far away from the sound as possible. She pinched her eyes shut, shaking her head. Stop it, she told herself. Don't let the dark get to you. She scrambled for her anchor—the one her work-appointed therapist had taught her as a means of calming down.

The anchor, her therapist had explained, was meaningless except in the significance you gave it. The words could be anything, but if you taught yourself to react a certain way when you thought of the anchor or said it aloud, it could, with practice, have an almost magical effect on your reactions, including those of your body. She hadn't taken her therapy very seriously at the time, but she nevertheless practiced using her anchor in times of stress, and, with time, it had begun to work. In her fright, however, she mentally continued to stumble over the words and images she associated with it and found herself more frightened the longer she sat there, scared in the dark.

That same rattling noise came from behind, louder this time, and she flinched again, moaning into her gag. The sound stopped, and then she heard something else. She had to fight the horror clouding her mind, but she finally heard it, clearly and without mistake.

Muffled screaming.

The effect of this recognition was instant. Relief swept through her like a cold wind, and her heartbeat began to slow. Some*thing* wasn't down here with her; some*one* was, and that someone was like her—tied up to something and gagged. No threat to her, and no help, either. She drove the thought of this person from her mind and focused on herself again.

She made herself relax back into her chair, testing the bindings on her chest. With her back flat against the chair, the straps over her chest were almost loose, slipping down a couple of inches. She tilted forward and they inched up slightly, but not quite to the same place they'd been before. She'd already discovered that her arms and legs were tightly bound, but now, not straining, they too had a little give, likely to avoid cutting off her circulation. The idea that she had a few millimeters of space that belonged entirely to her worked like a balm on her spirit. Her courage surged back, and her fright finally began to ebb. It wasn't much, but it would be enough. She could get out of this.

Again, despite the dark, she closed her eyes, breathing as deeply as she could through her nose. She needed a plan of action. Most obviously, getting one hand free would be enough. Her right wrist was throbbing, broken, so freeing her left from its binding was the best choice. Still, before she could try, she needed to get this gag out of her mouth. More than simply impeding her air supply, it was also distracting. For one thing, it made it obvious how dry her mouth was.

She had no idea how long she'd been here, or how long she and Bill had been driving, but her last memory of water was back in her own car, somewhere outside Santa Fe. The drug might have exacerbated her thirst, too. Underneath it, she could detect a kind of metallic tinge inside her mouth. Don't think about water, she told herself, but the idea overwhelmed her in its intensity. She shook her head and almost moaned again, the pain from the various punches so intense she could almost see stars. Beyond her thirst, the gag pulled her jaw back slightly so that her whole face was aching with the strain. Yes, she thought. Gag first, hand second. If she could just get this damn thing out of her mouth, everything would be much better.

She tested the inside of the cloth with her tongue. Her mouth was entirely dry, but she discovered some residual moisture there and probed it with her tongue, trying to absorb some of it. The sensation of the cloth was familiar somehow—a light cotton, probably a handkerchief, or something very similar. The idea that some brightly colored, paisley thing in her mouth was causing this agony made her angry for the first time since she'd come awake. She tried biting it, pushing it with her tongue, moving her jaw down even farther to loosen it—all to no effect. The back of the chair rose behind her head, and by twisting from side to side, she could feel the individual rungs. She paused at one and moved her head back and forth with the knot of the gag pressed against it. For a moment, she thought she was on to something. The gag actually seemed to loosen in her mouth. Then the light turned on.

She had no warning, no sound that proceeded it—like a door opening or the sound of a switch. It was simply on and so blindingly bright, she had to close her eyes, the pain making them water. She tried to open them, but her vision was foggy, and the light still hurt. Gradually, squinting, she felt her eyes begin to adjust and sat upright in the chair, peering around her.

She was facing a nondescript, concrete wall, very much like she'd pictured in the dark. She was perhaps five feet from it, close enough to have sensed its presence. The face of the wall was unfinished and unbroken, no windows or marks, and stretched some fifteen feet in either direction. Looking down, she wasn't surprised to see herself bound to a dining-room chair. By leaning as far as she could to the right, she could tell the chair was held in place with metal vises clamped onto beams that stretched the length of the floor in front and probably behind her. She'd seen this kind of thing before when she'd helped her brother put in hardwood floors. The beams were baseboard for a new floor—some kind of home-reno project in its earliest phases.

Her vision was finally beginning to clear, the pain and fog lifting, but she could see nothing beyond the wall and the floor— no doors, no windows, nothing. A sound behind her reminded her that she wasn't alone down here, and she craned her head and neck around, painfully, to see the other person.

It was Annie.

## CHAPTER NINETEEN

It was all Gwen could do not to scream. Annie looked terrified, her face paler than it had been before. Like Gwen, she was strapped to a chair held in place to the beams across the floor. Annie began to mumble and yell against her gag, twisting hard from side to side, and Gwen shook her head and mumbled back at her through her gag, trying to tell her to stop. Watching her struggle was the worst thing she'd ever seen. Terror surged through her, her earlier courage and plans dashed to pieces. It was one thing to attempt to free herself, yet another entirely to get Annie out as well. Before, she hadn't minded the idea of trying, as she'd rather be dead than trussed up like a sacrificial pig. Now that she knew Annie was here with her, they had to do everything they could to stay alive, and that meant not panicking.

Somewhere behind and to her left, a door opened, and then she heard the tread of footsteps as someone—no, some people—came downstairs. Gwen couldn't see what was happening, and she made herself stop, trying to look relaxed. Her heart was tight in her chest, her anxiety and terror so powerful they were almost suffocating.

"So you're awake," a woman's voice said behind her.

"I told you," Bill said.

"Shut up."

Bill muttered something, and Gwen heard the footsteps gradually make their way toward her. A moment later, a woman appeared in front of her, Bill at her side. Not having seen her before,

Gwen still knew this must be Susan, and not simply because of the circumstances. She'd pictured a woman exactly like this despite Annie's careful evasions and vagueness since she'd mentioned her name. Women like Susan could get away with anything. It was no wonder the police hadn't realized she was involved. Gwen even understood Annie's reluctance to turn her in, now. It would be hard to believe she was capable of anything criminal. She seemed professional, confident, and trustworthy, a little like a school principal.

Susan was older than her, but she was that relatively indeterminate age some women were lucky to look well into their forties. She could be as young as thirty, as old as fifty—only the slight lines on her forehead and at the corners of her mouth suggesting she was likely on the upper edge of that range. From farther away or wearing sunglasses, she could probably pass for much, much younger, even in her twenties. She was wearing formal business attire—a blue skirt suit, a silk blouse, and incredibly tall heels. Her hair was loosely curled, thick and dark, straying past her shoulders. Her dark eyes were almost black, even in the bright overhead light. Her features were straight and well-formed, not exactly pretty, but something in or behind her expression lent her face a strong appeal. Gwen sensed the allure there and something else—a warning, perhaps. She was, in a word, mesmerizing, like a dangerous but beautiful snake.

"My associate here," Susan gestured at Bill, "was stupid enough to drug you without knowing the correct dosage, after I specifically told him not to. We were afraid you might not wake up." She glared at him long enough for him to drop his eyes before looking back at Gwen. Her expression was lazy, unconcerned. Regardless of what she'd said, she clearly hadn't cared that much one way or the other.

"Get that thing off her mouth," Susan said. Her voice was low, almost a growl, but she uttered this command without any kind of rancor. She was clearly used to making demands and being listened to.

Bill pulled a knife from his pocket, flicked a blade open, and approached her. Gwen couldn't help but flinch, and she saw a slight lift at the corners of Susan's mouth. She was enjoying this. Recognizing that fact gave Gwen a little burst of indignant anger, and she made herself relax and sit up straight. She wouldn't allow this woman anything at her expense if she could help it.

Bill cut the gag from her mouth, and Gwen almost moaned with relief. She opened and stretched her lips, the pain in her jaw and neck so intense she could hardly make them function. The thirst was back, and that metallic tang much stronger now that the cloth was no longer masking it.

"You must be thirsty," Susan said. "Bill, give her some water."

Gwen saw what was going to happen a second before he bent down and grabbed and threw a bucket of water on her. She managed to close her eyes before it hit her. She sputtered, blowing some of the liquid from her nose and choking a little. She shook some of it off her face and opened her eyes again. Both of them were grinning at her.

"That was rude, Bill," Susan said, her grin still plastered on her lips.

"Sorry," he said, clearly not.

"Fuck you," Gwen said.

Susan laughed, throwing her head back with delight. "I like you. I can see now why Annie was drawn to you. You have some backbone."

"Untie me, and I'll show you some more of my attributes."

Susan laughed again. "No, dear. That's not going to happen. In fact, pretty soon, you're going to be begging me to let you help me. Do you know why?"

Gwen didn't respond, and Susan approached, leaning down close enough toward her that Gwen caught a whiff of her cloying scent—tea rose.

"I said, 'Do you know why?'"

Gwen could see that dangerous, predatory glint in her eyes again and realized she had no position here but that of obedience. She licked her lips, biting back an angry curse. "No. Why?"

"Because of Annie, silly. You want to help her, don't you?"

Gwen's eyes suddenly teared up, and she blinked, furious with herself for showing weakness. Susan saw all of this and smiled, standing up straight again and holding out her hands at her sides.

"Of course you do. And I can help you help her. But only if you do what I tell you to. Understand?"

Gwen was still fighting tears, but she managed to nod. "Yes. I understand. What do you need?"

Susan's smile brightened even further, and she turned to Bill. "See? What did I tell you? I knew it was better not to kill her."

He seemed suitably impressed, or faked it well, and nodded. "You were right."

"It's a little strange," Susan said, frowning down at her, "because you're not really her type. Annie tends to go for the cleaner-cut, feminine types. I know, and not just because she went for me. All her previous lady friends were like me. Still..." She stared at Gwen without blinking. "I guess I can see the appeal. You're a little bit of rough. I get that. And you're different, too, and not only because of whatever fucked-up gene pool produced you. You've got—" She turned back to Bill and gestured vaguely with one hand. "What's the word?"

He shrugged. "Moxie? Gumption?"

Susan laughed. "Odd choice, but close enough. Yes, it's that backbone I mentioned earlier. It's very sexy."

"I'm glad you approve."

Susan's smile evaporated, almost as if it had never existed. Gwen's stomach dropped with horror. All of her jollity was a ploy, a clever deception. Gwen's earliest impression had been correct: Susan was a snake, and if she kept trying to fight her, she and Annie would end up dead. She tried to make her face contrite, a little frightened.

"I'm sorry. Tell me what to do."

Susan gave her a tight, fake smile and nodded. "That's better. A little moxie goes a long way, as they say. Too much, and you're going to piss me off."

"I'll do whatever you want. Don't hurt her. Please."

Susan nodded, once. "Okay. I'll try. After all, I liked her too. We had some good times together."

Bill sighed, rolling his eyes, and Susan grinned again at Gwen and winked. "He has no idea."

"Can we get on with this already?" Bill asked. His face was slightly pink, and Gwen could tell he was more upset than he wanted to show.

Susan was obviously amused by his embarrassed discomfort. "Sure, Bill. Let's go get ready." She looked at Gwen again. "We'll be back soon. We have to set it up first. And for being such a good sport, I'll leave you like this. I won't even turn off the light."

Knowing what was required of her, Gwen managed a quick "Thanks."

Susan gave her that earlier bright smile. "No problem. We'll be back before you know it."

Gwen waited until she heard the door close before turning her head back and to the right again, making eye contact with Annie. She couldn't be entirely sure that they were alone. Bill could be standing at the top of the steps, listening to them, but she had to risk it.

Tears were streaming down Annie's face, and her pallor was stark and almost sickly. Gwen couldn't see any physical damage from here, but Annie's gag was tight and pulling on her mouth, much as hers had done, and the bonds holding her to her chair seemed much tighter than her own. Gwen had to blink back tears, swallowing her sorrow.

"Are you okay? Did they hurt you?"

Annie shook her head and then nodded. They hadn't hurt her, but she wasn't okay. The angle was awkward, and Gwen was forced to turn away again to spare her neck. Twisting that way put extra strain on her aching shoulder as well.

"Tap your foot once for yes, twice for no. Understand?"

There was a pause, and then a single tap.

"Great. Okay, first question. Do you know where we are?"

Two taps.

"You haven't been here before?"

Two taps.

Gwen thought for a moment, frowning. She knew Annie had

been to Susan and Bill's house in Dallas, and she'd assumed that was where they were now. Something occurred to her about her own journey here.

"Did they blindfold you on the way here?"

One tap.

"Ah, okay. So maybe I'm right. Maybe we're at their place. Do you think we're in Dallas?"

No response. Gwen wrenched her head back around, and Annie lifted her shoulders dramatically.

"Where did they pick you up? How did they catch you?"

Annie's eyebrows lowered and she shrugged again, clearly confused.

"Sorry—I should stick to yes or no questions."

Gwen faced forward again and rolled her neck a little to loosen it. With the gag out of her mouth and her thirst lessened, her other pains were starting to clamor for attention. She had to fight through them if she was ever going to get the two of them out of this. To do that, she needed information.

"Yes or no—did they get you in Dallas?"

One tap.

Gwen's body flushed with frustration. Why the hell had Annie come to Texas? She'd been safe in Roswell—no one would ever have found her there.

"After they got you, after they blindfolded you, was it a long trip? Were you in the car for a while?"

One tap.

"More than an hour?"

Two taps.

"Okay—so we're probably at their place in Dallas. It takes forever to get around the city, and they might live in a suburb or something, so we're probably still close to where they caught you. You've been here before. Do you think we're in their house? In the basement or something?"

No response, and when Gwen turned back that way, Annie's expression was still confused and a little frightened.

"Do you think this is their place?"

Annie shrugged yet again.

This was getting them nowhere. Annie was obviously overwhelmed and not thinking clearly. If the trip had taken less than an hour, logic suggested they were somewhere near the city. Had they picked up Annie at the airport? Had Annie arranged to meet with one of them? Gwen froze. The timing was strange. Unless Gwen had been unconscious far longer than she thought, things didn't add up.

"Was I already here when they brought you down here?"

Two taps.

"You mean you saw them bring me down here?"

One tap.

Gwen frowned. None of this made sense. If Gwen had been here before Annie, then she could blame the time confusion on unconsciousness, but if she came after Annie, that meant they'd caught her before Bill brought Gwen here. Annie had been in Roswell when Gwen had been captured—they'd talked on the phone less than an hour before he knocked her out. How had she gotten to Dallas ahead of her? But again, maybe she'd been unconscious longer than she thought. She shook her head, trying to dismiss the puzzle. No use harping on any of that right now. Annie couldn't explain with that thing in her mouth.

"I don't know what to do here. If I had enough time, I could probably get out of this chair, but then what? Would we try to escape? I can't imagine we'd get very far." She turned her head back. "Did you and Trixie get any of the money?"

Annie shook her head again before raising her thin shoulders dramatically. Gwen sighed, looking away again. "Well, that sucks. I was hoping. Then you'd have something to negotiate with. I'm sorry, Annie, but I think we're totally fucked."

Annie moaned loudly, and when Gwen looked back at her, she was shaking her head, almost violently.

"What? What is it?"

Annie emitted only a muffled jumble of sounds but kept shaking her head back and forth.

"I don't understand. What are you trying to say?"

Annie paused, clearly trying to enunciate as best as she could. "Nrrrr Annnn," she said.

"I don't know what that means."

"Nrrrrr Annnnn!" she said again.

"What?"

They both froze at the sound of the door opening, and Gwen turned back around, hoping they hadn't heard the two of them trying to communicate. The footsteps approached, leisurely, it seemed, and Susan and Bill finally appeared in front of her once more. Their casual pace was, Gwen could tell, another of their games.

"Okay, Gwen," Susan said. "Tit for tat. You give me something, and I give you something. Deal?"

"What happens after that? Are you planning to let us go?"

Susan and Bill shared a glance. "Maybe," Susan said. "It depends on how well this goes."

Gwen didn't believe her. In fact, she didn't really understand what all this cloak-and-dagger was about. Why capture them? Why hold them down here like this? After all, if Annie and Trixie hadn't gotten the money, why not simply kill her and Annie now? Still, she had no choice but to cooperate, at least for now.

"Okay."

Susan gave her that Cheshire, empty grin again, and Gwen's stomach dropped with dread. The next few hours or minutes could very well be the end of her life. Once Susan had what she wanted, whatever that was, she would kill her and Annie, both. The thought of her hurting Annie scared Gwen worse than she'd ever been in her life.

"Please," she said. "I'll do anything. Just tell me what you want."

Susan nodded, apparently satisfied. "Good. First, we're going to take you upstairs. Bill and I had to set up a special, unlisted phone. You're going to call that clever computer friend of yours, whoever he is, and tell him to give us our money back."

Relief filled Gwen, so overwhelming she almost wept. Trixie had managed to get the money after all. They might survive this ordeal. Gwen had to look down at the ground to hide her pleasure, pretending to think it over.

Trying to seem frightened, she met Susan's eyes. "All right. But what will you give me?"

Susan laughed. "Getting out of that chair isn't enough?"

"It's a start. But what about Annie?"

Susan frowned. "What about her?"

"Are you going to untie her, too?"

Susan seemed confused, but Bill laughed. "Do you mean you think she's—"

Susan silenced him with a sharp gesture. "Of course we will, but only after you make the phone call."

Gwen hesitated long enough that Susan shifted her weight to her other leg. Gwen knew she had to agree—even with the money to negotiate with, she could do very little. Still, the best way to make a deal was to ask for more than the first offer.

Susan chuckled, rolling her eyes. "Okay, Gwen. I can see you're not a person to fuck around with. I'll sweeten the deal a little. You make your phone call, and I'll untie her and give you both some medical attention. That wrist has to be killing you."

Gwen waited a beat, still playing their game. She wanted to look reluctant. "Okay, deal."

"Untie her," Susan said to Bill.

Bill undid the leather straps holding her in place, and despite the fact that they hadn't been very tight, the blood noticeably rushed back into her arms and legs. It took her a few tries to get to her feet, and the world gave a stomach-flipping lurch when she was finally standing. Both of them grabbed her elbows to stop her from falling over and then began to lead her toward the stairs. It took her a long while to climb them, her legs so stiff and unwieldy, she felt almost detached from them. Whatever Bill had given her, the aftereffects were still here. Standing up had sent whatever drug he'd administered coursing through her once again. She felt high.

The ground floor was nice, tasteful, every bit as comfortable as the mountain house near Santa Fe. The decorations here were less Southwestern and more genteel Southern, every corner of the house suggesting wealth and comfort. It was dark outside, further confusing Gwen's sense of time, but the clock on the wall suggested that she'd lost about twelve hours since the gas station this morning, provided this was the same day she'd been drugged.

She was led into an enormous living room and steered toward a lush armchair near a strange, overlarge telephone. She collapsed into the chair, her head whirling, and noticed that her vision had slight trailers as she moved her eyes to the phone. She closed them, the room still spinning, and fought against her lurching stomach.

"I told you, you gave her too much," Susan said, nearly snarling.

"Sorry. How was I supposed to know?"

"Exactly, you idiot. You didn't. Therefore, you shouldn't have tried to drug her on your own."

"Could I have a glass of water?" Gwen asked. "It might help." While her thirst was better than it had been before she'd been doused, that metallic taste was strong and bitter in her mouth.

"After. Make the call. When he answers, tell him who you are and then give the phone to me. Understand?"

Susan had said this, but Bill moved slightly, thrusting a hip toward her enough to draw attention to the gun holstered on his belt. Gwen nodded and reached for the phone, missed it, and reached again, aiming slightly to the left of one of the many phones floating in her vision. Her fingers finally touched the receiver, and she picked it up and held it to her ear. The numbers were dancing around before her eyes, and she closed them, fighting against the dizziness that threatened to pull her under.

"Jesus Christ," Susan said. "Tell me the numbers, and I'll dial."

It took her a moment to remember, and she said each one as loudly and clearly as she could. The beeping sound of each number was terribly loud in her ear, and she held the phone slightly away from her head as Susan finished. It rang on the other side several times before Trixie answered.

"Hello?"

"Hey, Trixie. It's me, Gwen." Her voice slurred slightly, but she couldn't help it.

"Gwen? Holy shit. Are you drunk? What's wrong with your voice? I was so worried. Where the hell are you? Your last call was almost eighteen hours ago. Annie—"

"Trixie, listen. Susan is here, and she wants to talk to you."

Gwen heard Trixie curse before Susan took the phone from her. Gwen settled back into the comfort of the chair, closing her eyes. In her current condition, she could do very little to help the situation. She could only hope that Susan would uphold her end of the bargain and bring Annie upstairs once she was off the phone. For now, she could only let herself sink into a peaceful, painless oblivion.

## CHAPTER TWENTY

Gwen woke up in a bed. The sunlight hitting her face was warm but filtered through a pale scrim over the window. She frowned, not remembering a window on that side of the bed, and when she tried to sit up, she moaned and sank back into the pillows. Her head was no longer spinning, but she ached all over. Still, the pain reminded her of where she was. She wasn't in her room in Colorado or California. She was back in Texas.

By turning her head slightly to the right and left, she could see most of the room. She was in a nicely appointed but rather small bedroom, a guest room, judging from its plain style and lack of decor. She saw a small dresser across from the foot of the bed, but no other furniture. The bed was soft and, for the summer season, overly dressed, with a thick duvet and a folded flannel blanket lying under her feet. Bill or Susan hadn't bothered to undress her; they'd simply laid her on top and left her here. Tilting her chin down to her chest, she could see the cause of the discomfort on her right ankle. It was fastened to the bed stand with a chain.

She sighed and let her head relax back again, closing her eyes. Crossing her hands over her stomach, she realized with surprise that her right wrist was in a cast. She looked at it, holding it up and twisting it in the dim light. When had that happened? Her memory after the phone call to Trixie was basically nonexistent. Like the time between the trunk and the basement, she'd lost it entirely. Whatever they were drugging her with completely anesthetized her.

Gwen used her left hand to explore the various cuts and scrapes on her face, most of them bandaged, and all of them cleaned up. Her fingers came away without a trace of blood. The cast was expertly done, obviously by someone who knew what they were doing. Had there been X-rays? Was Susan a doctor?

Gwen let this subject go, closing her eyes again. Either she would be told, or she could ask, but right now none of this mattered. She was tied up again, and though she felt better than she had riding in the car with Bill whenever that had been, the pain was here, whatever she did, no matter how she moved or tried not to. Judging from the light outside, it was much earlier in the day than when she'd made the phone call, which meant she'd lost at least another twelve hours lying here.

Her mouth was so dry it hurt, and the realization made her suddenly and rabidly thirsty. She snapped her eyes open, searching around herself wildly, and when she saw the pitcher of ice water next to her on a little table, she sat up quickly, forgetting her other pains, and grabbed it, almost knocking it over. Ignoring the little glass, she brought the pitcher to her mouth and started drinking, trails of water leaking out of the corners of her mouth and drenching her shirt. She had to pause halfway to gulp down air, and the break suddenly sent a shooting pain through her head from the ice. She ignored it and continued to drink, stopping only when her stomach started to heave. She set the rest of the pitcher back on the nightstand and lay down on the bed, almost crying with relief. Nothing, she knew, would ever taste as sweet and pure as that water.

She heard the snick of a lock, and the door opened a moment later. It was Susan, alone. She was wearing more casual clothes than before—a plain burgundy button-up and dark jeans. She tied her hair back, loosely, but a stray curl lay across her face on either side, by design, Gwen guessed.

"Oh, good. You're awake."

Gwen didn't reply, and Susan smirked. "I guess you're not in the mood for small talk."

"No."

"Good. Neither am I."

"Where's Annie?"

"She's sleeping in the room next to this one. I had my personal doctor treat both of you earlier this morning. He still makes house calls, if you can believe it, and he doesn't ask questions."

Gwen tried to struggle upward again, feeling distinctly vulnerable in her prone position, but the chain at her ankle didn't allow her to do much beyond sit up, straining her back and neck, so she had to lie down again.

"He came this morning?" Gwen asked. "What time is it?"

Susan glanced at her watch. "Going on noon now."

Gwen's stomach dropped, the excess water giving an uneasy lurch. She'd lost almost a full day. That, coupled with her lost time in the trunk of Bill's car, meant that, except for the hour or so she'd been awake last night, she'd spent most of the last thirty-six hours unconscious. She would have to do everything in her power not to let them drug her again.

Susan, as if reading her thoughts, grinned and sat on the edge of the bed. It was all Gwen could do not to kick her with her free foot.

"Listen," Susan said, "I get it. You don't trust me, but you're going to get through this. In a couple of hours, Bill and I plan to take you and Annie to the rendezvous we set up with your little computer friend, Trixie. She'll give us the money, we'll give her the two of you, and we never have to see each other again."

"Why should I believe you?"

Susan lifted one shoulder. "No reason, really, except that you have no other choice."

Gwen nodded at once. Of course she was right. And after all, Gwen thought, she might be telling the truth. If all Susan wanted was the money, and not some petty revenge, it was possible she'd let them go. Gwen and Annie would have to hide out for a while, maybe a year or more, just to be safe, but Gwen knew plenty of places they could do that. Everything, however, hinged on whether Susan would be satisfied with the money.

"Okay," Gwen said. "What do you need me to do?"

Susan smiled, the expression more genuine this time. "Not a

thing. Go where I tell you to go, and don't try anything. Do that, and this will all be over by dinnertime tonight."

Susan got off the bed, stretched her long, trim body, and then, as if remembering something, shook her head. "I almost forgot. You haven't eaten in a while. Do you want me to send up some food?"

As if the word "food" had brought her hunger to life, Gwen's stomach seized with deep, famished pain. She opened her mouth, ready to beg, but snapped it closed a second later. When Bill had drugged her, he'd used a needle, but that didn't mean they couldn't put another dose in her food. If she hadn't been so parched, she would have thought twice about the water pitcher, too. She had to fight with herself for several seconds to recognize the sense in this thinking.

She licked her lips and tried to steady her voice. "No, but thanks. I could use a shower and change of clothes. And a toothbrush, if it's not too much to ask."

Susan's eyes narrowed for a moment, but she nodded. "Sure. I'll have Bill take you to the washroom down the hall. You're thinner than I am, but I should have something you can borrow. I'll give you some plastic wrap for that cast, too."

"Thanks."

Susan nodded and turned to leave, but paused in the doorway, glancing back. "I hope you listen to sense, Gwen. Don't fuck this up. I meant what I said. I just want the money. I don't want to have to kill either of you. Annie meant something to me once, and since she likes you, I don't want to hurt her that way."

Gwen nodded. "Okay. I believe you."

Susan lifted an eyebrow, clearly skeptical, but said nothing more, closing and locking the door behind her.

Bill arrived about half an hour later to escort her to the shower. Unlike Susan, he didn't bother making nice, not saying a word and holding a gun on her the moment he unlocked her ankle. She managed to stand up, wavering as her head reeled and she found her equilibrium. She felt incredibly weak, and the various pains in her body were screaming for attention, but her head was definitely clearer than last night—the drug now out of her system.

In the hallway, they passed another closed door, and Gwen almost asked to stop and see Annie. One glance at Bill's face and she knew he would deny the request, so they continued without pausing. Bill seemed to think he was going to come into the bathroom with her, but once she stared at him without moving, he blushed a little and gestured with his gun.

"Go ahead, but don't try anything. I'll be standing out here listening. I hear anything, I'm coming in, so don't even try to lock the door or go out the window."

"I'm done with jumping out of windows. Did enough of that the other night."

He didn't smile at this joke, and Gwen eased into the bathroom and closed the door. There was, in fact, a lock here on the inside, but he was right. She had simply no reason to try anything. She hadn't gotten a good look outside, but they were at least a story off the ground. With all her various injuries, it would be stupid. Anyway, she would never leave Annie. But how would he know that? She started to take off her clothes.

She stood as long as she dared under the hot water, worried he would burst in. Everything was awkward with her cast, which, as directed, she'd wrapped in cellophane. She'd never realized how difficult it would be to wash her hair one-handed. The hot water, however, was wonderful, almost a revelation. She let it stream down her face and back, trying to loosen her sore shoulder. If she'd been awake when the doctor had been here, she'd have told him to check it out, as it hurt now even more than her wrist. Blood and actual dirt came off her body in surprising volume, and when she finally finished, she was grateful to see some clothes, a toothbrush, and new bandages waiting for her on the vanity by the sink. The clothes were, as Susan had predicted, almost clownishly large, but she'd been given a belt to hold up the pants, and at least they were clean. As she was fixing the last of the new bandages to her eyebrow—a deep cut that needed stitches—Bill pounded on the door.

"Hurry up in there. We're leaving in ten minutes."

"Okay. Almost finished."

She leaned down to the sink and drank as much water as she

could, cupped in her hands. She was still dehydrated and didn't want to have to ask them for any food or drink if she could help it. If Susan was telling the truth, Trixie could take them to the nearest restaurant for a big meal later. She smiled, not believing it for one minute. They'd be lucky to live that long.

When she finally opened the door, Bill and Susan were waiting for her in the hall. Susan smiled at the sight of her.

"Much better."

"Thanks."

"Bill—go get Annie. We need to get moving in case we hit traffic."

Bill walked over to the closed door, drawing out a key before unlocking and opening the door.

"Where are we going?" Gwen asked. She had to fight not to watch Bill in her eagerness to see Annie again.

"A state park outside of town. It should be fairly empty on a weekday, and it's close. I didn't want to drag this out more than necessary."

Bill and Annie appeared a moment later. Like Gwen, she was clearly wearing Susan's clothes, and the size difference was even more extreme on her. Now that she could see her clearly, Gwen thought it looked as if she'd lost some weight—her face was wan and sallow, seemingly thinner than before. Of course that was impossible, and probably an illusion brought on by the overly large clothes, but she nevertheless looked unwell. Her hair was dark with grease and sweat and tied into an unflattering knot on top of her head. The worst part of seeing her, however, was noting the fact that Annie's hands were bound in front of her. She was also still wearing a gag.

"What the hell?" Gwen said, taking a step toward them. "Why is she still—"

Susan put a hand on her arm, lightly. "Calm down. She's fine— aren't you, Annie?"

Annie's eyes met Gwen's, clearly terrified, but they flickered over to Susan, and she nodded.

"See?" Susan asked. "She's fine."

"You bitch," Gwen said.

Susan waved a single finger. "Uh, uh, uh. You said you were going to be a good girl, Gwen. Is that how good girls talk?"

Gwen had to fight back a retort, and she clenched her fists against her side, the fingers on her right hand digging in her cast. "No. I'm sorry."

Susan gave her bright smile. "Okay, then. We're keeping Annie tied up so the two of you won't talk. We have our reasons, and I don't have to explain myself. Just do as you're told, and you can untie Annie yourself later when we have the money."

As much as Gwen wanted to argue, she saw no point. She and Annie were close now, close to whatever was going to happen. They would either be free and eating shitty diner food in a couple of hours, or dead. Either way, fighting now would help neither of them.

"Okay. Tell us what to do."

# CHAPTER TWENTY-ONE

Gwen and Annie were directed downstairs and then into a garage. Bill and Susan debated for a while, trying to decide whether to take two cars, and finally told them to get into the back of Bill's car. As she slid in, Gwen saw a smear of blood on the front passenger seat from her ride up there, whenever that had been. Annie saw it too as she came in after her and started struggling, twisting in her seat and moaning through her gag. Bill slammed the door after them.

"Shh," Gwen said. "It's okay. That's my blood. I'm okay and you're okay. Let's just do what they say, and maybe we can get out of this."

Annie stared at her for a long time and then nodded before collapsing back into the seat. She did nothing as Gwen buckled her into the seat belt. Bill and Susan stood outside, still arguing. Annie's wrists were red and chafed from the plastic zip tie holding them together. The plastic tie was attached to her pants through one of the belt loops, ostensibly to stop her from removing her gag. Gwen massaged Annie's hands, and she stiffened and drew away as far as she could toward the door on her side.

"What? What's the matter? I'm only trying to help."

Annie shook her head, eyebrows drawn, and for a moment Gwen felt she was talking to someone else—a stranger. Despite all their time together on the road and in Denver, she didn't trust her anymore. Did she blame her for all this?

"Annie, I'm so sorry. I was only trying to help. I didn't know Bill would be there at the house in Santa Fe. He got the jump on me. I was stupid."

Annie stared at her and then rolled her eyes. "Nrrrr Annnni!" she said again.

"I don't know what you mean."

Annie didn't have a chance to try to explain further, as Bill got in the front, slamming his door.

"Fucking bitch," he said, clearly referring to his wife. He turned around, taking them both in. "You." He pointed at Gwen. "Keep your fucking trap shut. I've had enough chitchat from bitches today."

He pressed a button on a large remote, and the garage door began to open. He waited until it was about halfway up before gunning the engine and racing down the driveway, tearing onto the road so fast the momentum threw her sideways. Gwen glanced back and saw Susan standing there in the doorway garage before trees blocked the house.

"Why isn't she coming?"

"Shut up," Bill snarled. "I said I don't want to talk to you. Don't say another word, and I won't have to hurt you."

Annie whimpered slightly next to her, and Gwen put a hand on her shoulder to soothe her. Annie tried to shrug it off, and Gwen put her hand back in her lap, hurt by this reaction more than she should be. Annie was upset and didn't want to be touched—it was as simple as that, but it felt like a rejection. Gwen blinked back tears and stared out the window at the pastoral landscape sweeping by outside.

The drive was quick, less than half an hour. Gwen, upset, began to pay attention to where they were only when Bill began to slow down. She'd never have been able to retrace their way back to Bill and Susan's.

Bill turned into a dirt road off the small highway they'd been on, and a half a mile or so later, they reached a pay station for the state park. It was unmanned, but Bill got out and bought one of the three-dollar day passes in the little brown box and put it on his dashboard. All of this seemed out of character for him, but maybe he knew something she didn't.

The parking lot was almost deserted. Only three other cars were parked here, and Gwen spotted, with something simultaneously like dread and elation, that Trixie's classic orange Ford sedan was already here. Bill pulled into a parking spot far from the other cars, near the picnic area, and turned off his engine. It ticked and rattled for a moment as it cooled, and he turned in his seat.

"Stay here and don't try anything. If you fuck up this deal, I'll kill you and this nutcase."

He climbed out and slammed the door, walking over to one of the picnic tables. Gwen immediately rolled down her window, hoping to be able to hear what was going on. Bill stopped at one of the tables and sat down backward, resting back on his elbows. He was clearly trying to seem relaxed, but even from here, she could see anxious tension in his face—the same expression he'd had when he was trying to kill her. She hoped to God Trixie knew what she was doing.

She glanced at Annie, who was staring down at her legs, seeming uninterested in what was happening outside. Gwen shook her head, a little flare of temper heating her blood. It wasn't as if any of this was actually her fault. She'd been ambushed. Why had Annie come to Dallas before negotiating with them?

"Annie—"

Her head whipped up. "Nrrrrr Annni!"

Gwen took a quick glance outside to make sure Bill was still at the table and reached for Annie's gag. Annie wrenched her head back and away, shaking it fast and hard. Gwen held up her hands.

"Jesus, okay! I thought you'd want it off."

Annie shook her head again and hunched into herself, her shoulders curved and huddled, as if for protection. For Gwen, Annie might as well have slapped her. This time, however, rather than hurt, she felt betrayed.

"Fine. Fuck you, Annie. Let's get through this, and we never have to see each other again."

Annie shook her head, and Gwen focused back on Bill, forcing herself to pay attention. She needed to care about what was happening out there, but her anger and indignation were making it difficult.

Bill was still sitting at the bench, but some of his fake casualness had clearly evaporated, as he was now bunched up, elbows on his knees, one foot tapping impatiently.

"Come on, Trixie," Gwen whispered. This was not the kind of man to keep waiting. She barely knew him, but she could tell he could barely hold things together in the best of situations, let alone if his patience was tested. He wasn't wearing his holstered gun right now, but he probably had one or more on him somewhere. Another minute or two passed, and Bill, clearly fed up, jumped to his feet and started pacing. He was rubbing his hands together, almost as if he wanted to do something else with them.

Finally, Gwen saw movement at the far end of the parking lot and almost sagged with relief at the sight of Trixie walking toward them. She was wearing a neon-orange pencil skirt and a bright-green top that matched her heels—hardly the outfit to wear to hostage negotiation, but Gwen had never been happier to see someone. Bill spotted her too and stopped pacing, his face crinkling. He didn't seem to know who she was.

Trixie stopped on the sidewalk about twenty feet from his table. "Are you Bill?"

"Yes."

"Where's Susan? I was supposed to meet her."

"She's not here. And you weren't supposed to be here alone, either."

Trixie gestured helplessly. "We thought it would be smarter. Eggs in one basket and all that."

Bill lifted his hands. "Same here."

"Are they here?"

Bill pointed at his car, and Gwen waved. She saw Trixie's shoulders drop with obvious relief. "Oh, thank God."

"Do you have access to the money?"

Trixie paused, staring at him. "I do. I can give it to you as soon as I make a phone call."

"How the hell are you going to do that?"

She reached for her purse, and Gwen saw Bill tense, one hand going to the back of his pants. He had a gun there, but he didn't draw it. Trixie, seeing his movement, paused and held up her hands. "I have a phone in my purse. Can I get it out?"

Bill's shoulders relaxed a little, but he kept his hand on his gun. "Okay, but slowly."

Moving at an almost comically slow pace, Trixie unzipped the little purse at her side and pulled out a phone, which she held up for him to see.

"I need an account number," she said.

"Susan already told you that," Bill said, almost snarling. "She's the only one who knows about that stuff. Stop fucking around. Transfer the money to our account, and you can drive away with your friends here."

"What's to stop you from shooting me? Once I give you and Susan the money, why not just kill all three of us?"

Bill laughed and gestured around them. "Out here? In the open like this? Do you think I want to spend the rest of my life in prison? How stupid do you think I am?"

Trixie smiled. "Actually, Bill, I think you're a fucking moron. You just confessed in front of the entire police department."

She didn't wait for him to react. Instead, Trixie ran toward her and Annie, slunk near the ground and gesturing for the two of them to get down. Gwen bent toward her lap as far as she could and then reached over and pushed Annie down as well. Annie struggled under her hand, and as Gwen tried to explain, they began to hear shouting and the pounding boots of many people. Someone was screaming at Bill to throw down his weapon, and he was arguing with them. She was bent too far down to see much of anything, but a shadow appeared on her side of car. She could hear several people nearby.

"Stay down," a man's voice growled outside the car. Gwen

didn't know if he meant the two of them or Trixie, who, she assumed, was still crouched somewhere near the car.

Gwen heard Bill yelling some more, and then one or two people out there shouted in triumph, and more people were running around. She heard Bill curse and complain, but his voice sounded muffled, contained, almost as if something was restricting his mouth.

The shadow moved and fell directly on her. The man spoke again. "Okay. You can sit up now. Show me your hands, and don't make any quick movements."

Gwen obeyed, holding her hands up and out. A uniformed police officer bent next to her door, peering in. His eyes, however, were fixed on Annie, who was still twisted almost double.

"What's wrong with her?" he asked.

"I don't know." Gwen tried to keep her voice calm and quiet. "You can sit up now, Annie. Everything's going to be okay."

Annie was shaking all over, sobbing. Gwen put her hand on her back, trying to soothe her, and Annie shot up and started thrashing back and forth in her seat, panicking. The officer got up and held his gun low and ready, moving toward the back of the car and around to Annie's side.

"Annie, Annie!" Gwen said, hands out. "It's okay! Calm down. The police are here. You have to let them help you."

She continued to thrash around, as if she hadn't heard anything, and Gwen pulled away from her as far as she could, afraid of colliding with her swinging head. The police officer she'd talked to was standing outside Annie's door. Annie's window was up, so whatever he was saying was muffled, but his gun was still out and low. Several other officers stood behind him, hands on their weapons, waiting for his signal. Gwen was terrified he was going to open the door before she could calm Annie down. She wasn't about to watch these men shoot the love of her life.

Gwen unbuckled her seat belt and threw herself on Annie, squeezing her as tight as she could. Annie still bucked and struggled beneath her, but Gwen managed to avoid her head as it swung back toward her chin. In her terror, Annie had surprising strength, and Gwen could barely hold on. A steady stream of reassurances and soothing nonsense flowed out of her own mouth, but she focused on calming her. It was like trying to hold onto a hurricane. Then, almost as if she had been turned off, Annie sagged beneath her.

"Shh, shh, shh," Gwen continued to mutter. "You're okay, you're okay. Shh, shh…"

It took Gwen several seconds to recognize that it was over, and she moved back a little, letting Annie sit up. Annie's face was red and contorted, her eyes almost rolling in panic. She stared straight ahead, almost as if she couldn't see Gwen. Her hair had come loose from its tie, and lay in lank locks across her face. It was impossibly long—much longer than her hair had been before, and quite dark, hardly blond at all. Gwen pushed some of it back to clear her vision, and Annie didn't react, seeming dazed, shocked.

Suddenly but dimly aware of a commotion outside, Gwen looked up, searching for the source. Someone was screaming from behind what seemed like a solid line of police officers about fifty feet away, beyond the farthest picnic table. The crowd finally parted, and a small blond figure appeared amidst the taller, armed men.

It was Annie.

She was struggling to get through them, pushing them, but several of them held her back. Gwen could hear only the tone of her panic, not the words, clearly. But finally, a woman wearing a suit walked toward the group of officers holding her back. She must have said something to them, and Annie started running toward Bill's car a second later. The woman in the suit dashed after her, but no one nearby was fast enough to catch her.

A large, imposing moose of a man grabbed Annie's arm, almost as an afterthought, stopping her with little effort about ten feet from the car. Annie struggled for a moment and then relaxed, glaring up at him.

"That's my sister in there, you ass," she said.

The woman in the suit finally caught up, gasping, and waved at the police officers near the car.

"Step back, everyone," the woman said. "One of the women in the car is schizophrenic. Her sister's going to help us get her out safely."

Most of them stepped back and holstered their weapons, but the nearest officer, the one she'd talked to, kept his gun out and low and moved back only a few feet. Annie raced around to that side of the car and opened the door. Her eyes met Gwen's and then she was checking her sister, running her hands across her face and up and down her arms, looking for injuries.

"Oh, God, Beth," Annie said. "What did they do to you?"

Beth's face suddenly brightened, and she moved a little. Her eyes locked on Annie's and then filled with tears. Annie pulled her into a hug, and when she drew back, she reached up to remove Beth's gag. Beth let her without a struggle, and when it was off, she turned to Gwen.

"I'm not Annie," she said.

Gwen laughed. "Yes. I understand now."

"I'm so sorry this happened to you, Gwen," Annie said. "It's all my fault. I should never have let you go on your own."

"I shouldn't have left you. It's my fault, too. I was being pigheaded."

Annie's eyes briefly filled with tears, but she blinked them away, focusing on Beth again.

"Are you okay, honey? Did they hurt you?"

Beth shook her head. "No. I'm just scared. I don't like being tied up."

Annie laughed, clearly relieved. "No, sweetie. I guess you don't. But it's going to be scary again in a minute. That lady over there," she pointed at the woman in the suit, "is going to have to take me away."

"For how long?" Beth asked, sounding angry.

"I don't know yet, sugar, but hopefully not as long as last time."

"I don't want you to go."

"And I don't want to, but I have to, at least for a while. But you know what? My new friend Trixie is going to help you now, and Tom is on his way." She lifted her chin toward Gwen. "And you've already met Gwen. She'll help you, too."

"Tom's here?" Beth asked, peering around almost wildly.

Annie laughed. "He'll be here soon, if he's not already."

Beth continued to look around, clearly trying to see if she could spot Tom, and Annie took the opportunity to unbuckle Beth's seat belt. Gwen slid after them as they got out of the car, standing up and almost groaning with relief. She held her hands up for the police again and watched as the closest one finally holstered his gun. He stepped toward them, making everyone flinch, but indicated the zip tie on Beth's hands. He cut it off and retreated, joining his colleagues a few yards away.

The three of them were left on their own for a moment, and Annie gave both of them a long hug. Gwen, not satisfied, kissed her, hard, and Annie pulled away, laughing.

"We're giving everyone a show."

"I don't care. I had to kiss you."

Beth was staring at them, eyebrows nearly in her hairline, and Annie gave her another quick, one-armed hug. "Sorry, Beth. I should have told you. Gwen's my girlfriend."

"Really? I didn't know you had one."

"She's really special to me. And I hope, once all of this is cleared up, the two of you can be good friends. Like you and Tom."

Beth rolled her eyes. "Tom's more than a friend. You know that."

Annie grinned. "Yes. And Gwen's more than a friend, too." She looked at Gwen, grinning. "She's more than a girlfriend, even. I love her."

"You do?" Gwen and Beth asked at the same time.

Annie laughed again. "Of course, silly."

"I love you, too," Gwen said.

Beth squealed, throwing her arms around Gwen and squeezing her with that surprising, wiry strength. Gwen hugged her back, surprised now that she'd ever thought this woman was Annie. While they resembled each other very strongly, Beth was clearly different in every other way. Still, she had to give herself some credit. Most of these differences were only clear now that she was untied and ungagged.

The woman in the suit was pacing, somewhat impatiently, some ten or fifteen feet away. Trixie was seated on a nearby picnic table, talking to some police officers. How much trouble was Gwen in?

Annie glanced back, frowning. "We don't have much time," she said.

"What's going to happen?"

Annie shook her head, her eyes flickering toward Beth. She didn't want to speak in front of her. Annie would be arrested again, but what would happen next was probably anyone's guess.

"I tried to make it easy for you, Gwen. I told them I forced you to do most of it at the beginning, but I don't know how much they believed. I hope it's not too bad. Trixie intends to call a lawyer friend of hers, so someone should be there for you when they bring us in."

"Tom!" Beth suddenly shouted, and started running away. Annie tried to grab her but was too slow, so they watched as she dashed across the crowded picnic area. Several officers were escorting Tom, but he threw his hands in the air and caught her as she launched herself at him.

"She's in love with him," Annie explained. "She doesn't know he doesn't like her like that. If he ever tells her, I hope she'll understand."

"Ah." They watched them for a while, and Gwen recalled own brother when she was younger. She turned to Annie and took one of her hands. "I promise to help her, too, whenever all this is settled."

Annie smiled. "I know you will, Gwen. I trust you. You've already done so much."

Gwen laughed. "No, I haven't. You're right where you started. You're going back to prison because of me. You could have disappeared, run away, and instead you stage this huge rescue at your own expense."

Annie shook her head. "It wasn't for you, Gwen. It was for us—all of us. You, me, and Beth. Last night, when Susan told Trixie that she had both of you, I almost passed out. I knew then I had to turn myself in—it was the only way to help you both. That and I couldn't keep running away. It isn't in me. I thought I could do it, but I can't. We'll have to hope some judge will see reason."

"I'll wait for you, Annie. However long it takes. I swear it."

Annie pulled her into a hug and then whispered in her ear. "You better. You're going to have to take care of my money while I'm locked up."

Gwen reeled back, shocked, and Annie kissed her before she could say anything in front of the police.

# EPILOGUE

G wen stretched and set her book down on the little table next to her ice-cold daiquiri. The thatch umbrella above them was shading them from the sun, but the heat was still intense, almost uncomfortable. Too hot to read, anyway. She was wearing sunglasses, but the light off the white sand was blinding this time of day. The waves were calm today, the water that bright, greenish, almost neon blue that didn't look real. A breeze blew past once in a while off the water, deliciously cool, but it was infrequent enough that sweat pooled on her exposed stomach. She closed her eyes and adjusted her chaise lounge so that she lay almost prone and started to doze. Annie was already asleep in her chair, sitting upright. It was that kind of day.

It had been almost four years since they'd been arrested. Gwen hadn't gotten as much time as Annie. In fact, and entirely because of Annie's testimony, she'd been released fairly quickly, all things considered—less than a year. At the time, Annie had testified that she'd forced her to steal all those cars, and her lawyer had done a fair job of claiming that the rest of her actions had resulted from a kind of Stockholm syndrome. Everyone in the courtroom, including the judge, had been skeptical, but her lack of criminal record had helped sway her conviction and sentencing.

Bill had immediately confessed, partly, Gwen thought, out of spite for Susan, but mostly to reduce his sentence. After a brief, two-week period on the lam, Susan had been caught in San Diego. Presented with her husband's confession, she'd nevertheless remained tight-lipped and received the maximum penalty.

After a series of delayed appeals, Annie's sentence had been reduced and her conviction bumped down to accessory, in part because of Bill's confession. Most of the rest of the evidence to change her sentencing had to deal with the paper and digital trail Bill and Susan had left, which showed them in sole possession of the money from the day it was stolen. Had they not been as greedy as they were, Annie would still be behind bars. Annie's sentence had been reduced to seven years, with time served, which meant she'd been released six months ago.

Trixie had, in fact, managed to get most of the money. She'd made it seem like Susan had moved it herself before hiding it entirely, and, as Susan wouldn't confess to anything, let alone something she didn't do, she received the entire blame. In light of this development, Annie and Gwen agreed that a fifty-fifty split with Trixie was fair, and, in gratitude, Trixie had managed to grow their fortune significantly in the intervening years through smart off-shore investment.

Despite her time in jail, after giving her an official reprimand, Gwen's employer had kept her on. Gwen preferred to think her former immediate supervisor liked her, but she was probably desperate, and they were short-handed. Her bosses couldn't discount the whole situation, however, so they bumped her back down to local investigator, which meant a lot of stakeouts on cheating spouses and acting like a secret paparazzi at various events. She'd started with this kind of work as a PI and hated it, but she'd been glad for an actual job. Her employer had kindly transitioned her to the Dallas field office, closer to Annie, and eventually she could visit her nearly every week.

Beyond having something to do to pass the time, her job lent credence to their story: she and Annie didn't know where the stolen money was or where it had been. Gwen had spied a few police officers and agents tailing her that first year but didn't do anything about it. Thinking of them watching her watch other people amused her. They also weren't as good at it as she was. She'd never let herself be seen.

Tom moved closer as well, and eventually, among the three of them—Tom, Gwen, and Trixie—they were able to hire full-time care for Beth. They moved her out of the hospital into her own apartment in Tom's building, using their legitimate savings, so the police had no reason to investigate how they were paying for it.

Annie held up well behind bars, considering. Because of her education and background, she spent some of her time inside helping other inmates and prison workers with their money and taxes. She taught a few classes on professionalization, making résumés, dressing for interviews, that kind of thing, and seemed relatively interested in her occupation. Annie dealt with the situation as best she could, but occasionally one or both of them would lose it during a visit, terrified by what could happen to her while she was confined.

Three months before her release, Gwen and Trixie took a trip together, ostensibly to Mexico. They rented rooms there and paid some bribes to make it seem as if they'd stayed there the entire time. Instead, they hired a charter flight from Mexico City to Belize, all to cover their tracks. After a lot of driving around, they eventually found a series of remote cays near enough to a larger city for health care and shopping, but isolated enough to stay relatively hidden. They leased two houses on either end of the same cay. Only twenty residences were located on the cay, total, and each had its own section of beach.

They'd come here almost immediately after Annie's release, waiting just long enough for the police to see that they hadn't rushed to the cash. Whether anyone would come looking for them some day was another story, but Trixie believed that, with Bill and Susan as the sacrificial lambs, so to speak, no one had much motivation to try.

Beth had been here with them in Belize almost since the beginning. Her nurse was trained and dedicated—they all loved her. She came over from the mainland five days a week, and another lovely nurse spent the other two days there. Beth's part of the house had a separate entrance that gave her some independence.

Eventually, should things continue to go as well as they were now, she might get her own place somewhere nearby.

Gwen startled awake at the sound of a gull, very near. She sat up, resting her weight on her hands, and yawned, yodeling a little. The heat of the day had died down, maybe in part because the breeze had picked up. Annie stirred to life next to her, stretching, and Gwen watched her, delighted as always to see her in a bikini. Her little body was still milky white—she stayed out of the sun almost entirely—but she'd gained some weight since her release. Her curves were coming back, and her ribs and collarbones grew less stark as the weeks passed.

Annie yawned. "Did you say something?"

"No. It was a gull."

"Mmm." Annie stretched again, and Gwen stared at her without blinking. Annie must have sensed what she was doing, as she turned to her with a sly grin. "What are you looking at?"

"You."

"Uh-huh. And do you like what you see?"

"Yes. Very much."

Annie swatted her with her hat. "None of that, now. We have company coming."

Gwen glanced at her watch. "Not for another twenty minutes."

Annie's cheeks colored, and Gwen took that as an invitation, climbing out of her chair and into Annie's. They started kissing, and right as Gwen reached for the tie to Annie's top, they heard an engine approaching.

"Crap," Annie said.

They both looked toward the water. At the far end of their beach, they had a small dock. Gwen, Annie, and Beth used bikes to get around the island, primarily, but to reach the mainland, they needed easy access to the water. Gwen hadn't settled on a boat yet, but Trixie had one and used it when she dropped by. Today she was bringing their visitor over from the mainland, and Gwen could see Tom towering above her in the little boat.

"I should go get Beth," Annie said.

Almost as if they'd summoned her, they heard a shriek from

the house behind them, and they both laughed as Beth ran from the porch, across the sand, and toward the dock. Tom and Trixie were waving enthusiastically enough to tilt the boat back and forth, and Gwen and Annie laughed with shared joy.

"I guess I should get off you now," Gwen said.

"I guess you should."

Neither of them moved, and Gwen bent back down to kiss her. The others were still far enough away that they were still relatively hidden, and Gwen crushed Annie against her. Eventually Annie drew back, breathing heavily.

"You're going to get me going, and I won't be able to do anything about it."

"Cold shower?" Gwen suggested.

Annie laughed and pushed her shoulder. "Asshole."

"Okay—how about this? You can spend the rest of today thinking about what I'm going to do to you tonight."

Annie laughed again. "That doesn't make it any better."

Gwen leaned down for one more kiss, and they both froze when someone sighed a few feet away.

"Jeez, guys, get a room," Beth said.

"Really," Tom added.

Annie wiggled out from under her and jumped to her feet, rushing into Tom's arms. He picked her up and swung her around, the two of them giggling like kids. This was Tom's first visit here, and he already looked the part of a local expat—sandals, shorts, guayabera shirt, and a straw porkpie hat. Annie was hoping to convince him to move down here. Gwen had her doubts that he would go for it at all, or very easily. She'd promised Annie to help convince him this weekend. Maybe she could talk him into opening a business of sorts. He wasn't the kind to stay idle. Still, Annie's motivations were good. She wanted her whole family here, real and adopted. Gwen felt the same way.

Beth, for example, was already as close as a real sister. Standing there in Tom's shadow, she looked like an entirely different person from the one tied up in Bill and Susan's basement. Once sprung from the hospital, she'd cut all her hair into a pixie, and now that she spent most of her time outside, she hardly seemed related to Annie. Trixie was like the kooky aunt she'd never had. Her clothes and hair had always been outrageous, but here in Belize, that kookiness had taken on an entirely new level of wacko, now with locally made jewelry and clothing. All their neighbors here on the cay loved her. Even Tom was like a second brother to her now—closer in some ways. They'd spent many evenings together coping with Annie's imprisonment and Beth's initial transition to home care. She might not have gotten through any of it without him.

Annie, suddenly realizing she was still in the chair, held a hand out for her.

"Come join us, Gwen. We're thinking of eating at the little restaurant we like so much."

A prickle of tears made Gwen suddenly grateful for her dark sunglasses, but she blinked them away and levered herself to her feet. Annie's hand in hers was warm, comforting, and her fingers gave hers a slight squeeze. Annie was staring at her, her expression slightly concerned.

Gwen shook her head. "Just happy."

Annie smiled, her expression so dazzling that the natural beauty around them faded.

"Me, too."

The others had walked back toward the boat, and the two of them had to jog to catch up. As Tom gallantly helped all four of them climb in, Gwen realized they'd be able to convince him to come back and stay for good.

Their future, once so dark and uncertain, stretched in front of them with light and hope. Gwen pulled Annie into a deep kiss, and the others whistled and hollered. Gwen ignored them and kept kissing.

# About the Author

Charlotte was born in a tiny mountain town and spent most of her childhood and young adulthood in a small city in northern Colorado. While she is usually what one might generously call "indoorsy," early exposure to the Rocky Mountains led to a lifelong love of nature, hiking, and camping.

After a lengthy education in Denver, New Orleans, Washington, DC, and New York, she earned a doctorate in literature and women and gender studies.

An early career academic, Charlotte has moved several times since her latest graduation. She currently lives and teaches in a small Southern city with her wife and their cat.

# Books Available From Bold Strokes Books

**Femme Tales** by Anne Shade. Six women find themselves in their own real-life fairy tales when true love finds them in the most unexpected ways. (978-1-63555-657-5)

**Jellicle Girl** by Stevie Mikayne. One dark summer night, Beth and Jackie go out to the canoe dock. Two years later, Beth is still carrying the weight of what happened to Jackie. (978-1-63555-691-9)

**My Date with a Wendigo** by Genevieve McCluer. Elizabeth Rosseau finds her long-lost love and the secret community of fiends she's now a part of. (978-1-63555-679-7)

**On the Run** by Charlotte Greene. Even when they're cute blondes, it's stupid to pick up hitchhikers, especially when they've just broken out of prison, but doing so is about to change Gwen's life forever. (978-1-63555-682-7)

**Perfect Timing** by Dena Blake. The choice between love and family has never been so difficult, and Lynn's and Maggie's different visions of the future may end their romance before it's begun. (978-1-63555-466-3)

**The Mail Order Bride** by R. Kent. When a mail order bride is thrust on Austin, he must choose between the bride he never wanted or the dream he lives for. (978-1-63555-678-0)

**Through Love's Eyes** by C.A. Popovich. When fate reunites Brittany Yardin and Amy Jansons, can they move beyond the pain of their past to find love? (978-1-63555-629-2)

**To the Moon and Back** by Melissa Brayden. Film actress Carly Daniel thinks that stage work is boring and unexciting, but when she accepts a lead role in a new play, stage manager Lauren Prescott tests both her heart and her ability to share the limelight. (978-1-63555-618-6)

**Tokyo Love** by Diana Jean. When Kathleen Schmitt is given the opportunity to be on the cutting edge of AI technology, she never thought a failed robotic love companion would bring her closer to her neighbor, Yuriko Velucci, and finding love in unexpected places. (978-1-63555-681-0)

**Brooklyn Summer** by Maggie Cummings. When opposites attract, can a summer of passion and adventure lead to a lifetime of love? (978-1-63555-578-3)

**City Kitty and Country Mouse** by Alyssa Linn Palmer. Pulled in two different directions, can a city kitty and a country mouse fall in love and make it work? (978-1-63555-553-0)

**Elimination** by Jackie D. When a dangerous homegrown terrorist seeks refuge with the Russian mafia, the team will be put to the ultimate test. (978-1-63555-570-7)

**In the Shadow of Darkness** by Nicole Stiling. Angeline Vallencourt is a reluctant vampire who must decide what she wants more—obscurity, revenge, or the woman who makes her feel alive. (978-1-63555-624-7)

**On Second Thought** by C. Spencer. Madisen is falling hard for Rae. Even single life and co-parenting are beginning to click. At least, that is, until her ex-wife begins to have second thoughts. (978-1-63555-415-1)

**Out of Practice** by Carsen Taite. When attorney Abby Keane discovers the wedding blogger tormenting her client is the woman she had a passionate, anonymous vacation fling with, sparks and subpoenas fly. Legal Affairs: one law firm, three best friends, three chances to fall in love. (978-1-63555-359-8)

**Providence** by Leigh Hays. With every click of the shutter, photographer Rebekiah Kearns finds it harder and harder to keep Lindsey Blackwell in focus without getting too close. (978-1-63555-620-9)

**Taking a Shot at Love** by KC Richardson. When academic and athletic worlds collide, will English professor Celeste Bouchard and basketball coach Lisa Tobias ignore their attraction to achieve their professional goals? (978-1-63555-549-3)

**Flight to the Horizon** by Julie Tizard. Airline captain Kerri Sullivan and flight attendant Janine Case struggle to survive an emergency water landing and overcome dark secrets to give love a chance to fly. (978-1-63555-331-4)

**In Helen's Hands** by Nanisi Barrett D'Arnuk. As her mistress, Helen pushes Mickey to her sensual limits, delivering the pleasure only a BDSM lifestyle can provide her. (978-1-63555-639-1)

**Jamis Bachman, Ghost Hunter** by Jen Jensen. In Sage Creek, Utah, a poltergeist stirs to life and past secrets emerge. (978-1-63555-605-6)

**Moon Shadow** by Suzie Clarke. Add betrayal, season with survival, then serve revenge smokin' hot with a sharp knife. (978-1-63555-584-4)

**Spellbound** by Jean Copeland and Jackie D. When the supernatural worlds of good and evil face off, love might be what saves them all. (978-1-63555-564-6)

**Temptation** by Kris Bryant. Can experienced nanny Cassie Miller deny her growing attraction and keep her relationship with her boss professional? Or will they sidestep propriety and give in to temptation? (978-1-63555-508-0)

**The Inheritance** by Ali Vali. Family ties bring Tucker Delacroix and Willow Vernon together, but they could also tear them, and any chance they have at love, apart. (978-1-63555-303-1)

**Thief of the Heart** by MJ Williamz. Kit Hanson makes a living seducing rich women in casinos and relieving them of the expensive jewelry most won't even miss. But her streak ends when she meets beautiful FBI agent Savannah Brown. (978-1-63555-572-1)

**Face Off** by PJ Trebelhorn. Hockey player Savannah Wells rarely spends more than a night with any one woman, but when photographer Madison Scott buys the house next door, she's forced to rethink what she expects out of life. (978-1-63555-480-9)

**Hot Ice** by Aurora Rey, Elle Spencer, and Erin Zak. Can falling in love melt the hearts of the iciest ice queens? Join Aurora Rey, Elle Spencer, and Erin Zak to find out! A contemporary romance novella collection. (978-1-63555-513-4)

**Line of Duty** by VK Powell. Dr. Dylan Carlyle's professional and personal life is turned upside down when a tragic event at Fairview Station pits her against ambitious, handsome police officer Finley Masters. ((978-1-63555-486-1)

**London Undone** by Nan Higgins. London Craft reinvents her life after reading a childhood letter to her future self and, in doing so, finds the love she truly wants. (978-1-63555-562-2)

**Lunar Eclipse** by Gun Brooke. Moon De Cruz lives alone on an uninhabited planet after being shipwrecked in space. Her life changes forever when Captain Beaux Lestarion's arrival threatens the planet and Moon's freedom. (978-1-63555-460-1)

**One Small Step** by MA Binfield. In this contemporary romance, Iris and Cam discover the meaning of taking chances and following your heart, even if it means getting hurt. (978-1-63555-596-7)

**Shadows of a Dream** by Nicole Disney. Rainn has the talent to take her rock band all the way, but falling in love is a powerful distraction, and her new girlfriend's meth addiction might just take them both down. 978-1-63555-598-1)

**Someone to Love** by Jenny Frame. When Davina Trent is given an unexpected family, can she let nanny Wendy Darling teach her to open her heart to the children and to Wendy? (978-1-63555-468-7)

**Uncharted** by Robyn Nyx. As Rayne Marcellus and Chase Stinsen track the legendary Golden Trinity, they must learn to put their differences aside and depend on one another to survive. (978-1-63555-325-3)

**Where We Are** by Annie McDonald. A sensual account of two women who discover a way to walk on the same path together with the help of an Indigenous tale, a Canadian art movement, and the mysterious appearance of dimes. (978-1-63555-581-3)